FORN LJÓS

Books by Wynter Tickle

Forn Ljós

Incongruous

FORN LJÓS

Incongruous

Wynter Tickle

Paperback ISBN: 978-0-473-72048-3
Hardcover ISBN: 978-0-473-72314-9
eBook ISBN: 978-0-473-72066-7

Text, cover design, and illustrations by Wynter Tickle.
Typesetting and editing by Janis Hill.

Wynter Tickle Books
www.wyntertickle.com

To all sheep who aren't afraid of lions.

These pages contain descriptions of violence,
war, death, near death, survival,
other worldly beings, Gods, and danger.

Many creative liberties are taken with
Norse Mythology in this story.

CHAPTERS

YGGDRASIL

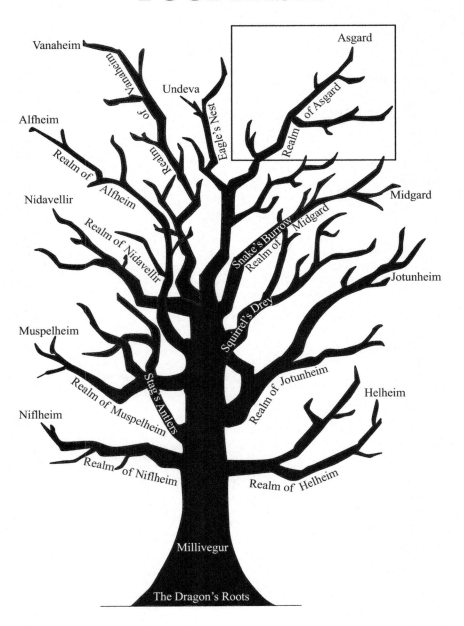

REALM OF ASGARD

Yggdrasil

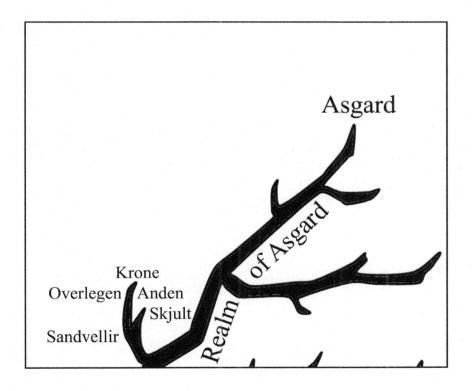

RUNES

⌐ Laguz

ᚺ Hagalaz

ᚠ Fehu

ᛟ Othala

CHARACTERS

OVERLEGEN

Alice Wood – Gale

Anjelica Starr – Firestorm

Apoint

Azar

Duana

Helena

Nora Frost – Honora

ASGARD

Ace Wilder – Blaze

Alec Monroe – Chameleon

Anakin Fjord – Devil

Ash Summers – Arrow

Heimdall

Loki

Odin

Sif

Thor

OTHERS

Ashia Rover

August Frost

Daymein Amolt

Freyja

Lavita

Nox Belmore

Pierre

Ray

Sage Marek

Sian

GUIDE

PLACES

Anden – Danish word – Prison world in the Kronevian Empire.

Asgard – Norse Realm – Head planet of the Asgardian Realm.

Bifröst – Bridge between realms – Norse mythology.

Krone – Danish word – Capital planet of the Kronevian Empire.

Midgard – Earth – Norse Realm –

Head planet of the Midgardian Realm.

Millivegur – Middle road – Icelandic word –

Unruled caverns located on Yggdrasil (Bifröst's path).

Overlegen – Danish word –

Military planet of the Kronevian Empire.

Skjult – Icelandic word – Planet in the Asgardian Realm.

Sandvellir – Icelandic word – Planet in the Asgardian Realm.

Undeva – Romanian word – Planet located north of the

Eagle's nest in the Asgardian Realm.

Vanaheim – Norse Realm –

Head planet of the Vanaheimian Realm.

BEINGS / GODS

Álfar – The race of Elves – Icelandic word origin.

Draugr – Undead being – Scandinavian folktales.

Freyja – Norse Goddess of beauty, gold, and war.

Fylgja – Norse supernatural being.

Heimdall – Norse God of war and the guardian of the Bifröst.

Loki – Norse God of mischief and deception.

Njord – Norse God of wind and sea – Rules Vanaheim.

Odin – Norse God of war and death – Rules Asgard.

Sif – Norse Goddess of grain and fertility – Thor's wife.

Thor – Norse God of lightning, thunderstorms,
and protection of mankind – Sif's Husband.

THINGS

Forn Ljós – Ancient light – Icelandic word –
Magically enhanced runes.

Gelu – Frost – Latin word – One of the Mutabilis.

Gjallarhorn – Heimdall's trumpet – Norse mythology.

Mjölnir – Thor's hammer – Norse mythology.

Mutabilis – Changeable – Latin word – The term given to the
weapons Gelu and Vorago.

Segredos – Secrets – Portuguese word – Segredos drive.

Smite/Smiting – The ability to wipe someone from existence –
Held by beings with access to dark magic, namely Gods.

Valknut – A symbol of Odin and Asgard – Norse mythology –
Appears as three interconnecting triangles.

Vorago – Chasm – Latin word – One of the Mutabilis.

Yggdrasil – Norse universal tree – The path of the Bifröst.

NOTE

Snorri Sturluson

Snorri Sturluson, who is mentioned a couple times in this story, was an Icelandic poet, historian, and politician. He lived during the 13th Century, and is still well known for his recordings of Norse legends and lore.

His work provides a lot of our modern day understanding of the early North Germanic cultures.

It is a possibility that when Snorri Sturluson wrote down the nine realms he may have altered them from the originals, likely due to Christian influences.

The original nine realms were believed to be:
Asgard, Alfheim, Jotunheim, Midgard, Muspelheim, Nidavellir, Niflheim, Svartalfheim, and Vanaheim.

After Snorri's work the nine realms are considered to be:
Asgard, Alfheim, Helheim, Jotunheim, Midgard, Muspelheim, Nidavellir (combined with Svartalfheim), Niflheim, and Vanaheim.

Forn Ljós takes place as a result of the change of nine realms. The addition of Helheim, and removal of Svartalfheim, acts as a catalyst for the events detailed within this book.

PROLOGUE

The Unspoken Event, Millivegur

Roughly 220 Years Ago

Duane, Head of Overlegen

Golden blood dripped down from my cold muscular hands onto the back of the wooden chair I was digging into. I didn't care for the stain I was leaving with each clench from my fingers. If they wanted to stain my people's reputation, I was going to stain their chairs.

I concentrated my anger on the wood, as I had been for the past hour, hoping that was enough to keep my raging emotions off my face. My cold blue glare was set like stone on the unconcerned woman standing at the opposite side of the large table before me.

'This is a mistake and you know it,' I growled, using my voice for the first time in this meeting. The sound of my grumbling words bounced off the walls and up into the domed skylight creating the perfect menacing effect.

'Snorri has confirmed the changes to the realms, his decision is final, Duane.' The woman's voice was full of infuriating nerves.

How dare this Midgardian not fear me! 'And why would that be?' My fury bit into each word as injustice fuelled my fiery rage.

'He's dead.' Her words were so simple and so emotionless as she twirled her hair along her finger.

'For how long?' My voice broke as my emotions choked me.

'Six Midgardian centuries.' The Midgardian running the meeting pulled her cloak closer as if to shield herself from my outrage as her words almost buckled my knees.

I wasn't the only one to be outraged by this as the other members filled the air with yells and insults. The disruption rattled the walls and the skylight but I didn't care. All I could do was pour my feelings into my hands, that way I may be able to get through this meeting without killing everyone. Not that *I'd* mind.

'When was it decided that Midgardians would negate the keepers of each realm?' The turquoise hand of my girlfriend placed itself over mine as she addressed the room.

Her magenta eyes fixed everyone with a momentary glare as she made her point. When only murmurs responded she let go of my hand and began to re-style her olive coloured hair. To anyone who didn't know her this action hardly meant a thing. But to me, that was a clearer sign than a sky painted pink. She was preparing for a fight. A grin formed on my face as I imagined all the ways we could destroy this universal tree and its multiple realms.

'I think it would be wise to calm down.' The smooth voice of the eldest member in this meeting momentarily shattered the fiery hate that was building.

Odin. I'd recognise the old God anywhere.

'Afraid that I'll smite everyone and take your realm?' I took a verbal shot at him, mocking the Gods as I did so.

However to my crushing disappointment the only response I got was the slight crease around his visible eyebrow. The old man's right eye was covered by a leather eyepatch, which to me, made him look like a rip off pirate. Not this grand powerful figure everyone else seemed to believe he was. His ridiculous golden robes annoyingly matched my hair colour, which was a similarity I did not want.

Trying to keep my focus on what I wanted I took my glare off of Odin and turned instead to survey the marble walls. White dripped into grey on each of the room's tiles. The teary colours adding to my stormy mood. Candles hung at knee height casting their light upwards to display the carefully etched designs of sacred animals and beings, or Gods of each realm.

A scoff escaped my throat as I failed to spot any representation of Krone or Overlegen on these walls. I had heard stories that the reason for this was my people's murderous culture. But the truth was they were scared. Rightfully so. We were powerful.

My eyes drifted to the curved, large wooden door that was sealing this room from wandering eyes and ears. If I could I would destroy these caverns. They served as the only place on the Bifröst's path that was unruled by any realm.

There should be no need for a middle ground. Diplomacy was overrated when one of us could rule everything. Sadly, that was a battle for another day.

Right now, Irie and I had one goal.

Before I could speak again a deep rumbling laugh filled the room. All heads snapped in the direction of a tall, frosty skinned man. His hair and eyes were the colour of a midnight ocean. Like all the rest of us he stood behind his chair, no one would risk not having an imposing posture during these meetings.

'Oh how I have missed the sounds of your poisonous voices, and the sight of stale anger in the eyes of those who believe they deserve more.' Jotunheim's ruler had never respected our power.

'Duane, Irie, do tell how you could overpower Asgard.' The threat of his words hung heavy in the air.

He knew exactly what we wanted, and even worse, he knew we had no means of responding. I caught a glimpse of a wicked smile spreading across his pale, blue face as Irie and I locked eyes. We couldn't answer without revealing something. But if we didn't answer we'd be weak.

Deciding for us, Jotunheim's leader continued speaking with his ridiculously smooth voice. 'So as to confirm, Asgard, Midgard, Jotunheim, Helheim, Niflheim, Muspelheim, Nidavellir, Alfheim, and Vanaheim are the chosen heads of realms?'

The woman at the head of the table nodded in conformation.

'And Krone or Overlegen are not?' He continued just to rub it in.

'Correct.' The Midgardian's voice did well to hide her discomfort.

Weak pathetic Humans. I wish I'd said it out loud but my voice was now far too croaky.

Everyone would know that despite being the weakest in the room Midgard still secured a realm over Krone.

I pulled my hands free from the bloody chair, not caring as my hands stung.

'Not to worry my dear.' Irie reached out her scarred hand wrapping it around my right arm. 'Save your power, they'll regret this later.' Her voice was quiet and soothing like a soft wind blowing an autumn leaf to the ground, slowly but surely achieving its goal.

'We'll take our leave.' Irie's voice turned back to bitter as she addressed the room. 'If Asgard could be so kind as to return us to Krone by the Bifröst?'

Odin didn't look pleased but didn't refuse her request as I let her lead me out of the room. As Irie turned back to close the large wooden doors our ears caught the Midgardian woman's voice once more before the doors clicked shut.

'Before the rest of you leave, we discovered something else in Snorri's research.'

CHAPTER ONE

August

'August Frost, you are from Overlegen are you not?'

I did not answer. Man, I hated this guy.

'And you are eleven without powers?'

I kept my expression blank as I stared past Apoint, the deputy of this planet.

We were outside by an awfully large willow tree. The way its large branches draped out in random directions covering this stupid congregation reminded me of the universal tree, Yggdrasil. Unlike the universal tree however there was nothing special about this willow. It wasn't cosmic in size. Its trunk and branches weren't abyss black with speckles of vibrant colours, and it definitely wasn't the Bifröst's path to each planet in the realms.

I sighed as I turned my imagination off. I had people to deal with or I'd become trapped on the worst planet on this branch.

All of Overlegen's people were here sat behind Apoint, their manipulated expressions bleak as they stared at me. *Why would anyone expect anything less from a planet raised to become conceited soldiers?* This planet wasn't the worst out of the three, on this twig-like side branch, but it was a close second.

'Dear August, you are being charged with banishment for failure to conjure powers,' Apoint spat his words as I suppressed a slight shiver.

I hated the word *powers*. Every culture had their own word to explain the abilities some are gifted with. However, on Overlegen and Krone they preferred the term *powers*. Seeing as everyone on both planets had a power, and those who didn't were banished to Anden, they believed the word suited them. I thought it was vain.

Joyful exhalations of air coming from my right increased in noise so I snuck a glance at Overlegen's cloaked hitman. He sat with a hood pulled over his head hiding all of his appearance except for a smug grey smile that I'd rather not see again. If my plan worked I wouldn't have to.

Out of the eleven main branches on this universal tree, nine of them were inhabitable realms, each named after the leading planet. I was located in the Asgardian Realm which was brilliant except for the fact that my sister had chosen the absolute worst branch in the realm to work in. I always imagined the planets lining the branches to be like leaves that never wilted or fell. In my mind the sooner I escaped this small side-branch the sooner I would be free of these terrible people.

'Is there anything you wish to say?' Apoint questioned me.

I stood. This was it.

Glancing to my right I met eyes with my two best friends, proof that there was good amongst evil. The one who stood closest to me was Anjelica Starr. She was a feisty blonde haired girl with pixie blue eyes and a soft splattering of freckles across her rounded cheeks. She had pyrokinesis and was also a lazy telepathic. Recently she had survived Overlegen's challenges, earning herself the title, Firestorm. Title earning was a major part of this realm's culture. They act as a class system along with being shields from various old magics and nasty Gods. All of which seem to be endemic to this realm.

On Overlegen, each year kids with *gifts,* or *powers* as they call it here, are put through tests to prove themselves a worthy part of society.

Alice Wood, my other close friend, had shoulder length brown hair and green eyes. She could control cellular regeneration and very lightly influence the wind. She had recently earned the title, Gale.

A breeze blew by and flicked my golden blonde ringlets across my face, snapping me back to what I had to do. My friends had been briefed and weren't in any danger, yet.

I approached Apoint and the rest of Overlegen's people who were situated below the stage that I was on.

I wasn't from Overlegen, I was Earth-born. Which meant that there was no *natural* way I could conjure powers. Apoint, along

3

with the rest of Overlegen, was choosing to ignore this. Typical. You would've thought they'd learn.

I heard a story that the last guy to be banished to Anden, for lack of powers, turned up fifteen years later with a nasty set of gifts and a bad case of revenge. Unlike him, I was not going to end up on the Kronevian Empire's prison world.

I met Apoint's eyes as I reached the front of the stage. His appearance was bland, just as you'd expect from someone in his position. His hair had almost been completely shaved off and his brown eyes were cold.

'Dear idiots.' I paused, mocking Apoint's previous attempt at formality, as I insulted his people. This wouldn't be the last time I did so. 'You are nowhere near as superior as you think you are.'

'What makes you think that? You worthless girl.' Apoint cut me off.

I held Apoint's gaze as a shiver ran through me. It was time to clue him, and the rest of Overlegen, in on the latest event perplexing me.

'Because, I am not from here and I can do this.' I closed my eyes for a second, focusing on the new cold feeling hiding in my core.

Once I had it in my grasp I snapped my blue gaze open and released an uncontrollable grin as cold swelled through my veins.

'Do what?' someone asked from the crowd rightly confused.

'Just kill the kid!' someone else yelled.

I ignored both of them and fixed my gaze on the river that was peacefully running to my left. I created a mental path from the river to this valley then traced it with my hand. As I did so the speed of the water in the river picked up before it leapt from its banks and attacked.

I met Apoint's stunned eyes as he tried to narrow them into a glare. Dipping my head, in a mocking gesture, I watched for a moment as the water charged towards him overrunning the valley. With Apoint and the people preoccupied, along with the hitman stuck in his own fiery situation, thanks to my friends, we quickly dashed off towards the edge of the planet.

⁕⁕⁕

Only two people were not there to witness my most recent unexplainable event. My sister, Nora, and the leader of Overlegen, Duana.

Duana's lack of presence at my banishment ceremony was disappointing as I would've liked to see her face when she realised what I'd been hiding from her, but it was probably for the better. I hardly had a clue how my gifts worked and Duana's presence would've just added to the pressure.

I do wish that my sister, Nora, had been there though. Ever since we'd left Krone, which was my fault, she'd changed. She had much less to do with me and hardly ever spoke to me about matters deeper than the usual small talk. I knew the reason for her distance wasn't the incident on Krone, she was set to leave anyway. Still, guilt burnt through me that the change in our relationship was my fault. I'd spent a couple years travelling with her after she got her new job, whatever that was. But it had left me feeling homesick and like I didn't belong.

Duana and Nora appeared as Anjelica, Alice, and I walked down the slope of a hill. They were waiting for us across the grassy fields that ran towards the cliffs where the planet dropped off into space. It was starting to turn into night and an amethyst sunset had begun. The sinking sun shed a purple glow onto the few trees that stood silently on the lonely hills. This planet was truly beautiful but its serenity failed to hide the cruelty that took place here. I missed the stormy oceans of Earth. The long hanging grey fog on a chilly morning, and the chaos that ruled over the planet.

As we got closer to Duana and Nora, I was able to make out their expressions.

Duana stood with her arms folded, her blue eyes filled with the same anger that her father's were rumoured to carry.

While my sister, Nora, would not meet my gaze. Sadness and annoyance clawed at my heart. Despite how close we'd been, the aftermath of Krone had left me alone.

Bye Nora. I thought, holding back the only water I despised – tears.

'Honora, will you help sort out the flooding?' Duana asked with a wicked smile, that drew attention away from her sandpaper blonde hair.

I frowned, but remained silent, as Nora headed for the trampled path that wound its way up a grassy hill, eventually leading towards the newly sunken valley. There was nothing Nora, or anyone, would be able to do about the flooding. No one here had a connection with water and, if my guesses were correct, my sister was able to teleport. However, it was unlikely that she would be able to teleport liquids. Just like my gifts, I wasn't sure how she'd gotten hers.

Nora didn't offer me much more than a slant of her head to say goodbye as my eyes followed her until she was out of sight.

'So you have powers now?' The sour voice of Duana drew my eyes back to her.

The wart on the left side of her eye twitched as she spoke.

I nodded in response, being careful not to speak. Duana's gift was that of controlling the actions of those who opened their mouths to speak in her presence.

'Well, where did you steal them from?' The threatening question was little more than a whisper.

I shrugged, once again denying her a vocal response.

'Oh August. You could've been on the winning side. Where do you think you're going to go now? How will you even get there? Don't you know how the untitled are treated?' She couldn't help but laugh a little as she bombarded me with questions.

I frowned at the absurd notion of titles and the fact that she thought I cared. I did, but what annoyed me was that she knew it.

'Firestorm, Gale, what do you two think you are doing?' Duana spoke to them as innocently as she could but not without a sprinkle of her condescending attitude slipping in.

'We're leaving.' Anjelica was bold enough in herself not to fear Duana's manipulation, despite not having complete control or understanding of her gifts either. Even if hers was biological.

'And why would you possibly want to do that?'

'You know what you did you domineering b-' Anjelica's sour remark was cut off by Alice grabbing her wrist and yanking her past Duana.

I sent Duana one last glare before joining my friends.

None of us looked back as we got closer to the cliffs. The air was much cooler over here, causing shivers to ripple over my skin.

Taking a deep breath I committed the musky scent to memory as a warning. Overlegen stunk heavily of oakmoss, a smell that I couldn't wait to never come into contact with again. I drew in another deep breath this time surveying the abyss below as I did so. The lightless gaps between planets and stars looming in the forefront of my mind. I was beyond grateful that I wasn't doing this alone.

When I'd told them my plan Anjelica jumped at the opportunity to leave, she wouldn't survive here much longer. While Alice's parents had encouraged her to escape with us.

'You ready for this?' Alice asked, from my right.

I gave her a nod and a small smile.

Space was well known for being cold and suffocating. Luckily for my friends, biologically they were able to withstand a quick tumble through it provided they land in a wormhole and don't burn up in an atmosphere. I, on the other hand, had no idea whether I would survive this. Being Human, I didn't have a natural tolerance for space or any drastically different gravitational systems. In fact, it was both a miracle and a mystery that my abilities hadn't killed me yet. I let my eyes fall one last time to the cold, musky grass. I had made my decision, it was a surprisingly easy one. However, the consequences I was blissfully unaware of, as my friends and I leapt into the twinkling unknown, would be the difficult part.

CHAPTER TWO

Four Years Later

August

Crash! I fumbled out onto a cold, wooden floor and hit my hand against an extremely sharp blade. 'Ouch,' I mumbled, as I climbed to my feet and looked around.

I was in a rectangular room with wood panelled walls. The windows were huge and displayed the calm waters of the planet. In the centre was a desk. It was golden and vibrant making it seem out of place in the rustic room. Two big, brown doors stood with silent dignity opposite me. I turned and looked behind me as Alice and Anjelica fell through a wormhole and into the room.

'Bifröst, Asgard,' I gasped, as Alice opened her mouth.

'Anjelica,' Alice whispered, and ran over to where my friend was sprawled on the floor with her leg oozing blood.

'I am completely okay,' gasped Anjelica, as she forced herself to stand.

'No, you're not,' came a new voice.

I turned in shock to see who I assumed was Heimdall. He was small in stature but his muscle mass made up for it. He carried the Gjallarhorn and beamed at us with a full set of gold teeth.

'Welcome to Asgard,' he said joyfully. 'Odin will be here to greet you soon. May I have a word with Miss Frost outside?'

Anjelica narrowed her eyes at Heimdall as she adjusted her position, trying to make it less obvious that she was bracing against the wall.

'No you may not, speak to me instead.' She headed towards him.

I wasn't entirely sure that was a good idea, but as Alice and I had both dealt with the nobles on our previous planets, it was in fairness, her turn.

Anjelica hobbled towards the door as her shoe laces began to unravel themselves. She pushed the large door open and gestured for Heimdall to move outside. He had other ideas though and only moved a foot.

Frustrated, she ploughed forward to lead the way outside.

Smack! She hit the floor face first. Heimdall lifted up his foot and I noticed Anjelica's shoe laces now pressed flat against the floor.

'She needs a healer and I really need to speak to you.' Heimdall stared past me as he spoke.

⚘⚘⚘

Asgard's wind was chilly and carried with it the smell of salty water, no doubt picked up from the sea on either side of us.

Asgard's two suns swung in and out from behind the clouds, not shedding any lasting warmth. Heimdall and I stood on a small island that was only large enough to hold the hut that I had just left my friends in. I noticed an ancient looking bridge only a few feet away from where we stood. It arched up before curving downward, tying this island to the land that I could only just make out on the other side of the sea.

'Why have you come to Asgard?' Heimdall asked me as I tugged my jacket closer for warmth.

'It was an accident,' I said slowly, wracking my brains for any useful information on Heimdall.

'Hum,' he muttered. 'Miss Frost, how did you come across your abilities?'

Four years later and I still didn't have an answer, not to mention Heimdall's questioning was making me uneasy so I returned a question. 'Don't you have heightened senses?'

He chuckled. 'You're not the easiest person to keep an eye on.'

I titled my head, unsure what he meant by that. Before he could explain though, four figures emerged walking down the nearest arch of the stone bridge. My hands flexed at my sides as I watched the figures get closer.

'That'd be Odin.' Heimdall's voice took on a softness as he noticed my tension.

From what I knew about Asgard, Odin would be accompanied by Loki, Thor, and Sif, if anyone.

'They're in there?' The woman, presumably Sif, asked me bluntly, pointing towards the hut I was just in as she marched past Heimdall and I.

I didn't respond, unsure what sort of welcome we would receive. Sif didn't care for my lack of response as she continued with her hostile swagger in the direction of my friends. Once she had passed through the monstrous doors I turned my attention to the rest of the group.

Loki was the exact opposite of Heimdall. He was tall, lean, had a white smile and, other than his windswept hair and scars, he carried a deceiving grace.

'How do you do?' He held out his hand as his sentence trailed off, silently asking my name.

'August,' I said, and shook his hand.

Loki's grip tightened to an uncomfortable point. Refusing to bat an eyelid at this, I responded in kind. Despite the slight pain flaring in both of our hands, Loki smiled.

His grin made me uneasy but he released my hand and turned to say, 'Who's next?'

Thor walked over chuckling. He was far more built up than the others, his extra muscle giving him an over exaggerated swagger.

'I have a trick,' he said.

At that moment Anjelica (fully healed), Alice, and Sif came outside and stood with us at the start of the bridge, which surely must be the origin point of the Bifröst.

The colours of the rainbow bridge were subtler than I had imagined, only occasionally catching the light on its cobbled surface.

'Let's see it then,' came Angelica's voice in response to Thor.

He stood a little straighter as he prepared his next words.

'If any one of you three have the strength enough to carry my hammer then you may stay here momentarily. If not, get out. Asgard doesn't need your troubles here.'

The overbearing God shared an unspoken conversation with Loki as he made a show of untying his hammer, Mjölnir, from his belt. Thor raised an eyebrow in question at us.

'Seems like a fair price for a moment to catch our breath.' Alice accepted for us.

Gravely, Thor handed Mjölnir to Anjelica, her eyes widened at the opportunity. She couldn't stop her lips tugging up into a smile as Thor let go of his symbolic weapon and took a step back. Anjelica looked around with a huge grin. Her blonde hair being blown violently across her face as the wind started to pick up.

'Now give it back,' Thor said bluntly, taking another step away from Anjelica.

I stared blankly at him wondering what he was up to.

Anjelica took a step forward but misplaced her weight and collapsed to the floor. She scrambled back up in a grump and dragged Thor's hammer back to him.

He walked towards Alice next. His heavy footsteps shaking the Bifröst. Alice put her hands up and backed away.

'I'd rather not,' she mumbled, but Thor didn't grant her a choice shoving Mjölnir towards her.

She grabbed the hammer and he stepped back. Once she'd heaved herself out of her hunched posture her glare met Thor's eyes at full force. He gestured for her to walk over to him. She sighed, taking a foot off the ground, mistake, as soon as she lifted it she dropped the hammer.

Bang! It shook the bridge as it landed.

'Sorry,' she whispered, and backed away.

Thor reclaimed his hammer and came towards me, but Loki beat him there. He put a hand on his nephew's chest keeping him at bay. 'I think we've seen enough.'

I had never met any Asgardians before but from what I had heard about Loki he was egocentric.

So, why was he being protective?

'No, it's alright, I will give it a try,' I said.

My friends and I could use a place to catch our breath. Both Thor and Loki looked at me. Thor's long red hair waving in the wind while Loki's short brown hair was already too wind swept to move any more. Loki hardly stepped aside as Thor extended his tattooed, iron gloved hand moving Mjölnir towards me. I braced myself for the weight of the hammer. Thor, by far, was the strongest one here.

How was a fifteen-year-old meant to carry his hammer?
It must weigh a ton!

I needn't have worried. Thor passed it at a weird angle and it slipped right through my hands. I reached for its leather wrist strap to stop it from hitting the ground. I braced myself for my shoulder to be jolted out of place, but it wasn't. It hardly even felt as if I was lifting anything. I grinned, at least there was truth in some stories. Only the strongest can wield the hammer but anyone could carry it. Oh, if only Duana could see me now, an Earth-born titleless nobody, holding Mjölnir. I glanced up at the expressions of those surrounding me.

Anjelica was eyeballing Sif with a smug look on her face. Heimdall stared at me with a neutral expression, and Odin turned away when I looked at him. While Loki was staring at Thor, with reticent smiles spreading across their faces. I handed Thor his hammer back.

'Feel free to stay as long as you need,' said Odin keenly, rubbing his hands together as if he was cold. 'I unfortunately have to go. Loki and Thor will show you to the guest house.'

'You don't actually have anything to go to Odin,' Loki said, accusingly.

Odin hobbled over to his brother, getting up close to whisper in his ear. Loki was still standing in front of me so Odin's whisper didn't serve him as well as he might have hoped.

'Forever you shall be known for your misdeeds, failures, and injustices so don't for one second think you'd be worthy enough to call me on anything!' Odin ended his brutal speech with two quickly whipped smacks to Loki's thinly defined face.

'Pleasure seeing you three.' Odin smiled innocently towards us.

I didn't return the smile nor did my friends. Anjelica was glaring needles, and even polite Alice didn't offer a reply.

Odin's square cut beard and his gleaming blue eye added to his look of a weathered warrior but there was nothing about this man that suggested he actually was. I stared at him confused. The image I had developed of Odin was very far from the truth.

He shifted his weight ready to leave but turned to me one last time. 'It is a shame really.'

I hesitated in my reply as I spotted the provoking glint in his eye.

'You'll never get a title now.' He shook his head as the disappointed words left his mouth.

That was it.

Smack!

My hand struck him across the face faster than I thought possible, leaving a red mark.

Why was everyone bringing this up? Did I really just smack the head God of Asgard?

I took a deep breath to cool myself down, as I tried to figure out how I'd become so wound up.

'Not quite strong enough to be noteworthy but good try,' Odin said, chuckling as he hobbled away.

I knew that I should have been thankful for his response but the way he spoke reminded me of Overlegen, which triggered my temper. Usually I was pretty cool minded but I was just about done with arrogant men and women who had far too much power.

I started to move towards him, fuming, but two cold arms wrapped themselves around mine holding me back. Loki.

'I know you don't care for the consequences of this action but you ought to,' he whispered plainly.

Anjelica, also being a vengeful soul, charged after Odin. But out of fear of Odin hurting her, Alice placed a calm hand on the back of our friend's head and she collapsed exhausted from whatever Alice had done.

Alice and Thor had to drag an angry looking Anjelica up onto the bridge and towards wherever we were staying. Alice had somehow exhausted her.

I started to relax when we reached the highest point of the bridge, soaking in the glazed brown view of Asgard. I didn't want to get ahead of myself but this was the best reception we'd ever received from a new planet.

Several turquoise rivers dissected the beautiful green and brown land. My gaze followed one of them to a large, deep blue lake that sat nestled just below large, dark snow-capped mountains. These mountains cast their formidable shadows towards the largest castle I'd ever seen. It sat soaking up the sunlight in its lonely valley. I couldn't make out many details but from what I could see it had several towers fending off the shadows from the looming mountains. The turquoise moat of the castle ran smoothly below a lowered drawbridge. Not far from this a gate glinted as if it were made of gold.

From where I walked I couldn't make out much more of Asgard's landscape. As we began to reach the final section of the Bifröst, Loki struck up a conversation with me. I didn't contribute much, it mainly consisted of him explaining certain features of Asgard emphasising the best place for jump scares. I tried to pay attention, my friends and I had learnt that it was best to know as much as you could about a planet before winding up there. Unfortunately, we learnt that lesson the hard way every time, so it was nice to have a quick rundown of Asgard.

'Do you have any weapons on you?' Loki asked.

I brought my hands up to shoulder height. 'I'm trying to understand how to use my gift.'

'And how's that going?'

'Brilliantly,' I said sarcastically. *I almost always revert back to martial arts.*

Loki grinned, then with immense care he pulled out two throwing stars from his cloak's pocket. One was gold in colour while the other appeared silver. Both eventually faded into a faint blue before reaching the sharp ends at the seven points.

I smiled at the beautiful weapons which reminded me of snowflakes. Loki handed them to me as if handing over a burden. His shoulders drooped as I took them.

This stirred a slightly uneasy feeling as we entered a golden flowered meadow. Sif led the group towards a small, slightly isolated, house.

'Don't touch or try to remove the glowing shape in the centre,' Loki said, as Thor and Alice carried Anjelica into the Asgardian guest house.

'And you're giving these to me because?' My question was received but went unanswered as Loki's attention was purposely diverted to Thor who was now heading towards us.

'Did I just see Loki being nice? Man, that is a rare sight. I feel so honoured.' The God grinned mockingly.

I took the hint and walked away from Loki and Thor, not wanting to be anywhere near the two bickering Gods.

⋙⋘

Asgard's suns rose and the warm light swam through my vision until I flicked my eyes open and got up. After donning a blue armoured t-shirt, my black leather jacket, and matching coloured jeans, I stalked quietly out of the room and into the wooden floored hallway.

Scampering past Alice's room, who was undoubtedly still asleep, I spotted Anjelica as she swung the bathroom door open, making me jump just a little. She didn't even notice me as she returned to glaring at herself in the mirror while attempting to brush her hair.

I kept walking until I reached the kitchen where I ripped off a corner of an Asgardian bread loaf. It had been baking in the oven when we arrived yesterday, leaving the house with the wonderful scent of baked bread. Asgardian bread was soft and melted a little in your mouth.

Enjoying the blissful food, I left the kitchen to locate my boots and Loki's weapons. They were by the door, just where I'd left them. After putting my boots on I reached and cautiously picked up the throwing stars Loki had gifted me. The metal wasn't the soothing cold I was used to. Despite being left out overnight they were warm as if they had been next to a fire. Deciding to research this later I tucked them through my belt and headed outside for a breath of fresh air.

It was nice to take a moment to absorb the fresh green and brown scenery before Anjelica joined me outside. She was wearing a hoodie and a maroon skirt, paired with her knee high boots and a sword tucked through her belt. She had obviously given up on brushing her hair and it was down.

'What did I miss?' Alice asked, leaving the wooden cabin.

She was wearing a very pale yellow armoured t-shirt and dark grey trousers. An axe was strapped to her back and she wore comfy running shoes. Her brown hair hung at shoulder length.

'Nothing really,' Anjelica responded.

I turned away from their conversation to look across to the other side of the valley. Morning dew hung on the grass and flowers, filling the air with a refreshing chill as the sun slowly melted it away. I couldn't remember a time when I was able to feel this peaceful.

Odin's chestnut palace was on the far side of the meadow. It sat shining in the early morning light. Its carefully cut edges cast small shadows onto the ground. Though my peaceful state shifted when I spotted two people by the moat.

Being cynical, by nurture not by nature, I watched slightly suspicious of the two casually dressed people wandering discreetly up to the palace. They cast subtle sweeping glances between each other, and their surroundings, before heading out of my sight.

I was so absorbed in their concealment that I didn't even notice Sif's approach until she spoke. 'Come and visit our training grounds.'

She had her long golden hair tied back in a braid and her arms folded. I got the feeling she didn't like me that much as she eyed me before turning rudely on her heel and heading back from where she came, as if she expected us to follow her. We did.

I walked at the back of our small group in silence while Sif chatted to my friends, mainly Alice. Anjelica watched her feet as she plodded along the dirt path and contributed to their conversation when she felt it was least convenient for Sif.

I gripped my left hand trying to massage the nerves out of my fingers while admiring the two beautiful forests that shouldered the path. To my left were dewy ferns that ran their emerald fingers across the soaked trunks of towering eucalyptus trees. The forest was too dense to see more than a few trees in and the only noises to be heard were that of screeching birds. While on my right was a more spacious woodland. The golden bark of the hibernating coniferous trees reflected off the beautiful pillows of snow that lay waiting at their feet. The smell of fresh snow relieved the tingling in my fingers and so I moved to walk along the edge of the wintery forest.

'What causes the difference in climate?' Alice asked, trying to keep the awkward conversation flowing, while Angelica decreased her pace until she was walking next to me.

'I could not tell you,' Sif answered gracefully, allowing the conversation to die.

'I would've thought Thor's wife would be nicer,' Anjelica whispered.

The crunching of my black combat boots on the snow and our distance were the only things disguising Angelica's words.

I grinned before responding. 'The nerves in my fingers are going off.'

'Ah yes, your sixth sense.'

'Seventh.'

'Which, may I remind you, is only accurate half the time.'

'Hey, you're the one who said you didn't like her.'

'No, I said she was mean.'

'So you think she's fine?'

'Well no, but I haven't really talked to her.'

'You just were.'

'Was I though?'

I sighed, fighting a smile. Most of our conversations were like this. A back and forth of disagreement just to subtly reach the same silent conclusion.

Anjelica wore a giant grin on her face as she stared at the back of Sif's perfectly styled head. I didn't even bother to wonder what she was thinking. Finally we reached a giant opening, a sort of pebbled courtyard surrounded by sections, which I guess represented the four seasons. There were groups sword fighting in the shade by two overbearing oak trees. Asgardians crouched alone playing with fire and weapons. In the direct solar heated heart of it all was a small mountain of rocks with a spear impaled through its centre. We followed Sif around as she briefly gestured to the different parts of the training grounds, which I hoped at least Alice was paying attention to. I was too busy focusing on how the light bounced off the bronze metal of the spear and reflected upon the trees that stood marking the sections of the seasons; one with green leaves, red, no leaves, and blossoms. This place was absolutely breathtaking. Warning flashes of Overlegen's serene scenery flashed through my mind but I pushed it away. I wouldn't let my worry ruin Asgard. For now I just wanted to enjoy the beautiful and surprisingly comforting place, before all of Helheim inevitably broke loose.

'Wow,' Alice said, 'I love it.'

'Have fun.' Sif smiled for the first time before she walked away leaving us alone in the middle of a place none of us had ever even fantasised about.

'Training, we haven't trained properly since Overlegen,' Alice said with a sad smile, as if realising for the first time how long we'd been on the run for.

'We should challenge someone.' Anjelica was starting to get excited. 'Isn't that what you're meant to do in these places?'

'Who?' I asked, looking around for anyone who looked like a challenge.

'Them.' Alice pointed.

I followed her finger and eyed up our competitors. They were a group of boys sitting outside the Autumn section. One of the taller ones sat on the centre of a log, with a huge grin on his face, leaning forward forearms resting against his thighs. His gaze followed back and forth as his scruffy brown haired friend talked loudly with his hands.

The guy next to him was repeatedly striking two rocks against each other, his hair darker than my jacket. The fourth member of their group was sitting on the ground in between two rocks. He was paler than the others and had fluffy blond hair. They looked about our age.

Deciding to challenge them, Anjelica, Alice, and I, approached. I met the deep blue gaze of the taller one as his attention shifted to us. He had slightly tanned skin and wavy dark brown hair. He wore a denim jacket which sat snug around his athletic shoulders and blended in with his shirt and dark jeans. His blond friend stood to face us and I was shocked by the intensity of his hazel eyes.

'My friend here reckons she can beat you guys in a fight.' Alice smiled at them with her diluted green eyes.

'Which one?' the guy in denim asked.

'Either.' Alice shrugged.

'I don't think so.' The messy haired guy swept the fringe, that was attacking his forehead, out of his pond green eyes.

'Wanna bet?' Anjelica said, provoking a toothy smile from the guy.

'Why not a challenge?' The guy striking the rocks put them down.

He too had green eyes but his were darker than his friend's. He wore grey jeans and a deep red shirt that pulled attention away from the blond's black and white outfit. Out of the group he was built with the most obvious muscle.

'Who are you?' the guy in denim asked, looking at me.

'August. These are my friends, Alice and Anjelica.'

He got up and walked over to me without a word or gesture in response. Pausing once he reached me, he held my gaze for a while.

'Are you the August that screwed over Krone's leader?'

I stared at him, truly shocked. Not even Anjelica and Alice knew too much about my time on Krone.

'That would be me,' I answered, cautiously.

This was the longest time my friends and I had been welcome on a planet in a while and I didn't want to ruin it. Tense, I stood still as he took a step closer to me, stopping within the perfect distance to be a threat, but instead a large grin appeared on his chiselled face and he offered me his hand.

'I'm Ace, it's nice to meet you.'

Relieved, I took his hand and returned the smile.

'I'm Alec.' His blond friend waved at us. His freckles curving up with his smile.

'Ash.' The ex-rock striker dipped his head.

'And you are?' Anjelica asked the messy haired guy.

'Wouldn't you like to know,' he teased.

'That's Anakin,' Alec answered for him.

❧❧❧

We all headed towards the Spring section of the court, which led to one of the forests we'd walked past. The boys stopped walking when they reached a large body of lime green solution that to me looked like one of the sulphur lakes that resides on Earth. The crusty yellow surface was releasing a red steam that turned clear not long after it was evolved. Neither of my friends made a comment but I heard Alice take a deep breath.

'Really man?' Ash punched Anakin lightly in the shoulder.

Anakin offered his friend a contemptible smile before turning to face us.

'So basically, you have to find a way to cross the pond using either your abilities or, if you don't have any or they're not relevant, ingenuity. Good luck.' And with that perky ending to his serious explanation Anakin placed one perfectly white shoe onto a thick clump of purple that had only just materialised.

With each step Anakin took another thick, purple clump formed just large enough for his foot and just buoyant enough to stop him from sinking into the acidic waters.

'That's got to be bacteria,' Anjelica muttered.

'But it's purple,' Alice responded, only loud enough for Anjelica and I to hear.

'Bacteria can be purple,' Anjelica defended herself, not matching Alice's volume.

'He can communicate with living organisms,' Alec told us, trying to hide his amusement.

My eyes followed Ash as he wandered over to one of the oak trees that stood near the sulphur pond. He grabbed a fallen branch off of the grassy ground and came back towards us just as Anakin reached the other side. Crouching at the side of the pond that gave him the easiest reach into the middle, Ash pushed the branch into the acidic water. Hastily, he ran back over to us then jumped from our side of the pond onto the branch that was slowly disintegrating. Ash made the jump perfectly balanced, to my surprise, as he'd jumped way too far for anyone else to use his tactic. He bent his knees to make the second part of the jump, and I watched, eyes wide, as he reached the other side. Barely. His shoes skimmed the sulphur but otherwise he'd made it.

'Sorry bro.' Anakin helped Ash up who just brushed him off with a relieved flash of his teeth.

I looked at Alec to ask what Ash could do.

'Enhanced speed and strength,' Alec answered, before stepping up to the edge of the pond.

Alec closed his hazel eyes, his blond fluffy hair stopped moving in the wind and then he morphed into a dragonfly. I couldn't help but blink as a little sparking sound filled the air. The noise being the only sign that something had happened. Gracefully the emerald dragonfly, with sequinned wings, fluttered at breakneck speed across the pond.

'I've always wanted to meet a shapeshifter.' Alice grinned in awe.

Alec in dragonfly form reached the other side of the pond easily but kept flying until he landed on the branch of a nearby tree. We all stared in sheer veneration. The large eyes of Alec glanced around.

'That's so weird,' I mumbled, to no one in particular, looking at the pink coloured lump at the end of dragonfly Alec's abdomen.

Then, without warning, Alec was sucked backwards into the mouth of an extremely well camouflaged chameleon, shrouded by the leaves of the tree.

'Huh!' I gasped as Anakin ran over to the tree.

'Alec!'

'What the?' came the voice of a shocked Anjelica.

'What's going on?' The sound of Alec's voice confused me but pulled my attention to the empty space next to Anakin where Alec morphed out of chameleon form.

He had a large grin on his face and had a hand on Anakin's shoulder as he bent over his knees laughing.

'Welcome to Asgard,' Anakin gasped out in between laughs.

Alice folded her arms. 'That was not funny.'

'I mean-' Anjelica stopped herself from finishing that sentence.

Taking my thoughts from Alec's prank and back to the challenge, I stared at the large sulphuric pond hoping an answer would present itself. My friends and I had gifts that gave us benefits in fights not getting places.

Anjelica must've been thinking the same thing as she poked me.

'What am I meant to do? Set it on fire? What are you gonna do? Make a wave?'

'Freeze it?'

'That might work. It would have to be really thick and cold ice though.'

Anjelica and I continued staring at the lake as we conversed.

'And we'd have to run.' I giggled as I said the words, and Anjelica joined me in laughing at the impracticality of our idea.

'Alice? Have you got anything?' I asked, as Anjelica and I turned towards her.

She stood with her arms folded and a blank expression on her face as she shook her head in response. Looking past her I watched as Ace emerged from the tree line with a thick rope in his hands. His serious expression flashed to amusement when he realised I was watching him.

'I'm guessing none of you have seen rope before,' he teased lightly as the others also turned to watch him leave the tree line.

'You're the cousin of the prince not the prince himself. That means you're just as special as the rest of us,' Anakin teased back from his side of the pond.

Ace cracked a full smile in response to Anakin. Their inside joke didn't carry any weight for my friends and I, so we went back to plotting. That's when a thought struck me.

'Ace.' I wandered over to where he was.

'August.' He greeted me with a smile then returned to unravelling the coiled rope.

'I'm not entirely sure what your plan is with that, but potentially we could help each other out.'

He paused looking back at me. 'Are you suggesting we work together?'

'I might be.' I shrugged.

'And why would you want to do that?' His eyes flicked behind me to Anjelica and Alice who were no doubt on their way over.

'Well, based on the fact that your friends were surprised when you emerged with a rope, and the fact that you're not already across the pond, I'd say you're in a similar situation to us.'

I gestured to myself and my friends.

'Brilliant minds, unfavourable circumstances?'

'Sure. What do you say?'

'Alright. What have you three got?'

Ace dropped the rope the second he agreed, the only sign that he was glad to be ditching his original plan.

'Fire, a gentle breeze, and ice.' Anjelica gave him half the picture.

'I've got telekinesis...' he responded, with a slight hesitation cutting off the end of his sentence.

He wasn't giving us the full picture either.

'Explains the rope.' Anjelica nodded at him while Alice and I shared a glance questioning the logic of our friend.

'Permission to move you to the other side of the lake?' Ace asked Anjelica and Alice.

'Please,' was Anjelica's response.

While Alice just shook her head obviously not comfortable with the notion of letting someone control her movements. I didn't blame her.

'Oh Ace, just so you know, I have weak telepathy and I can set you on fire so don't try anything, okay.'

'Wouldn't even think about it.' Ace reassured her before raising Anjelica up off the ground by twisting his hand around, he then proceeded to fly her across the large pond.

'No way man, no teamwork,' Anakin grumbled.

We ignored Anakin's cheap remark. Ace looked back to Alice once Anjelica had reached the other side. Inclining his head in question. She took a deep breath then gave him a nod. Once again Ace used his hand to control his telekinesis and brought Alice to the other side. I was far from an expert in gifts but I had the impression telekinesis was a mentally controlled thing. Once Alice was safely on the other side Ace looked at me. I extended my arm, thankful for the cold feeling surfacing. I blew three cold sheets of ice across the sulphuric surface.

'Fancy a skid?'

'So that was fun but you promised me a fight.' Anjelica pressured Anakin after everyone had made it across.

'Let's go to the Autumn section, there tends to be less people there,' Ash suggested.

He was right, it would be hard to fight with so many other groups dotted around.

'That's because everyone always slips on the dewy leaves,' Alec explained, as we all walked past the large spring tree and back into the centre of the court towards the section that had an orange glow.

The warm colours from the trees and cluttered floor was absolutely stunning. I turned around slowly, admiring the scenery, Asgard was a truly amazing place.

'No killing, maiming, or using abilities.' Alec laid out the rules clearly.

'Once someone defeats you, you're out,' Ash added.

'Ooh, last chick standing, love it.' Anjelica grinned.

'What makes you think one of you three will win?' Anakin attempted to annoy her.

I turned away before she could respond and headed into the woods as everyone began to disperse subtly into the surrounding trees. Once deep enough, I put my back to a tree and glanced around the sunset forest. It was the kind of silence that is only heard in the dead of night. The kind that makes you pull your covers closer and squeeze your eyes shut until dawn breaks. But I kept my breathing normal and quiet. *Why am I so competitive?* I heard the crunch of footsteps to my left so I set my eyes there, watching silently as a figure rounded a large tree.

CHAPTER THREE

August

It was Alec. His fist shot out as he came to stand directly in front of me. I ducked and stepped forward ramming my elbow into his guts. He reared downward on the impact and I narrowly avoided being headbutted as I pulled back. Without taking another moment to recover, Alec sent a leg swinging towards my side. Sacrificing for the sake of my next move, I took the impact as I stepped in. He managed to parry my elbow with his arm but it didn't matter. I relaxed my elbow into a grab and spun him off balance. Not giving him time to fight, out of the angular position that I was holding him in, I swept his legs out from under him. The ground was so soft, hardly letting off a thud from the impact, which made me feel better about using that particular move. I dropped with a half-hearted punch and hovered just above his neck.

'Where did you learn to fight?' Alec asked, staring up at me.

'Oh you know, the two planets that hate Asgard the most,' I answered genially, offering him a hand up.

'That bodes well,' he responded playfully, as I pulled him to his feet.

We shared a respectful nod before he turned back toward the clearing and I continued forward through more leaves and trees. My careful footsteps were halted by the sound of voices.

'Is that all you've-?'

'You-'

It sounded like Anjelica to me, so carefully I continued towards the sounds. It was Anjelica and Anakin. What a shock. They were wrestling in the clearing at the entrance to the Autumn section. Alec and Alice sat on a nearby fallen tree. Like me, they were watching. Ash, Ace, myself, and the two throwing sloppy punches in the clearing, were the only ones left. Anjelica kicked Anakin in the leg and he responded by grabbing her wrist and twisting her into a wrist lock. Anjelica was forced to let Anakin throw her onto the soft ground as she had no clear desire for a broken wrist, but the second she hit the ground she kicked his legs out from under him. Ash walked quickly past them and joined Alec and Alice on the tree.

Wait, that must mean that... A warning tap to my shoulder verified my assumption. Ace. Before I could do anything my oxygen supply was put under pressure. Relaxing into his grip I let him take my weight. Twisting ever so slightly I kicked his closest leg, knocking him off balance, and thus freeing myself. He was more prepared for my escape than I realised as he landed a smooth elbow to my side. Breathing through the pain I kicked outwards, changing my direction at the last second to make contact with his stomach. He went with the momentum choosing to crumple and roll backwards.

Damn it! I'd been trying to master that move for ages and he made it look so easy. My moment of annoyance and admiration gave Ace the upper hand, and he scored a kick to my thigh before I even processed that he'd come back into distance. Our forearms smashed into each other as I parried his next attack. I fired back with my free arm but Ace didn't care to block. He leant away as his foot flew into my shin. Once again, ignoring the pain, I kept my arm across his chest and swept his legs in the other direction, knocking him over with ease. Unlike Alec, Ace gave me no chance to hit him while he was down. He rolled swiftly into a sitting position and charged to the side, grabbing a shiny object before he stood.

Crap, is that a sword? Ace moved the concealed weapon into view, displaying what I was up against. *How had I not spotted the sword?* I reached for my belt and pulled out the only weapons I had on me, Loki's throwing stars. *This was going to be interesting.* Ace stepped forward pointing his blade at me. He was letting me make the first move. *Don't mind if I do.* Carefully, I threw the spiked star at his left shoulder. Ace deflected with ease and took a step forward with a slash. Stepping out of distance, I aimed my last throwing star and sent it spiralling for his shoulder. He side stepped with a smooth parry, but to both of our confusion the other throwing star came hurtling through the gap back towards me.

What? It kept flying straight for me. I sidestepped but it arched, slowing its spin mid-flight as it continued towards me. I waited until it was within an arm's reach then reached for it hoping to catch it just as the leading point rotated. The second the warm metal stopped spinning between my fingers Ace's sword sliced through the air again. This time I ducked, checking with the back of my arm as I threw a punch into his stomach. I stood just in time to see my second star come hurtling back towards me. This one I didn't catch as gracefully. Blood dripped from two of its points as it stilled. I didn't have time to worry about this, I wanted to win. My next few attacks hit their mark, as I avoided Ace's blade with ease. After another duck, and hit to his guts, he decided to attack as I reared back. This caught me by surprise but my reflexes managed to throw both my arms up before his blade could reach me. Only it never did. Instead I was thrown backwards into a tree by a hit from the pommel of his sword. He'd feinted, and I'd bought it! Frustration rippled through me as oxygen left.

'Had enough?' Ace asked as he placed his sword at my neck.

I wish I had a sword. Then we would see who'd had enough. But all I had to work with were throwing stars. A rather uncommon weapon. No wonder Loki wanted rid of them. They're unhelpful and they chase you around. Deciding to try to use them like knives

I brought my hands closer, but they felt heavier than before. Confused, I snuck a glance down. In my hands were two perfectly cut blades, shaped similarly to Katana. I did a double take, this couldn't be real. It was. Now grinning, probably from ear to ear, I brought a blade upward and smashed Ace's away from my neck. He stumbled back, somehow managing to mask his surprise as a gleam entered his eyes. We slashed at, and parried each other for a while, covering quite a large portion of our surrounding area as we did so. Frustratingly, he was even better with a blade than he was without one. Fortunately for me, I had an advantage. I sprung forward with a one bladed attack. This was a new tactic. He kept his eyes on my spare blade as we fought.

I'll have to make it more complicated. Increasing the speed of my movements I changed lines with each new attack and riposted quickly after my parries. Eventually his eyes focused on the blade in front of him. Perfect. I stepped forward, holding his parry, and with my free sword pressed it to his neck. I knocked his sword from his hands as he held my eyeline with a reticent expression.

The sounds of insults up ahead brought my eyes to the clearing where Anjelica and Anakin were sprawled on the leafy forest floor. Both locking each other in uncomfortable looking positions.

'On three,' Anakin whimpered.

'Three,' Anjelica cried, and they both tapped out at exactly the same time.

Shoving each other as far away as possible in absolute disgust. I looked back at Ace.

'Had enough?' I returned his courtesy.

'No,' Ace said, with a tilt of his head and a quick flash of a sneaky grin.

I felt a check on my left sword arm and a pang in my leg before finding myself staring at the autumn canopy. I wasn't winded which meant that I had obviously dropped my weapons to allow myself a proper landing.

Did I really just lose to an Asgardian? I sat up quickly, too quickly. Causing the autumn scene in front of me to fall into a slowly descending spiral which put pressure on my eyes. I closed them and dug my fingers into the damp earth while I waited for the blood to drain out of my head.

'You're from Midgard aren't you?' Ace's question forced my eyes open.

Frustrated, I climbed to my feet, and began brushing the leaves off of me.

'Humans are not the only species to get dizzy. What makes you think I am one?'

'Well you're not from Overlegen that's for sure-' Ace was cut off by the look on my face, not that I knew what it was, but it was enough to stop him midflow.

It wasn't that I was ashamed to be a Human. It was more that in this realm it was considered a weakness, and that was not something I needed piling onto everything else. Not after what my friends and I had been through. It was hard enough being three teenagers on the run, desperate to escape that dreadful branch. We also had to deal with the fact that we were being hunted by Overlegen's high ranking officials, and I didn't have a title, which made safety here rather elusive.

'August, if I meant offence either you would be in tears right now or I'd be lying unconscious on the ground. Seeing as your eyes are dry and I'm still conscious you can trust I didn't mean it as a weakness.' Ace's words washed over me like a deep breath.

My shoulders relaxed and I detached my hand from the tree that I hadn't realised I was balancing against.

'Here.' Ace extended his two denim protected arms towards me. In his hands were my new swords.

'Thank you.' I flashed Ace a small smile before taking back my weapons.

෴෴෴

I spotted Loki as soon as we walked out of Autumn and into the main clearing.

'Excuse me guys,' I said, and headed towards him at a fast pace.

He stood with a hand on his hip facing the large spear in the centre of the rock pile that had caught my attention earlier.

'What's with these?' I asked, holding up the weapons I'd returned to throwing star form.

Loki spun around as if he'd been expecting me. Instead of responding he just shrugged his coat hanger shoulders.

'Everyone paints you as a selfish villain, isn't this the opposite?' I questioned, not settling for no reply.

'Well you have to confuse people once in a while,' said Loki mischievously, still not giving me a clear explanation. 'No one can beat you if they don't understand you.'

His words seeped into my memory. They surprisingly made sense. I screwed up my lip, still not sure about Loki.

'So why did you give them to me?'

'I didn't want them anymore. You seem like you can handle them.'

I held his gaze for a minute, hoping that he'd offer up an answer, but he didn't mind the silent questioning. It seemed I was losing fights today. *Probably just tired.*

'Thanks, I guess.' I offered Loki a small smile before walking away.

Heading back in the direction of my friends, my mind trying to calculate every possible reason Loki might want to give away shapeshifting weapons.

The boys had kindly walked us back to the guest house on their way home. Upon returning we had realised that there was a large thermal pool behind it.

Anjelica, Alice and I now sat in it talking while watching the suns set. We had told the boys we'd probably see them tomorrow and had a quick dinner before venturing into the pool. The warm, slightly bubbly waters were another of Asgard's relaxing features.

'Did you two see those men sneaking into Odin's palace this morning?'

The glance Anjelica gave me, in response, told me she suspected the same as me.

'What?' Alice asked.

'You know Alice, it's Overlegen's standard attack procedure,' I said.

'Well let's go, we don't need to stay,' she reasoned.

I looked away and took in more of our sunset surroundings. Normally we would but I wasn't leaving here yet.

'Why do we care?' Alice asked, understanding my silence.

We hadn't been here long and weren't a hundred percent sure we could trust anyone.

'Alice,' Anjelica remarked in a shocked manner. 'I thought I was the cold one.'

'No, you're fire, not ice, that would be August,' Alice responded, not in the mood for funny banter.

We sat silently in our own thoughts taking in the scenery as the two suns left the sky and the last light of the day began to fade. For the first time in our four years, of running from Overlegen's hunters, I actually felt safe and slightly relaxed. Even if Loki had given me a strange gift, and there was an imminent attack coming. For the first time I felt like we'd stand a chance if we stayed to fight.

Long after the stars had replaced the suns we all retired to our rooms. I lay staring up at the ceiling, or the art on the walls, for a while. The cabin wasn't much in comparison to the rest of Asgard's extravagance but it was still fitted with everything one would need. The beds were even comfortable! My mind, however, was far too busy to let me sleep. I continued tossing and turning for a while before I got up and wandered into the kitchen. Not long after I sat down on the wooden chair right next to the kitchen counter did Alice come to join me. She poured two steaming cups of tea before taking the seat next to me.

'Thanks,' I said, as she handed me the warm mug containing liquid comfort.

'Do you think Apoint is running the attack?' Alice asked, getting right to her point.

'I don't know. Tomorrow I might try snooping around Odin's palace, in case they left a mark,' I responded, the warm liquid making me feel a bit drowsy.

'Should we fill the boys in?' Alice questioned casually.

Surprisingly, a warm feeling flowed through me when I thought about today's events but my logic gave my answer to Alice.

'No, we don't know them.'

I took another sip of my tea. It wasn't too sweet and it was the perfect temperature. Just what I needed.

'We might need them,' Alice muttered, before taking a sip.

How did she go from not wanting to help to wanting to get everyone involved?

'Agreed, but let's be sure before we alert the Gods.'

She gave me a warm smile in agreement.

'Would you stay? If you could?' She looked up from another sip as she spoke.

I pondered her question while taking another sip from my mug.

'Would you?'

'It would be nice not to have to run any more. We are only fifteen. There are adults who haven't been through half of what we have.'

'How boring.' I attempted to lighten the mood a bit with a half-hearted joke.

Alice flashed a brief grin.

'Do you regret leaving your family?' I immediately regretted asking her this.

We normally avoided the conversation of parents, especially when Anjelica was around, but I couldn't help but feel a bit sad for Alice. Especially now if Overlegen was on our doorstep and we might actually stay this time. Anjelica and I didn't have much choice but to leave, but Alice, she chose to leave so that she could help us.

'Well, between your desire to prove yourself and Anjelica's moronic ideas, I would just feel like I was missing out. And besides I don't feel like being used for my powers until I had no emotion left to use.'

I gave her a warm smile.

'Don't forget you contribute to a rather significant amount of the trouble too.'

She almost spat out the sip she'd just taken.

'How so?'

'You rub people the wrong way with more ease than Anjelica and I combined,' I reminded her.

This time there was a strong flicker of pride in her green eyes as she smiled back at me. I finished off the rest of my tea before saying good night to Alice and heading back to my room.

⤷⤶⤷

Banging on the front door dragged me out of my sleep. Quickly I got dressed into a similar outfit as yesterday. Grabbed my throwing stars, which were in sword form, and opened the door. As it swung open Heimdall and Thor were revealed, standing there rather impatiently. Both of them looked equally concerned.

'What's wrong?' I asked cautiously.

Bracing myself for another randomly catastrophic event that would send us tumbling off yet another planet. We'd spent years attempting to get off Overlegen's branch, on Asgard's Realm, and when we had finally escaped it was due to an accident.

'We haven't seen Loki since yesterday evening,' puffed Thor.

His red hair a mess and his general dishevelled appearance told me he hadn't slept. I looked between them, confused but a little relieved. It is well known throughout the universe that Loki disappears from time to time.

'I know,' Heimdall said, seemingly reading my mind. 'But more than 20 people have also gone missing.'

Oh. 'What does this have to do with me?' I asked, on the edge of becoming defensive.

'We found this,' Heimdall said, holding up a short sword.

Engraved on its hilt was an O and L linked together in an almost overlap – Overlegen's symbol.

I looked up from the sword and saw movement behind Thor. He turned to follow my line of sight and spotted him. Loki. He strode toward us, looking mad. No, not mad, his hair was a mess, foam was forming in his bloodshot eyes, and his mouth was screwed up in pure rage. He carried his shoulders closer to his ears than normal. He took long heavy steps, flailing his hands as violently as possible, and haze was coming from his ears. The God wasn't mad, he was fuming.

I opened my mouth but shut it as Loki pointed.

'No. I'm going to get my darts, revisit those bastards and I'm sure you'll hear about it later.' His words were spat violently at us.

Thor extended his arm, blocking Loki from walking past. His calmness met his Uncle's raging storm.

'Uncle!' Thor said, with a hint of threat in his voice.

Loki glared at him before turning to me, his gaze cold.

'Next time you abscond from a planet, don't come here!'

Despite my urge to, I didn't step back.

'I needed to give you those weapons but don't think for one second it's because I want you and your friends to survive.'

What on Earth is that supposed to mean?

'The nerve of those people to come here and harass me. Me!' Loki continued venting.

The second he took his eyes off me I tuned him out. I needed a clear head, and Loki's rant would not give me that.

'Knew it.' Anjelica grinned.

Her voice bringing me back to our current situation and the arrival of her and Alice. Loki stopped ranting and we all turned to Anjelica.

'We're under attack from Overlegen.'

CHAPTER FOUR

August

Not long after those words had left Anjelica's mouth, a long deep trumpet like sound swept gradually through our ears, bouncing off of every solid object it could find. Before I could fathom what was happening Odin, Heimdall, and Sif stood before us, while the warriors of Asgard began to hasten over. Everyone was dressed head to toe in the most spectacular silver armour. It was form fitting to allow for movement and covered pretty much all of the vital areas. I spotted Ash, Ace, Alec, and Anakin in the crowd of warriors that was gathering, but none of their gazes met my own. I turned my attention to Odin who stood close enough to Thor for me to see him fidgeting with his armour in my peripheral. Throughout the universe, though specifically on Earth, there were many stories about the great feats of Asgard. Each one different and possibly not entirely true, but they all told tales of the skill and tactics of the Asgardian warriors. So I waited in anticipation for Odin or Thor to speak, bubbling with childish excitement at getting to witness one of those future stories.

'My people,' Thor started, his voice bold, 'the military planet of the Kronevian Empire has decided to test us. So we'll show them what we are made of!'

A few grins and cheers erupted from the crowd as we all waited for Odin's plan. But the God's blue eye of wisdom remained fixed on nothing somewhere in the distance. I wasn't the only one to follow his gaze, trying to work out what had grasped his attention. But there was truly nothing noteworthy. Odin was broken. As the vexatious silence continued a small light became doused for me as the truth of reality swept me into a metaphorical wall.

When did I let childhood stories lull me into this lack of clarity? These people weren't heroes, they were simply warriors. The descendants of Gods, other brave souls, and the Gods themselves, all just doing their best to live and protect what matters to them. I took one last awe filled look at Asgard before I let the place of hope and skill fade into fiction. Thor was, at this point, desperately prodding his father in an attempt to get his attention, while Loki hadn't changed from his fuming state. Once again my friends and I had to save ourselves, and the rest of Asgard, in the process.

'Remember the battle on Skjult?' I asked Anjelica and Alice, who were thankfully still standing next to me.

'Oh brilliant! I loved that tactic but I'm not sure we can do that final bit here,' Anjelica said, looking around disappointedly at the end of her sentence.

'We'll just do the first half.' Alice amended Anjelica's idea of the plan.

'You lot come with me,' Anjelica barked, pointing to the group of Asgardians gathered closest to Heimdall.

Not wanting to give up their home they didn't even hesitate to follow Anjelica towards the Bifröst. Whenever we used this tactic she always stole the best job, cutting them off at the feet so to speak. I glanced at Alice knowing full well what move she wanted to make.

'Let us help.' It was Anakin backed by Ace, Ash, and Alec.

'Then two of you come with me.' Alice hardly gave them a second to process before dashing off in the opposite direction to Anjelica.

Her group consisted of Ash, Anakin, and a large portion of the remaining Asgardians. I surveyed the remaining group trying to gauge any other plays we could make.

'Heimdall?' My eyes stopped on him.

It took me a while to fully realise that he was here.

'Why aren't you at the Bifröst?'

He didn't answer, but he looked towards Odin, and I got the message.

'We should go that way.' Odin spoke for the first time this morning.

The nerves in my fingers flared up as I watched Odin and Heimdall dash off.

'Loki you're with me and them,' I said, gesturing to half of the remaining warriors.

'The rest of you go, get your people to safety.'

As everyone scattered I went over to Ace and Alec.

'If the plan works they will flock to the Bifröst. See if you can trap them there and blow them to Helheim.'

I almost smiled at my mischievous twist to the plan that had just formed.

'How do you expect us to do that?' Alec asked.

'Be creative.'

⤢⤻⤢

Loki, the remaining warriors and I, hurried towards Odin's chestnut coloured palace. The golden gate which I had spotted earlier was, in fact, made of spears. Much like the bronze one that stood at the centre of the training grounds. The gate stood open and the drawbridge was lowered over the turquoise water that looked even more appealing up close.

'Is Odin's palace normally this accessible?' I asked the Asgardian, who was keeping pace next to me.

'No, this is not a good sign,' he answered, worry flooding his tone.

Picking up our pace we sprinted into the main room of Odin's stone palace. The floor was made of polished wood, and large decorated pillars adorned the vast empty room. The occasional artefact or weapon pinned to the walls stood isolated even from dust.

'The battle's out there, why are we in here? And why did you want me to come with you?' Loki asked, purely to be annoying.

I kept walking forward with my eyes on the iron doors at the other end of the large hallway we'd just entered.

'Because you would've come here anyway.'

Loki stopped walking and stared at me. 'I thought you'd be above all of that cliché Loki crap!'

I turned to face his glacial gaze, still heading away from him.

'First, you've got to prove that *you* are.'

'You'd argue with a God?' Loki asked, with a trace of approval pleating its way into his words.

I didn't respond. The one thing Overlegenians desire more than causing bloodshed is gold. That way they can kill a planet through violence and poverty. They teach this tactic religiously and it's only ever failed once.

'Through those doors.' The warrior to the right of me pointed.

We burst through the heavy doors into Odin's vault. Loki in tow. Just as I had thought. Two bodies lay cold beside the empty door frame which was surrounded by an army of metal smithereens.

Silently we broke off into groups, each of us heading to a different section of the fortress-like vault. Entering any of them wouldn't be an issue as all of the doors had been torn off. I followed Loki through the farthest door frame.

For future record never let Loki choose the door (frame) you walk through. Relaxed and confident, I walked into the room only to see a Jotnar glaring at me with glowing eyes the colour of which I could not recognise. The giant must have been at least 100 feet tall. I looked up confused.

How would it have even gotten in here? My answer was on the ceiling or merely the absence of ceiling. *How did I miss that?* The storm coloured giant turned, plucking a gold cabinet out of the floor, then snapping it like it was not more than a twig, before throwing it over his shoulder. Loki and I ducked out of the way.

'Excuse me.' It was Loki who spoke.

The Jotnar turned back to us. 'Name's Pebbles.'

Pebbles had a thick, dark grey hide and was dressed in chain mail and leather. He had two boar-like teeth protruding from his lower lip and curving toward his large nose, which had puffy scarring around it. His eyes appeared to have sunk back into his skull likely due to protuberant eyebrows. Thin white lines worked their way down his face to his nose where they disappeared into the puffy scars.

'Pebbles, can you please leave?' Loki asked politely, as if he wasn't even slightly scared.

'Only after I squash you.' Pebbles didn't hold eye contact as he continued rooting around the rubble filled room.

'What?'

'Pebbles wants to kill you,' I clarified, finding my nerve.

'I know that,' Loki spat.

'And the kid,' Pebbles added.

'That's just cold,' Loki tutted.

'Thank you.'

I pulled out one of the swords Loki gave me as Pebbles set his full attention on us. The Jotnar grinned, smashing his arm down, fist closed, right onto where I was standing. Managing to roll out of the way just in time I threw my sword arm outwards, the blade just scrapping through his skin. I watched, waiting for blue blood to come gushing, but instead a thin gold liquid dripped out of the slice.

'That doesn't make sense,' Loki shouted, after seeing it too.

'He's not a real Jotnar.' I realised.

This was an Overlegenian creation.

'Overlegenians,' Loki spat, 'they're so cheap.'

The sound of clapping came from a dark corner beside Pebbles, and I watched as an averaged height bald man emerged from the shadows. Apoint.

'Nice to see you again, August,' he teased, with bitter intent behind his words.

'You've changed,' I responded sarcastically, referencing his now completely bald head.

'Funny.' He didn't sound as if he had appreciated my comment.

'I've got the oversized troll, you deal with the Overlegenian.'

Loki purposely brought up trolls to upset Pebbles – real Jotnar are also known as troll hunters. I didn't need another excuse to attack Apoint so I charged.

Due to the lack of subtlety in my attack Apoint was able to easily side step but unfortunately for him my reflexes were faster than his brain. My left hand struck out to the side, my sword cutting a clean line down his face. He didn't scream, to my annoyance, but instead traced two gloved fingers over the cut as he reached for his sword. He flicked it against my face but I managed to stumble back before any more than a scratch was done. He tried again. I parried but the metal twang disappeared all too soon. Assuming I had miss judged my parry I put distance between us, quickly. But I hadn't misplaced my sword, instead the contact had shattered his blade.

'Wow,' I gasped, taken back.

'You're welcome,' came Loki's voice as he dodged the Jotnar, ripping into its ankle with a dagger that he must have taken from a warrior.

Weaponless, Apoint turned to his last resort, words. 'Names mean everything in this realm, so tell me August, what's your title?'

I bit the inside of my lip, some people are just pure evil.

'What's your gift?' I asked mockingly, knowing full well he had been drained of it by an Álfar long ago.

'At least I have a purpose and place in this realm,' he bit back.

'What's that? Hunting people who pissed you off?'

'I defend the reputation of my planet and people, and yes sometimes that means I get to wipe out trouble like you and your petty friends.'

Hating this conversation, I gave into the comforting cold feeling. Ice formed slowly around his mouth and hands, rendering him silent and stuck.

'August,' Loki commented, blocking a clumsy attack by angling a cabinet over his head. 'Pebbles is better at fighting than I expected.' Loki ducked another haymaker.

'HOW DARE YOU OFFEND ME!' Pebbles screeched.

Loki looked up at him confused. 'What?'

'YOU OFFEND ME!' boomed Pebbles.

'Did I say something or perhaps is it just my existence?' Loki's outwardly mocking comment seemed to have projected from something in his heart, but he kept weaving and slashing at Pebbles as if his voice had never faltered.

'Your words. They hurt more than your puny little weapon.' Pebbles crouched down to try and flick Loki in the head.

Fighting the urge to laugh I ducked in to help Loki fend off Pebbles. The fake Jotnar lifted up a leg to grind Loki to pulp against the fancy flooring. Loki rolled away and I jumped up and hit Pebbles in the nose with the hilt of my sword. I wasn't aiming for the nose, but due to his slow movement out of his squatted position, that was what I hit. I narrowly missed being thwacked by Pebbles' hands as he brought them past my falling body and towards his nose.

'This is not over.' The muffled voice of Pebbles sounded as my feet connected with the ground.

The fake Jotnar then rose to his full height before crumpling. His entire being folded before dispersing into dust and pebbles across the floor by our feet. I shot Loki a questioning glance as a breeze collected the remains of Pebbles and swept them up and away.

'If you haven't already had the ways of old magic explained to you, don't think that'll change today.' The notorious God at my side responded whilst recomposing himself.

I looked back to where I'd left Apoint.

'Are you kidding me?' I yelled in frustration. He was gone.

Internally irritated that Apoint had managed to get away, I led Loki back into the main vault where the, thankfully, large remainder of our party was waiting.

'Only lost two and the enemy has been dealt with.'

I recognised the owner of the voice to be the brown haired warrior who had spoken to me on our way in here. I nodded in acknowledgement, not quite feeling ready for words yet.

I'd had him. We'd almost been rid of him. Almost.

'Half of you should remain.' Loki gave the warrior the order to protect Asgard's, or Loki's, treasure.

I nodded respectfully at the man then followed the rest as they headed silently out of Odin's vault and back out into the Asgardian sunlight. I was relieved to see the green grass and stone streets of Asgard free of Overlegenian assailants. Our plan must be working. In which case it would be best to go and help at the Bifröst where any remaining Overlegenians would be fleeing through the wormhole.

⋰⋱⋰

'Just in time for dinner,' stated Odin, appearing from the shadows by the Bifröst's sort of control room.

His timing couldn't have been more perfect as the last of the remaining Asgardians, Anjelica, Alice, and I had just started to head back to our homes.

Heimdall eyed Odin as he made his way up the bridge to join us in the fading sunlight.

'You, you were hiding?' questioned Loki, who despite glaring, let his blood brother approach him.

Odin put his hands on Loki's shoulders, his eyes taking in Loki's.

'Brother.'

With that lonely stretched word Odin pushed and Loki toppled from the bridge. There was nothing to catch him. Nothing to save him as he fell into the calm waters below. I leant over the bridge watching as Loki hit the blue surface. As soon as he connected with the sea the blue pulled back around him, providing a hole just large enough for Loki to slip through. Dismayed, I watched as he fell through the sea and toward the rest of the lonely and cold realm below.

'Uncle!' Thor's yell was full of panic as he ran from the cobbled bridge towards the hut containing Asgard's wormhole, Mjölnir in hand.

Odin turned grinning. 'One less trickster for the rest of us to deal with.'

I glanced at Anjelica in horrified shock. She was simmering but everyone else had fallen into a stuporous daze.

Loki wasn't that bad. He was misunderstood, and still being held at sword point due to behaviour a millennia ago. Sure he was troublesome but he was a large part of Asgard.

Pure and cold silence filtered out the sun lit air as Thor returned, his steps pounding heavily on the bridge. His head was bowed, shoulders slumped and the usual battle eager expression was completely erased from his face. 'He's gone.'

'Lighten up everyone, he's disappeared countless times before, it's never affected us.'

'You. Affected you.' I heard Anakin grumble quietly, more to himself than his God.

My gaze remained fixed on Thor as movement near his feet caught my attention. Glancing down I watched as a green substance, resembling seaweed, flung itself tightly around Thor's right ankle and leg.

'Thor,' I let out a warning.

Sif ran to help him, her hands reached out desperately towards her husband, but it was too late. Thor was pulled back harshly against the side of the bridge before being flung over. Mjölnir was all that was left by the time Sif reached where Thor had been. The green slime didn't intend on leaving it there. Once again Sif failed to reach out in time as her husband's prized possession was flung strap first off of the Bifröst.

Both Gods had been lost to space. Both Odin's closest relations were gone and he just stood there. Laughing.

Anjelica and I shared a quick glance before we approached Odin. His eyes scanned us, not sure what to make of our approach. We marched him off the bridge before ramming him up against the side of the Bifröst's control room. I held Loki's gift, in the form of knives, against his throat as Anjelica pinned him down.

'Explain yourself,' Anjelica barked at him with disgust.

Odin shrugged so I dug my knives in a little deeper.

'Heimdall wasn't here to protect Asgard as you *needed* to talk to him. You are the most powerful God here and you hid throughout the entire battle. Some of your people have died. You could've stopped that from happening by helping!'

I stopped waiting for his explanation, instead he just sighed.

'You two have quite the tendency for violence. Clearly you haven't learnt anything from your previous *adventures*.' He added emphasis to the last word to make us seem childish.

Odin's eye looked past us to Heimdall.

'You and Sif escort them off the planet.'

Was this really our destiny, to be thrown from every planet?

Heimdall didn't move. He just stood there, his pink eyes tarnished. Sif grabbed my arm with a tight pinch and two men grabbed Anjelica and Alice. Sif walked me towards the door but Odin stopped her.

'Sif, why don't we send them off the bridge?'

It wasn't a suggestion, it was an order. My heart leaped into my mouth. I had abandoned many planets but I've never been pushed off of the Bifröst.

'Odin.' It was Ace who spoke. 'Did you remove your eye or did Mimir?'

'Mimir did,' Odin answered casually, 'but I don't see its relevance here, boy.'

Something changed in Ace's blue stare as Odin uttered the word boy.

'Really? And what did he do to the water you drank?' Ace asked with no emotion, but I could sense his eyes start to glisten with salty water.

'I don't understand how these questions are relevant boy. I am the king of Asgard.' Odin gestured to himself egotistically.

Realisation spread across Ace's face and he whispered something to Alec. Alec gave a subtle nod and approached rather quickly. Snapping his fingers in Odin's face as he reached the God. A snapping noise filled the air as Odin transformed into a tall thin man with knotted black hair and piercing cold eyes. Everything about this guy was a smudged mess. He had dark patches under his eyes and cheek bones. His clothes were dark and tattered and it looked as if any colour on his person had been rubbed out.

'What!' Sif shrieked, outraged, immediately releasing me.

Ace was in front of the impostor in a split second.

'He drugged it, you imbecile.'

Smack! Ace left a red handprint on the imposter's face as punishment, while his other hand gripped the guy's jacket holding him in place. I stepped forward to get a better look at the imposter. As I got closer to his smudged thin features I was hit with recognition.

'Azar.'

The imposter smiled at me. His face twisted with his sneer as he exposed only a few of his teeth.

'Where is Odin?' Anjelica asked him, her tone furious.

'Not here.' Azar gave a wicked wink to my fire hearted friend before daring to speak again. 'Traitor.'

This lone word outraged Anjelica enough to extend her leg, thrusting her heel into his chest. Despite the pain that kick must have caused, nothing but a smug twinkle rested on Azar's face as he too toppled off of the Bifröst.

I was so tense I wanted to scream. We had been tricked and now Asgard was weak, tired, and angry, while Loki and Thor were lost to space and Odin was missing. This truly was the farthest Overlegen had ever taken things to get back at or kill my friends and I.

Surely this was more than just about us? No one bothered to move or speak for a while so I joined them in silence. Staring at the weapons Loki had gifted me while I tried to process yet another strange situation.

'Those weapons of yours are called Mutabilis,' came Heimdall's fascinated tone.

I didn't respond.

'May I see them for a second?' Pondered Heimdall.

I gave them to him, hesitantly. He examined the handle and then changed them into throwing stars. I watched his every move refusing to take my eyes off of them.

'They have names on the blades.' He noticed.

'This one,' claimed Heimdall, holding up the throwing star on the right, the one that glistened silver, 'is called Vorago and this one is Gelu.' He added, holding up the gold based one.

'Cool,' I responded, taking them back protectively.

'Alice.' Heimdall beckoned.

Heimdall pulled out a leaf shaped blade, with a green handle, from his pocket and handed it to Alice. So that's his motive. Heimdall wanted us to go get Thor and Loki. Anjelica, Alice and I had done something similar before, we'd manage to do this. The only thing was that this time we'd be facing the planet that had been hunting us for longer than I'd like to acknowledge. Other than the battle we'd just had this would be the first time we'd actually be heading towards our enemies.

I closed my eyes and sent a wish to anyone who was listening. *Please don't let Thor and Loki be on Overlegen, or Krone, or Anden.* Despite not being super eager to head knowingly in the direction of Azar, the kidnapping, if that's what it was, was sort of our fault. Besides Loki and Thor had welcomed us nicely to Asgard, allowed us to stay, and given me strange weapons. I suppose we owed them a rescue.

I opened my eyes to find Heimdall's pink ones waiting intently. I offered him a nod. He placed his hand on his heart, his way of saying, 'thank you.' Anjelica, and Alice approached me.

'I guess we're the only people they can spare.'

Alice, surprisingly, had a playful tone as she made it clear she and Anjelica were helping.

From the corner of my vision I noticed Ace, Ash, Alec, and Anakin now stood in a circle, rapidly whispering to each other. When they had finished their intense discussion they all turned in unison to face Heimdall.

'We want to come too.' It was Anakin who spoke. 'They're our Gods and extended family,' he continued, with a glance toward Ace.

Heimdall nodded. 'Be careful. Most planets are no place for teens.'

'Well, we've already been to a few,' Anjelica bragged.

'I can tell,' Anakin commented.

'Do you have an idea of where we should start looking?' Alec asked Heimdall.

'Sources say that Azar has been to Vanaheim fairly recently. So I suggest trying there.' Heimdall's voice sounded as if he was miles away.

'Oh and August.' He turned his gaze from the stars to me. 'Njord is away so Freyja will be sat on that throne.'

My heart beats became uneasy under the calm pressure of Heimdall's warning.

CHAPTER FIVE

August

The Bifröst dropped us off in Vanaheim. Its roaring green hills sloped downwards towards the proud, unworn buildings that had been fashioned into architecture so beautiful that even the sun didn't want to look away. We followed a seemingly innocent river as it wound its way towards Njord's palace.

When we finally entered the marble monstrosity we found Freyja sitting vainly on the throne, examining her jewellery. She had long wavy hair that blended from brown down to red and eventually into blonde as it wove around her fragile shoulders. She had fair features but cold eyes that sat close to thread thin eyebrows.

Windows were positioned against the stretches of wall on either side of the room, and the floor was painted more decoratively than the ceiling, which was a bland, lonely pink.

'What are your names, friends?' Freyja asked, not looking up from a ruby necklace. Her voice even and fair.

'My name is Anjelica-' My friend started but was cut off by the conceited Goddess.

'-No,' interrupted Freyja, 'your titles, you should know better than to give your names here.'

Anjelica shot me a worried look that I shrugged off. Hopefully this was the only realm obsessed with politics and obscene formality.

'I am Devil,' started Anakin, and then continued naming the others, 'Chameleon (Alec), Blaze (Ace) and Arrow (Ash). Then there's Gale (Alice), Firestorm (Anjelica) and...'

'August,' Freyja spoke mockingly, finally looking up from her red necklace. 'I was hoping we wouldn't meet again. Shame about your friend though.'

She grinned. Her blunt sentence hitting my nerves, just as she'd intended. The cold feeling began to surface in my stomach, but I couldn't give into my gifts, just yet.

'I suggest you leave, you titleless-' Her long manicured nails tapping on the arm of her chair allowed her final insult to drift off.

'Freyja what's your title?' I asked, to aggravate her. It worked.

She slammed her fist down into the arm of her chair, shattering a crystal nail in the process.

'I am a Goddess,' she shrieked, fighting the urge to stand.

I bit my tongue, trying to disguise my joy at the fact that the Goddess wasn't above petty irritations. She brought her hand up to cup her forehead but in doing so triggered a small arm compartment into opening. It clicked, the sound softly filling the large room.

Without shifting her head position she silently pushed the compartment back into its previous position, before returning to our conversation. As if she hoped I hadn't noticed the movement.

'Girl, don't make me repeat history. Wait outside.'

I rolled my eyes. It's not like I wanted to be in here with her either, but Thor and Loki's lives were at stake. I turned, pretending to leave but stopped before I reached the stupendous wooden doors and closed my eyes. It took me a moment but I found the cold feeling hiding in the pit of my stomach. Focusing on it I coaxed it into my fingers until my nerves were uncomfortably cold. I could feel the surge and rhythm of the river outside, the crash of water against slimy rocks called like a siren, but my mind slipped past it. Freyja was my primary concern. A dehydrated brain has been known to affect memory and I didn't want to deal with a repeat of last time so I focused on the water in her body and willed it out.

'August really?' Anjelica's eyes pierced me as Freyja slumped back into her chair, sweet pouring like waterfalls off her skin. 'I could've used my telepathy!'

'She's going to die!' Alice grumbled at me.

'I didn't remove that much water, just enough to make her memory fuzzy.' I frowned at Alice.

Freyja was a Goddess, it would take more than the limit of my gifts to hurt her. Walking past them I headed over to her chair.

'August.' Alice came towards me, her tone on edge. 'She's a Goddess, you can't just render her useless and then go rooting through her personal effects!'

I took a deep breath. Alice had to be kidding me right now.

'Thor and Loki got thrown off of the Bifröst because we stayed in Asgard too long. Heimdall sent us here. She tries to make that compartment seem as insignificant as possible, and she'd rather argue with me than discuss why we are here. I can't be the only one who wants to see what is in there?'

I gestured to Freyja's throne as I reached it.

'You're not.' Anakin supported my statement, his words suggesting Alice back down.

Alice heeded his warning, retreating away from Anakin who was standing at my back. Turning back to Freyja's chair I clicked open the compartment. Just as before it slid forward with ease. Inside was a small, neatly folded piece of paper with an ink heart drawn lightly on the outside.

'Read it out loud.' Alec's voice broke the silence, like a stone through a window.

Freyja my dear,

I have the snake and the storm. Could use your light to blind the eyes of our enemies. You know where to find me.

Xx A.

I stopped reading and let my hands soften their grip on the note as I remembered seeing Freyja's photokinesis for the first time. The coral blue flash of my friend's hair and then a blinding cold light.

'Photokinesis,' Ace whispered.

'What's that?' Alice asked, a small dose of worry seeping into her words.

I bent down and picked up the note that had slipped through my fingers. Quickly, I folded it back up and placed it away. Anjelica wouldn't meet my eyes as I walked back to where I was before.

'Control of light.' Alec was the one to answer Alice's question.

I nodded my thanks to Anakin before willing water to flow back into Freyja, the borrowed cold feeling sinking with it.

The temporary Queen of Vanaheim sat there like nothing had happened. Anjelica elbowed me lightly. I smiled, and elbowed her back. Our silent and slightly violent way of showing we were still on the same team.

'I thought you knew about Freyja,' I whispered to her, while looking at the faces of my other counterparts.

'I forgot,' Anjelica grumbled. 'It appears that Alice did too though.'

Both of us locked gazes on Alice, who was standing a little further forward. She had her back to us which was probably a good thing.

'Either that or she thought I'd kill Freyja for it.'

'I would've.' Anjelica's response had us both fighting not to laugh, and we were losing miserably.

'I know.' I grinned, trying not to imagine the many different ways Anjelica would go about revenge.

'But I still would've liked an opportunity to practise my telepathy,' she whispered back, when she'd finally composed herself.

'Freyja, where are Thor and Loki?' Ace spoke with no emotion in his voice, though the look he was giving Freyja was enough to make even me shiver.

A long pause followed until finally Freyja recovered her nerve.

'Have they abandoned you?' Her silver voice coating her words. 'How will you survive on your own?'

'Heimdall hears all. We know that you know where they are.' Ace's words were plain and harsh.

'I am not obliged to help you.' Freyja's words, however, did not do such a good job at hiding her emotional state.

'No? But as a Goddess you are obliged to help Thor and Loki.' Alec wisely added, knocking that excuse right off of her tongue.

Freyja scowled.

'The only reason you wouldn't be obliged to help is if someone you love is involved in the matter.' Ace carried on.

'Unless of course Azar is your-'

'-Stop.' Freyja cut off the end of my sentence. 'Blaze, August, get out!'

I paused long enough to whisper to Anjelica as Ace made his way over to me.

'See if you can get a location.'

Her eyes flicked to meet mine for a brief second, a slight twinkle of excitement swirling around the blue. Once Ace had reached me I fully turned towards the door and matched pace with him. Steaming with irritation from having to breathe the same air as Freyja. I held my head high as Ace and I walked loudly down the marble hallway until we exited into the gravel courtyard. From there we made our way up towards the hilltop overlooking the palace, and most of Vanaheim's lands.

'How did she know you?' Ace asked, as we walked through the long grasses.

'She tried to kill my friend,' I answered blandly.

He stopped looking at the view and turned all his attention to me. 'I'm sorry.'

I met his blue gaze, a small bubble of pride forming. 'I said, she tried.'

He grinned, his breath disguising a small laugh as he exhaled.

'How did you and Alec know that Freyja was obliged to help Thor and Loki?' I asked, curious.

'Gods have rules, they are not meant to publicise them but sometimes Loki can't help himself,' Ace said, as a sad expression gripped his face.

After a moment he shook himself free from his memories and turned the conversation back onto me.

'Why are you three being hunted by Overlegen anyway?' His question was belated but still caught me by surprise.

I guess coming to think of it only Heimdall would have known for sure. When he noticed it was taking me rather long to respond he spoke again.

'It's okay.' He turned his gaze back towards the hill we were climbing, as I looked up at him.

'No, it's not.' I started my response causing him to turn back and face me.

He and the others deserved to know.

'I flooded a valley during my banishment ceremony, which the Deputy – who happens to be head of military – was running.

Anjelica verbally insulted the planet's leader, and Alice chose to deprive them of her healing talents when she left with us.'

Ace lifted an eyebrow as I spoke but broke into a full laugh as we reached the top of the hill. Ignoring the view I stared at him, not realising that our story was that funny.

'I'm so sorry,' he mumbled, between laughs. 'They've spent years chasing teenagers across planets only to kidnap the Gods of Asgard when they realised that they couldn't catch you. All because you embarrassed them.'

I nodded before adding another detail.

'You should see what else they've attempted.'

This spurred his laughter on even longer and somehow his hysterics brought a laugh out of me. I'm glad someone was finding amusement in this.

'Unless they have a secondary motive behind all of this, Overlegen is the incarnation of pettiness.' The last part of his sentence had me smirking.

Aside from Freyja, Vanaheim was stunning. The lovely green hills sloped gently across the terrain. The grass was the purest green I had ever seen and the water of the nearby river was almost perfectly clear. We both sat, smiling, in silence, watching as the others finally emerged from Njord's palace.

Alec and Ash waved as the group began heading up the hill towards us. Ace and I stood, brushing any strands of grass off of our clothes as Alec, Ash, and Anjelica joined us. Alice and Anakin were only just behind, not bothered about keeping up.

'We know where they are,' came Ash's voice, as he and the others reached us.

'Where?' Ace asked eagerly.

'A planet called Sandvellir,' Alice said, squinting in the sunlight. 'Though she seemed to give it up rather easily.'

Anakin and Ash looked towards Anjelica as if implying she had something to do with that.

'What happened to Freyja?' I angled the question towards Anjelica.

'Ask no questions, hear no lies.' Anjelica grinned, clearly having too much fun today.

'But seriously, it was a bit easy.' Anakin reaffirmed as a humming entered the air around us.

The continuation of our conversation was suddenly overwhelmed by the unmistakable sound of an engine. I turned my head to the sky as an elegant looking ship plummeted towards the ground not far from us.

'Take cover,' Ash said, and we all dived for the shelter of a large nearby tree.

We'd just made cover as an ear-splitting bang filled the air along with the sickly smell of oil lit flames. As the dust, and thrown up dirt, began to settle, I took a scan of the group. Everyone seemed uninjured. We had all taken shelter behind the largely exposed roots of the tree. Twisting around I glanced up above the root. There was an unusual lack of debris lying on the ground and other than a few small fires there wasn't anything else visibly wrong.

'You better not have scratched my ship, Sian!' A voice rang across the hilltop startling me.

I couldn't tell if it was my ears ringing from the crash or if his voice actually echoed for a while after he spoke. Still peeking over the root I watched as a guy, with carrot coloured hair, pointy ears, similar to those I'd imagine on Álfar, and a pair of round distinctly Earthian glasses, left the crashed spacecraft. He immediately began to survey the ship in a disappointed manner. Not two moments later did a shorter guy, with a full head of pine green hair, come to join him outside.

'Of course I scratched it Pierre.'

'This is coming out of your wages.' The Álfar looking guy, Pierre, pointed at Sian who just shrugged.

'Who are they?' Anakin was also peeking over the tree's root at the two men.

They were unlike any beings I'd seen before. Pierre had strange tattoos that wound their way up his neck, stopping just before his brightly coloured hair. The patterns of which I couldn't make out. Small metal hoops also hung from his ears, nose and even the bottom of his lip. I winced imagining what it would feel like if they were ripped out during a fight. Sian's eyes were squinted and appeared to be sunken in, allowing his green eyebrows to appear more bold. He also had a hoop on his bottom lip and no visible cartilage in his ears. Both of them wore basic, loosely fitting clothes. Unlike Pierre, Sian wore no jacket allowing the tattoos on his arms to be visible.

'Ace, do they look like pirates to you?' Anakin leant to the side, giving Ace a clear view of both Sian and Pierre.

'Oh yeah, they're pirates,' Ace responded, with a hint of apprehension after taking one glance at their tattoos.

'How do you know what pirates look like?' Alice asked, unable to hide her curiosity.

Wondering the same I turned to look at Ace. Anjelica, Alice, and I had been to some dodgy places and never run into Pirates. *So how had he?*

Ace went to say something but changed his mind allowing Anakin to cut in. 'He's got a history with Pirates.'

I frowned. *That didn't make any sense.* On Asgard, Anakin was joking that Ace was connected to royalty and now he was claiming he was a pirate!?

I looked at Ace for confirmation but he gave almost no reaction. His only response being a small, humour filled smile that only added to his mystery.

'Boys.' The voice of a new person distracted everyone's attention.

I followed the new voice to its source; a winged lady with cotton-like blonde hair and tiny green eyes stood at the entrance of the spacecraft. 'It's not that bad.' She brought hands up to her face as she spoke. Her long white nails contrasting against her strongly pink skin.

'Whatever, it wasn't all my fault.' Sian headed towards the entrance of the ship.

He shoved past the woman as he headed back which caused her to turn and glare at him, exposing the two sets of dragonfly wings that sprouted from her back through slits in her dress.

'August.' Alec tapped my shoulder in warning as the sound of footsteps met my ears.

Quickly, I ducked back behind the tree. I couldn't see what was going on behind me so I sat facing Ace and listened.

'What exactly is going on here?' Freyja's unmistakable voice was the first to speak.

'We've crashed.' The rude reply was distinctly masculine leading me to believe it was Pierre who responded.

'Obviously,' Freyja sounded, heavily agitated.

Hopefully that was thanks to our visit.

'We'll be out of here shortly.' This time a silky feminine voice responded to Freyja. The winged lady.

There was a long silence that carried through several long moments. We all sat perfectly still unsure of what was going on.

'And what would be your name?' Freyja finally spoke again.

'Lavita.' The winged lady gave Freyja her name, not her title, without falter. There was also a certain attitude to her voice.

'Lavita is it?' Freyja sounded like she recognised the name. 'I hope to see you out of my realm.'

'Oh of course. Which realm do you head?'

Alice almost gasped at the openness of Lavita's dig. Freyja didn't grant the winged lady a response. Despite the grass, I could still hear Freyja's feet meet the ground as she walked away from Lavita and Pierre. Thinking she had left, I snuck a glance over the root to see Freyja whisper something to her guards before disappearing down the hill.

What was that? I hadn't caught a word. Anakin caught my eye as I glanced around. Once he was sure my attention was on him he mouthed, 'kill them.'

'They could give us a ride,' Ash whispered to the group, as we all shuffled into a tighter circle.

'Or we can take the ship once they're dead.' Anakin volunteered the alternate option.

'Anakin.' Alice ruled out that option.

'What? They're pirates.'

'Including her?' I asked Ace. They'd said something about wages, she might have hired them.

'It's unlikely that she's a pirate.' Ace gave me a clear answer, his eyes free of their usual cheek.

'We might not need a ship though.' Alec added another angle to our situation. 'Heimdall can always open the Bifröst up for us.'

'So, are we going to let them die or help them?' Ash drew us back to the threat of Freyja's guards.

'One pirate and one fairy against six guards.' Anakin counted for us.

'Let's help them, and then work out our next move,' I suggested.

Once everyone had given a nod in agreement we stood and leapt over the tree's root charging towards the guards, who now had knives drawn. The guard closest was too slow with his knife giving me time to kick him in the leg before sending a hard punch into his temple. The guard fell face first onto the hard ground. I paused a moment making sure he was out before I turned to check on the others. The other guards had also been knocked unconscious.

'Where did you..?' Lavita looked around with a panicked expression.

'Thank you.' She offered as realisation flooded her features.

She extended her hand towards me. I shook it, but she didn't let go. Her grip just tightened. I stared at her confused. Unsure whether to tighten my grip too, like I had with Loki, or fight my hand free from hers. Instead small vortexes of water appeared from her fingernails and wrapped themselves around my hand. I felt a weird sensation in my mind but there was nothing I could do as my thoughts were wrenched away from reality.

❧❧❧

I flashed back to Earth, before my gifts. *Why was my mind here?*

'Focus.' The unknown voice had strength.

Strength enough to force me to sit down. Scooping up a pile of sand into my hand I watched as it drained through my fingers. It left a dehydrated feeling on my skin when it had gone. I shivered as a cold breeze blew by. Deciding to move I stood brushing the sand off of my jeans and took off down the beach. Every movement was predetermined, I didn't have any control here. This had already happened. A few metres of calm water to my left met my attention and I spotted a white glint. I had nothing other than my curiosity with me so I plunged into the cold water and headed towards it. The light disappeared when I got to the spot, causing me to curl my lips up at the anticlimactic venture. I looked back at the beach and shivered as another cool wind blew by.

So what. I thought to myself, bent my knees, and submerged my entire body into the ice bath of the Mediterranean. Eyes stinging and lungs freezing, I reached for the shiny object and brought it out of the water. It was a perfectly rectangular rock. Smooth and well-aged. Cut from the front there was a crevice in the shape of the symbol:

$$\Gamma$$

The symbol's bright blue light startled me as it cleared the water's surface. The warmth of the blue was one of the most beautiful colours I'd ever seen. Despite having been in the sea, the rock was rather warm, strangely so in fact. Gradually, it began to heat up my hand. It's heat increasing until I felt my skin start to burn. Reacting to this I dropped it back into the clear waves of the Mediterranean.

⋙⋘

My vision blurred before I was greeted by the questioning eyes of Lavita. Their green being pulled into contrast from her magenta skin.

'Your name miss?' she asked elegantly, finally letting go of my hand.

I didn't know what to tell her. I would rather not give this stranger my name but I had none other to give. I frowned, realising that this was the first time I'd given myself permission to want a title.

Damn, this realm was getting to me. I missed Earth. Lavita smiled, raising her eyebrows at me.

'Riptide.'

The title came out of nowhere but it seemed to fit.

'Would you and a few of your friends like a lift?'

I couldn't respond. I was too shocked. *What had Lavita done to me? Where did Riptide come from? Was it even possible to appoint yourself a title?*

'Quite possibly,' Ash answered, as I squinted trying to process everything that had just happened.

'We'll give you a minute.' She grinned, and headed back towards her ship.

My feet stayed planted as my friends formed a group around me. I tried to decide how I felt about letting the hired pirates and Lavita give us a lift, but my mind remained as blank as a fog covered land.

'Isn't Sandvellir that place we went a couple years ago?' I asked Alice and Anjelica, trying to distance myself from the absence of my intuition.

'Yes,' Anjelica replied.

'The one with the giant reptiles?' It seemed the only thing I could process was my history.

'Yes'

'With absolutely no hills?' I kept going along this bland thought path, desperate not to give into the annoyance of not being able to think about the now.

'Yes'

'They won't be there'

'Nah.'

'Hang on, how come you three get to make all the decisions? We don't even know you.' Anakin raised a fair point. 'I mean they could be in on this,' he continued.

Ace and Ash shared a look.

'Are you saying I'm untrustworthy?' Anjelica asked mockingly.

'Are you saying you're not?' came Anakin's quick response.

'Heimdall asked us to get Thor and Loki back so we are.' Alice clarified the situation.

'They only went missing because of you three in the first place.' Alec combated Alice.

'That's why we are helping.' I joined the discussion.

From here it escalated to the point where our once logical discussion turned into a competition to speak, everyone raising their voice to be heard. I took a breath and several steps back. The contrast between my frighteningly foggy mind, and the loud chaos in front of me, bringing my eyes to water.

'Enough!' Anjelica's voice echoed through my head and everyone else's, sending us to the ground.

I grasped my ears as I dropped to my knees. The sound became a thought in my head and it hurt. My eyes poured until I couldn't see anyone else, but I knew they were all sprawled on the floor. My head throbbed, and I held in the urge to scream. The word *enough* turned into a torturous white noise, I couldn't think. Save the one word that managed to slip past Anjelica's blockade of pressure. *Ice.* I struggled as I placed two fingers on my temple. Fighting past the pain ringing through my head I tried my hardest to focus on the cold lying in wait for my call. Excruciating numbness pleated itself in my skin and I let out a sharp scream. The cold offered a pleasant relief from the incapacitating noise.

A sudden rush of gratitude for my sister shot through me. Though my childhood wasn't anything it should've been, for the first time in my life I was glad. At least I had learned ways of surviving most would never figure out.

The ringing pain had now fully subsided and I managed to stand. Rubbing the water away from my eyes until I could clearly make out everyone sprawled on the floor, squirming in pain.

Thank this strange universe I have gifts. I turned my attention to Anjelica who was standing, arms by her sides, fingers outstretched.

Her eyes were distant and I wondered if she'd sent the screeching noise through her own mind as well. Freezing her wasn't an option as everyone would be stuck in the pain. Any tactics involving water would be too risky as I would not hurt, or risk killing her, so that left one thing: distract her.

Finding momentum, I charged towards Anjelica tackling her to the ground. It worked and her focus was completely disrupted. A swift glance told me that the others had been freed from the pain, but none of them were moving yet. Anjelica's eyes were still looking far away as we both got to our feet.

Damn it. She sent a punch flying towards my nose. Only just managing to cover my head with my arm I sent an elbow towards her nose. Not thinking straight she didn't even attempt to protect herself. I grimaced as my elbow connected with her face. *Sorry.* She stumbled back, hands flying to her nose.

'Anjelica-' I didn't get to finish my sentence as her foot connected with my stomach.

I should've seen that coming. My hands flew out, managing to grasp her ankle as pain flared in my core. Pinning her ankle against my hip I pivoted, forcing my body to face the other direction, my hands following this movement. She was airborne for a brief moment before she came crashing back down. Thankfully, that did the trick and her eyes returned to normal, focusing on me.

'You did it again.' I informed her in case she hadn't realised why I was attacking her.

'Crap.' She stayed down for a minute waiting for everyone else to recover.

I went over to Alice who was sitting a few paces to my right. 'You alright?'

'Yeah.' One hand rubbed the side of her head as she gave me the other to help her stand up.

'Ow,' Alec murmured, as everyone began climbing to their feet.

'Sorry, I'm working on it,' Anjelica claimed, as she too got up, pretending not to notice the death glare Anakin was sending in her direction.

CHAPTER SIX

August – Riptide

Once I was sure that Anjelica was unlikely to try her telepathy again I melted the ice in my head. The relief from the cold was freeing.

'So,' Ash prompted, 'what did we decide to do?'

'Haven't the faintest idea,' Alec said, while massaging his temples.

Ace and Anakin stood side by side, arms folded, with neutral expressions resting on their faces. While Alice remained standing farther back from Anjelica, probably suspecting another loss of control.

I went to offer a solution but the overwhelming feeling of sickness changed my mind, so I kept my mouth shut for fear of throwing up. A waft of burnt toast began to overwhelm my senses and an increasing feeling of light-headedness triggered alarm bells. After all this time I was surprised I could still recognise the smell. My eyes went wide as black crept across my vision. Not wanting to blackout I slowly made my way to a tree and leant against it. The tree was close enough that no one thought anything of it. Which I was relieved about as I wasn't sure I would be able to respond to questions of concern. I stayed there bracing against the tree for a while, fighting the blackness off through gritted teeth but I was losing the fight. I caught one final whiff of burnt toast before my eyes closed.

◈◈◈◈

When they opened I was in a dark, damp, dimly lit room. The walls were made of concrete and on the floor were reflective tiles. There was a wooden door, and no natural form of light, trapping the stench of slime in this already creepy room. I approached the far end of the chamber and gasped, there was Loki! He was bound to the wall, chains on his ankles, wrists, and around his waist. His greasy hair hung down by the sides of his face covering half of his eye on one side. He appeared to be unconscious. I looked around the room and saw a key on the top of a set of boxes. I went to grab them, but instead I watched horrified as my hand passed directly through the keys and the boxes.

Where was I? What was happening? My head bombarded me with questions that I couldn't answer. I heard a groan and turned toward the left side of the room. This side had a lone wooden desk, unaccompanied by pens or paper. On the wall, tied the same way as Loki, was Thor! He was wearing his usual armour but it was in tatters and his hair looked extremely knotty.

Walking up to the door, in another desperate attempt to work out my situation, I reached out for the handle. My hand passed through like I was grabbing at steam. *Was I dead?* I didn't get time to fully comprehend that last thought as the sound of a cough behind me caught me off guard. I spun, freaked out.

There, in a dark corner, stood Azar. He had red on his hands and was wearing a dark cloak over grey jeans and a matching coloured t-shirt which was splattered with, what I imagine, to be blood.

'Good to see you again.' He smiled, his tone making it plain that he had been expecting me.

'You're lucky.' Azar threatened as he ran his gooey fingers through his oily black hair. 'If you were really here I might try to kill you.'

'How am I here?' I questioned, keeping my distance from the hitman.

Azar laughed. 'Sit down.' His pale bony hands gestured to two chairs that I hadn't spotted before.

'I can't, I'm not here,' I reminded him.

Azar scowled at his own stupidity for a brief moment. Moving on, he approached the chairs and sat, crossing his legs before draping his arms across the back of the chair.

'None of this is personal Frost.' Azar used my last name causing the air between us to feel colder.

'How is this not personal?' I spat the words out harshly.

'Everyone has goals in life.' His response was as bland and as meaningless as his expression.

I fixed him with a glare. It must have been as cold as I intended because he flinched briefly, then readjusted his position, like the look I'd given him hadn't bothered him at all.

'Do you know what my goal is?' He tried again.

'To make a name for yourself that is so dark your targets will drop dead upon hearing it,' I responded, with a bitter guess.

Azar grinned, his pale teeth crooked and aligned poorly, much like his moral compass. 'You know me better than I thought.'

'I've heard your story.' His smirk remained but died down ever so slightly at my words.

'Not from me you haven't.'

'Well, why don't you tell me after you get to your point.' I crossed my arms, somehow the cold air in this room was getting to me.

'My goal is to serve Overlegen, and Overlegen has a rather large goal.'

I waited, unsure whether a prompt, or no response, would get him to reveal what it was.

'For millennia those in authority have been recording secrets Frost. Dark, treacherous, and heavily protected secrets.' He paused, his cold silver eyes trying to read my face.

I did my best to remain cold and not let any worry creep across.

'I know you know of the flash drive I'm referring to.'

I kept my glare set on him, but not physically being in the room was the only reason I wasn't taking several hundred steps back right now.

'How?' I couldn't even bring myself to finish the rest of the sentence.

Azar's smug expression told me he knew what I was going to ask but all he offered me was an enraging wink.

'Many have tried to set eyes on this flash drive. Many have died. Being a superior race, we from Overlegen are too smart to send one of our own after it. We need someone we know, who has powers enough to protect it, and who knows where it is. August, we need you.'

I forced myself not to react as those words left his mouth. *His spies must be seriously good if they'd figured out that I know where it is.*

'There is nothing in it for me.' I made a show of shrugging off Azar's spiel.

'There are only two ways out of your situation,' Azar spat.

I studied my nails.

'Escaping from the tree's top realms or death.'

'Where are you going with this?'

'Like you, Anjelica never learned how to use her powers, and Alice, quite frankly, is useless unless you're dying and still have your head intact.'

That earned him a glare.

'And you can't even trust those Asgardians. There's no way you can survive Overlegen.'

I leant forward as if to say something but remained quiet.

'But if you help me, you can undo the trouble you caused for Asgard, and get you and your friends the hell out of here.'

Silence took over the conversation as I processed his words.

'How exactly will you get us out of this realm?'

'That's for your sister and I to worry about. She owes me a favour.' Azar's words hit harder than any strike to the chest or stomach.

I couldn't even fully process what he'd just said. *What did my sister have to do with Azar? Hopefully not the same thing Freyja did. Did he know what her gift was?* To me, it sounded like he was confident he did. But, then again, surely he couldn't be certain. She'd never told anyone, not even me.

'What favour?' I managed to force the words out in an extremely pathetic voice.

'I could've gone after her for the drive, left you to try to survive Apoint on your own. But I haven't done that.'

'Why?' The word was so forced, my breath hanging on his answer.

'Because, she asked me to give you a chance.'

Confusion was the next emotion to gut punch me. *Did she think she was helping me out?*

'If you think providing me with an escape from your boss is enough to get me to help you, why kidnap the Gods? Also, what makes you think I can't just go ask my sister for help?'

'Come on Frost, use that brain of yours. It seems to have kept you alive thus far.'

I frowned, trying to narrow my world down to Azar's words, in hopes of blocking out everything else I was thinking and feeling. *Just get through this now, process later.*

'Leverage.' It dawned on me. 'You got scared I wouldn't want to leave Asgard. For whatever reason you won't divulge, you won't get the drive through Nora, you need me, but all you can offer is freedom. You're worried I would turn you down.'

Azar nodded, looking up at me through his dark ghostly eyes.

'For the most part you are correct. As for your sister, she's on Overlegen. She doesn't even know where you are, and she isn't looking, so do tell how you would get to her?'

I gulped knowing he was right, and hating it. Regardless of whether or not he was lying about getting us out of here, we would have to get him the drive to trade for Thor and Loki. Which was something I really did not want to do. Finally, I made up my mind and met his ghostly eyes.

'I don't believe you.' My lack of snark seemed to faze him for a moment, but nothing more than a moment.

His only response was to grin, a long slim snarl displaying his teeth.

'You and your superiors have been after me and my friends for years. Don't think I'm just going to help them so that they, or you, can kill us in the end.'

'Then help Thor and Loki.'

I will. But not by helping you. 'How'd I get here?'

'Someone in your midst is working for me.' Azar and I both knew his response came too fast to be a lie.

My hands went cold, bone cold.

'The Segredos drive, midday, tomorrow, Undeva.' Azar ended the conversation, tapping his ear as he spoke. 'Show her my story. Might help if she understands who she's dealing with.'

I already knew who I was dealing with, so I continued glaring at the murderer sat across from me. To my disappointment I didn't get time to say anything else as the scene in my head blurred morphing into something else.

I was sitting tight up against a wall, with a death grip on the curtain hanging in front of me. Something wasn't right, I wasn't *me*. Glancing back at my hands I fought shock as I stared at the extremely pale, long, and bony appendage.

Now fighting panic I turned to look at the reflection in the window, my eyes meeting the silver ones of a young boy! He was pale with a familiar smudgy appearance. His nose was long, and his eyes were almond shaped, only just bold enough to distinguish themselves against his pale skin. Much like the defining traits of Azar. I tried to scream but no noise came, instead I shifted back around to stare at the curtain. *Oh no! I was living Azar's memory as if I was him!* A gruff inner voice began ranting in my head. *How on Earth was this happening?* By the time I had stopped silently panicking, enough to listen to what was being said in my head, Azar's younger self had stopped ranting. Both of my hands – his hands – wrapped around the edge of the curtain as flashes of red and simmering heat began flooding in through the window.

Tears even began pricking in my – his eyes. Then, as I finally managed to relax into Azar's memory, I was completely swept into his thoughts and feelings.

'In here, quick.' My heart tightened as shouts entered my house.

I had little time to worry as not long after the heavy footsteps of soldiers filled the room. The curtain, my curtain, was ripped off the wall. It fell dramatically, revealing me to the bloodshot eyes of the three soldiers.

'Do you have a power yet, kid?' The question was blunt but I was glad to hear it, it meant they were Overlegenian.

I shook my head to answer, I was only eight. *How long ago was this?* I kept shaking my head until he responded, my voice far too coarse to use.

'You know what to do, we'll be outside.' The sentence wasn't aimed at me so I remained where I was as two of the red stained soldiers left, leaving me with the tallest out of the three. The remaining soldier knelt down to my height, placing a comforting hand on my shoulder.

'Not to worry kid, I'm going to get you out of here.'

I looked up into his brown eyes.

'I want to help.' My statement was honest despite the fact that I was shaking in my bones.

'You can't, our attacker is Overlegenian. We're at war with our own kid.'

No way. This had to be about the guy who came back to destroy the planet after they banished him.

The soldier used the hand he had on my shoulder to pin me against the wall as he drew a knife from the sheath in his boot. My eyes caught on the blade, rather than worrying about my looming doom. The metal glistened a perfect lime green, and the perfectly sculpted edges carried no trace of blood or dirt. I gulped, feeling the cold blade press against my throat. My fear finally catching up with me. This was not the fate I wanted. I could feel my frustration start to rise and I decided to meet it halfway. Sinking down into my feelings, bubbles of anger began to eat away at the fear in my quivering bones.

'What are you doing?' I managed to scream through my tears.

'Being merciful.' He grinned. Actually grinned.

But that would be the last thing he ever did. I was sick of being powerless. No longer would I be shoved around, picked on for my looks, status, lack of title. No more. My emotions had finally consumed me. I could feel lumps of it, dark green and sticky, suffocating my thoughts. Only then did I notice the blade was no longer at my trachea. The soldier had slumped onto the floor, green goo pouring out of his nose, eyes, and throat. Shoving him away, my emotions laid down a plan. I was going to be the one to destroy the enemy, I would earn a title, and I would show up even my high ranking parents.

As fast as I could I made it to the front door and flung it open. But as soon as the red smoke touched my lungs I let out a high pitched scream. The air was scorching. The type of hot that inflicts pain as it enters and exits your lungs. All I could feel was my breath as it clawed its way down my throat. Hunching over, with my bony hands on my knees, I fought the thick lumps of oxygen into my mouth and waited for my body to grow accustomed to the baking pain.

'It's the kid.' One of the soldiers alerted the other to my arrival.

I stared past both of them at the bark of an ashen tree. Anyone else may think that I had two choices here, but they would be wrong. There was only one choice and I'd already committed to it. My maddening anger had me balanced precariously on the edge of an emotional cliff. One small gust of wind and I would fall. *Or would I rise?*

'We have no choice, kid. It is protocol.' Both soldiers looked at me with sympathy, like they actually felt bad for their actions.

But they were just following protocol. Protocol. I would spit on the word if I had any saliva left in my mouth. Right now I didn't care for rules, I only cared for violence. I shoved myself from the top of the cliff and let myself rise into the consuming mirk of my own power.

Bubbling with numb pride, I made my way through the red fog up towards the military office. I had captured the suffering screams of my first victims in my mind, should I ever need a reminder of what I am capable of. I was well on my way to becoming who I wanted to be. A fearsome, merciless man whom the realm fears. Absolutely nothing and no one was going to stop me.

The second I reached the bricked building of the military office I kicked in the wooden door. Watching as it smashed open to expose a singular rotting hallway. Nothing accompanied the walls, or the floor, and two doors were positioned at opposite ends of the underwhelming passage. Just passed the two doors a kid with a typical Overlegenian look sat drawing on the wall with a blade. I said nothing to him but made a loud approach. Sweeping my eyes across the wooden board stuck over the brick wall, I paid close attention to the inadequate drawings of a man destroying a planet.

'They won't listen.' The boy spoke without looking up from his etching. 'I told 'em. Without my plan they're dead.'

I looked at the plain boy beside me, he was definitely older but not by much. Not wanting to speak unless necessary, I waited 'till his brown eyes met my silver gaze then pointed to the door behind him. He nodded. I walked around the boy towards the beige door.

'Title's Apoint.' I stopped. Briefly halting my mission at his words. *That's Apoint!?*

'You're not old enough to face trials.'

'Yeah well, I'm second in line. I'll do what I want.'

I snorted. One day I would be considered above that.

'Your drawings are hideous.'

'I have vision though, admit it.'

I ignored him placing my hand on the door, but before I pushed it open I turned back, remembering not to be hostile to everyone.

'Your plan isn't as hideous.' With that I stalked through the doorway.

I spotted my mother and father standing at the opposite end of the room to the King and his daughter.

'Son?' I chose to ignore the voice of my father and get straight to the point.

'I'm going to get rid of your attacker, and then, when I get back, I would like to receive a title,' I barked my order at the King.

He stood three times my height with a crown on top of his blond head.

'Is that so?' he responded, intrigued.

I could easily spot the anger that so famously circled his blue eyes. I couldn't care less about the details of this rather bland room, or the expressions of those in it, so I kept my eyes focused on the King.

'Duana, if you still see fit, you and this boy may go and track down the whereabouts of Amolt.'

The King broke my gaze and locked eyes with his daughter, who appeared to be four or so years older than me. She too was blonde, blue eyed, dressed like royalty, and carried the obvious tinge of anger. I too looked exactly like my father whose glare I could feel fixed on the back of my greasy head.

'Will you really send children to kill this traitor?' My mother's voice filled the room but I refused to turn and look at her.

My goal was to stare down the King until he gave me what I wanted.

'Well, track him down at least. If they think they can achieve, where the rest of the planet has failed, then I don't see why not.'

The King's answer was final, thankfully both my parents remembered that.

'I'll get a title?' I questioned, just to be sure.

'You'll get more than that if you achieve kid.'

That was all I needed. I marched out of the room, not offering my parents a glance and headed back down the hallway, Duana running to catch up.

'Do you have a plan?' she asked, as she finally caught up with me.

'Destruction.' That was the only word I offered her as we burst back out into the burning air.

⁂

I sat up gasping at the clear air. Overwhelmingly glad I was finally back in my own body and mind. I was still under the tree, but now everyone was huddled around me. I filtered through what had just happened trying to find my words. My mind felt confused, unsure who I was or what was happening as I tried to detangle myself from Azar's memory.

'Azar,' I started, before anyone could ask me anything.

I paused, giving myself a moment to try and remember what our conversation had been about. 'He wants the Segredos drive by midday tomorrow on Undeva, or Thor and Loki will die.'

I watched as Anjelica and Alice's expressions turned to disgust.

'What does that mean?' asked Lavita.

I hadn't even realised she, Pierre, and Sian had come back outside.

'The Segredos drive contains everything you need to know about everything,' Alec explained slowly.

'What if you need to know nothing?' mumbled Pierre to himself.

'Then you don't need it,' Alice answered him anyway.

Needing room to breathe, after all that had just happened, I forced myself to my feet. Offering a smile to the group, most of whom were still looking at me with worry written across their faces, I removed myself from the conversation. Allowing myself a brief moment of nothing I slowly walked towards the edge of the hill, taking in the cool air as it bit into my skin. The second I made it to the edge my brain spurred into action. The Segredos drive had been made by the universal government to collect important intel and enable blackmail in tough situations. Rumour has it that there are two Segredos drives, and, unbeknownst to me, my sister somehow got her hands on one. Though I was rather sure I knew where the other may be.

The evening wind started to pick up a little and my conversation with Azar had left me cold inside. I decided to sit on the peak of the hill and watch the sunset on Vanaheim's ridiculously stunning city. The harmless orange flame touched on every stationary thing in the green valley, and as the sun finally began to disappear it dawned on me that this long day was far from over.

The conversation behind me went quiet so I snuck a look to see why. Everyone was still huddled together in a circle, obviously the conversation had just turned stale. I turned back to my view but as I did so Lavita's green eyes met mine. The smile pricked on her face lit a small flicker of panic in my gut, but was distinguished by the calming breath of darkness unleashed over the planet shortly after I put my back to her.

'You lot are overcomplicating this.' I heard Anakin's voice above the low whispers from the others.

'Do elaborate,' Anjelica asked, probably folding her arms as she spoke.

'August can go pick up the Segredos drive from wherever and then we just make a trade with Azar. No big deal.'

I turned from my beautiful yet dark view to look at Anakin.

'Dude, we can't give a megalomaniac one of the most powerful objects in the universe.' Ace's words smacked Anakin in the face.

'It won't really affect us though.' Anakin pointed out, causing subtle smiles to splash themselves onto the faces of the group.

They were, however, quickly banished when Anjelica realised that giving our enemies the Segredos drive would hinder our survival. Before another argument could break out I got to my feet and wandered over. I could worry about Azar's spy and my sister later. Right now I need to figure out what to do about the Segredos drive(s) and Azar's deal. Besides, in my experience, the spy would slip up soon enough. I joined the circle, standing in between Anjelica and Anakin.

'If it is as simple as Anakin thinks then not all of us are needed.' Alice's voice brought a cowboy tension to the conversation.

Everyone's eyes were darting back and forth waiting for someone to make the first move. Despite dealing with Freyja together there still was a subtle distrust in the group, that was ever so slowly boiling.

'Then you two can go.' Anakin broke everyone's thought process. His comment directed at Anjelica and Alice.

I looked at Anakin with a defiant expression on my face, although also wondering why he'd elect for me to stay.

'Fine, but we do it my way,' he grumbled.

'Which way is that?' Anjelica asked.

Anakin turned toward Ace and asked, 'What do you want to do?'

Ace raised a slight eyebrow at Anakin but answered him nonetheless.

'Ash and I should go to Sandvellir, just in case Freyja didn't lie. The girls can go to Undeva to track down Azar, and Anakin and Alec can collect the Segredos drive. That way, we have it, not Azar.' Ace's chestnut hair blew sideways as he stood centre of attention.

'You should probably take Alice,' I said to Alec and Anakin, having a faint idea of which location they were about to be sent. But also because I wanted someone I knew I could trust there when they found it.

Alice nodded, no doubt slightly annoyed.

Anakin turned to me. 'What's the location of the Segredos drive?'

'Which one?' I asked purely to be difficult.

The reason for my soon to be tiresome behaviour wasn't for Anakin, it was for Azar. Whoever his spy was, I wondered if they even knew there were two, and if so, did they already have one?

Azar asked me because he doesn't know where at least one is. So I grinned. Imagine how annoyed he'd be if I gave his spy the location of the one he already knew about. *Providing that he already knew.* Anakin grabbed my shoulders, pinning me against the tree behind us. His strength surprising. I frowned, not at

Anakin, I was either going to have to guess which location Azar possibly already knew about or try to guess which location held the least valuable information on the drive. Grass like vines wrapped around my wrists and ankles to stop me from moving.

'The real one.' The words flowed from Anakin in his most threatening tone.

I looked him dead in the eye. 'They're both real.'

Watching Anjelica from the corner of my eye I saw her turn away and start to laugh.

'Why are you being difficult?' he asked, risking a glance at Anjelica who fought to compose herself in time.

'Don't think I won't kill you, Godnappers!' Two more veins began to reach out for Anjelica and Alice.

'Anakin.' I managed to pull my hand up to his wrist, drawing his attention back to me.

'Give me a second, Azar just pulled me out of my physical form.'

He would be the third person in my head since we got here. Anakin's harsh green eyes softened and the vines started to pull back.

'Sorry August, I forgot what that's like.'

The sudden deterioration of his anger startled me as, for the first time since I'd met him, he appeared to have dropped his brash guard.

Think. If Azar knew that Nora knew where one was then maybe he might know of the one closest to her. But then again the person he hated most in this universe was guarding the other, assuming I had that location right. So both options were equally probable. *Ah never mind.* We'd probably have to get both to make sure that Azar couldn't get them later. At least that way we could make the trade if we had no other choice.

'The drive is in Antarctica, Midgard.'

He let go of my shoulders. 'Crap, why'd I ask?'

'Because you have a quick fuse and can't handle not knowing.' Anjelica provoked him again.

'Not in the mood, smoked brains!' Anakin fired back at Anjelica holding his glare on her before turning back to me.

He offered me a weak smile before shoving past Anjelica towards Alec and Alice.

'Let's go,' he grumbled, storming off.

Alice shot me a look that said, *really?*, before heading down the hill with Anakin and Alec, who was now trying to cheer up his smouldering buddy. *Sorry Anakin.* I regretted giving Anakin a bit of a hard time but Azar had wound me up more than I'd realised. I stayed standing in front of the tree for a moment longer. *Had I just made a mistake in giving up the location?*

'You alright August?' Ash's voice shook me out of my own thoughts.

'Yeah. I just can't seem to think straight,' I answered, still a bit wound up or chilled, I wasn't sure.

'Don't worry it'll pass.' Unlike Anakin's, Ash's green eyes carried flecks of grey which were sprinkled around.

'So, where are we taking you lot?' Sian's voice called out from the entrance to the ship.

'One sec' Sian.' Anjelica smiled, as she walked towards Ash and I as we made our way over.

'Isn't Antarctica where *he* is?' she asked, in a hushed voice.

I nodded as a response and heard her smile, 'poor Alice,' before walking away.

I was about to follow Anjelica into the ship when Ace grabbed my hand.

'August.' His grip was tight. I spun around rolling my wrist as I did so, freeing it from Ace's lock.

'And the other one?' Ash's question somehow took me by surprise, but I knew exactly what he was asking. They wanted to get the other one.

'Nowhere I'm going soon,' I responded, with a wary tone.

'We're here to help you,' Ace said, as he moved around Ash to face me more squarely.

'I think you'll find I'm here to help you.' I corrected his statement.

'Well then help us, help you, help us,' Ace responded, causing me to smile at the strange but present reference to Earth.

'Why do we even need to get it?' I pushed to see if they had the same logic as me. I couldn't trust my brain right now.

'Don't you think it'd be better if we had both instead of risking Azar getting one?'

Well we had the same logic, but that did mean I was about to give up the second location of something no one should ever know the location to.

'Overlegen,' I told them. 'Find my sister, her name is Nora Frost. Tell her that you've found the dark side of the sun. She'll know what that means.'

They both nodded, their faces conveying neither grave nor joyful expressions.

'Shall we?' Ash said, gesturing towards the open entrance to the spacecraft, seeming more than happy to be done with that conversation.

'Sorry about your wrist.' Ace offered an apology as we boarded the silver vessel.

'Sorry about your wrist.' I grinned, as the metal door slid shut, sealing us in for better or worse.

'No you're not.' His words smiled as he said them.

Sian and Pierre were in the cockpit while Anjelica, Ash, Ace, Lavita and I all sat together in the main area on the ship. A tight room with pink coloured walls and gold curved revolving chairs. There was a conversation happening but I was ignoring it. Something seemed off about our lift's timing, and Azar's words were still in my head again. *'Someone in your midst is working for me.'* My thoughts dragged me back to Freyja's reaction after learning Lavita's name. No, it couldn't be Lavita. Azar obviously kept Freyja in the loop, and Freyja had ordered her men to kill Lavita and Pierre. Sian. What if he was? No. I changed my mind immediately, that theory didn't make sense. Unless, it did. He wasn't there when Freyja's men were ordered to kill the others. He is unassuming apart from his green hair. I sighed, unsure.

'We are here.' Pierre wandered over to us.

'Start to land,' Lavita said to Pierre, while staring at Ace.

She got up and gestured for us to follow.

'When we land that door will open,' she said, pointing to a grey door at the back wall of the ship's cargo bay.

She left the room smiling and stalked gracefully back into the main room.

'You alright?' Anjelica asked me.

I stared at her questioningly, I was fine. 'Just thinking,' I replied.

She nodded and went to say goodbye to Ash and Ace.

Anakin. He was the only one who heard what Freyja had told her men to do. *What if he was..?*

My thought was unable to be finished as the door opened, revealing the dark shaded scenery of the extremely empty planet. Undeva, like Vanaheim, had green hills that were dispersed evenly across the countryside, but in the far horizon was a dark imposing mountain line that was guarded by thick forests on its foothills. I could hear the loud bickering of waterfalls and the constant clash of running water but there was no source in sight.

Anjelica jumped out of the ship onto the dark tinted planet, landing steady on her feet for once. I went to follow when it hit me. Anakin was wrong.

It wasn't, *'kill them.'* Was it? It must've been, *'kill him.'*

I turned around to warn Ace and Ash. Too fast, my hair whipped across my face and the evil wind from Undeva was quick to pull me off balance. Ace's sturdy hand grabbed my arm and steadied me.

'Lavita is Azar's spy,' I said, before thanking him.

'Azar has a spy?' Ace voiced the question but it was clear that Ash was thinking the exact same thing.

'I may have forgotten to mention that,' I replied, quickly glancing between them.

'So that's why you're being so cynical.'

I flashed Ace a quick smile as he released me, allowing me to fall out of the ship onto Undeva's grassy surface. Ace and Ash quickly jumped, landing on either side of me.

'Did I miss something?' Anjelica asked, as she turned away from surveying the view to see Ace and Ash.

'We're swapping rides,' Ace answered her.

⊰⊱⊰⊱

There was a large sign sitting just in front of the trampled path that we were heading towards. The large bold letters read: 'Undeva is protected by G.A.P.S. Due to this no one may tamper with, or inflict damage on, this planet's surface.'

'Well I guess that explains the absence of any signs of inhabitants,' Anjelica mumbled, as she plodded along.

'That somehow makes this place that much creepier.' Ash pulled his hands out of his jacket pockets as he spoke, glancing around.

'It is a bit strange that G.A.P.S. would bother protecting a planet this far out,' Ace added.

I had only ever heard of the Galactic Association of Perfected Security once. Nora had mentioned them but I couldn't remember what she had been talking about. We followed the grassy path to a set of mud stairs that lead onto a hill. Thankfully, the steps weren't as slippery as they looked, enabling us to make it into the entrance for the underground planet without slipping.

Undeva was not stunning underground. A theme of brown and various dark blues swallowed the light supplied by strange starlike shapes that hung from the mud ceiling. We stood on a mud path that forked into three. One was blue stone, while the other two were mud. One of the mud paths lead into the city while the other towards our right, which appeared to be a market of sorts. Most of the buildings were made of mud with the occasional visible brick or wooden plank. Everything was constricted within the blue path which took up a decent amount of space between the clay looking walls and the city. There were the odd concrete or semi glass buildings but they were mostly located at the other end of the city to us.

I bet Azar was in one of those.

'We should head to the market, someone there will have a spacecraft,' Ash sounded hopeful, despite the grim city.

'Stay alive you two.' Ace fixed Anjelica and I with a surprisingly serious look before he and Ash began heading off.

'You too.' Both Anjelica and I called after them.

'Blue path?' I asked Anjelica, liking the idea of going around the outskirts of the city.

'Blue path,' she confirmed.

It was miles of blue surrounded by the brown and grey tones of this creepy place. We were getting rather close to the far side of the city, that contained the more upper class looking buildings, when a couple came into view. They were casually walking towards us. Anjelica and I averted our eyes as they passed us. Even once they were out of distance we didn't even attempt to start a conversation, though we easily could've with the amount of odd things piling up. We knew better than to distract ourselves from our surroundings on a strange new planet. So we continued on in silence as we passed depressed tortilla coloured buildings, none of them more than two stories high. There was no plant or animal life in sight, and for the only city on the planet it was preternaturally quiet.

Suddenly, the muffled sound of heels on stone met our ears. We didn't say a word to acknowledge the footsteps, instead we carefully increased our pace. Anjelica snuck a glance back, pretending to fix her hair.

'The couple's back,' she said coldly, both of us knowing what that meant.

'Let's see what they want.' Anjelica made the call and we stopped walking, turning around to face them as they approached.

The two women's facial expressions hardened as they grew closer. There was no mistaking that the scowls on their faces were a silent threat.

'Quietly?' I whispered.

'Nah, I wanna hear 'em scream,' she whispered back.

'What if there are more?'

'Do you see more?' she responded, teasingly.

I scanned the environment. I didn't and she knew it. She started walking briskly toward them. I didn't. We were doing it her way. She shoved past them and only stopped after they reached me. They both pulled out knives and held them to my throat.

'We need you to come with us.' Were the only words I made out through their thick accents.

One day I would like to see what would happen if we pulled this move and they went for Anjelica instead.

'Any day now,' I remarked coldly to my friend.

The couple shared a look and then returned their gazes to me. Before they could do anything their hair burst into flames. The woman to my left screamed, her hands flying in a panic to her head. Her partner, however, let a pained expression cross her face but no sound left her mouth as she took off.

'YOU BITCH!' The woman remaining turned to face Anjelica.

'Is that a code phrase?' I asked, trying to prove my previous point.

The woman pulled a strange face at me and then returned to screaming. Anjelica gave me a smug look.

'Girls don't move.' The words belonged to a masculine voice, which was accompanied by the clicking of several lightning throwers.

I put my hands up and turned to face the man. He had dark navy skin which carried a mystical quality. White freckles accompanied his cheekbones and moved slowly but swiftly around his face. The man even had a singular blue horn on the left side of his head which was surrounded by his bouncy azure hair. But by far the strong livid coloured bat wings were his most unusual feature. Other than him, we were surrounded by people dressed in an intense dark blue, all of whom, save him, were holding lightning throwers. I glared at the gun looking weapons. They were similar to technology we had on Earth but the inventors thought it would be far more useful to shoot electrically charged rods. These weapons were considered cowardly and amateur to use leading to their disparagement in the Asgardian Realm. Which meant that these men were working for Overlegen, the only people brazen enough to use something in spite of Asgard.

'Told ya so,' I whispered to Anjelica, as she dared to join me in the middle of the circle that had formed.

CHAPTER SEVEN

Ace – Blaze

Ash and I crept through the outskirts of the dark woods that were spread across Overlegen. We had managed to negotiate with a strange looking local on Undeva. He happened to be headed towards this branch and agreed to give us a lift. Although, he did not seem too eager to hang around and so left rather abruptly. Thankfully it was a particularly dark night so we didn't give much thought to concealment as we trekked silently through the trees. I could hardly see Ash in front of me and we had no solid evidence that we were heading in the right direction. Yet we still walked on.

Snap! I was looking over my shoulder before I could even process what the noise was. I couldn't see anything but the dark figures of trees.

'Twig?' Ash mouthed at me and we both looked down to check our feet.

Pine needles. *Snap!* The sharp noise found its way into my ears again. We were being tailed. Ash and I shared a nod before silently heading in the direction of the sound. Engaging with my telekinesis I lifted Ash ever so slightly off the ground, pushing him forward without a sound. The fingers in my right hand curled upwards toward my palm as my abilities held him in place. Careful not to lose my balance and drop Ash, I followed with caution so as not to alert our tail.

*Snap! T*here it was again. The source, just past the trees in front of us. I released my abilities and let Ash make his own way for the next few centimetres. We crouched down behind the two large trees and looked at the small path Ash had made previously. Empty, apart from a small bird. The dark coloured creature was hopping around oblivious to its audience. I relaxed, false alarm.

'You two look like you're up to something.'

Slowly we turned, staying crouched down to not impose too much tension. In front of us stood a Human girl. It was easier to distinguish Humans from other species as they rarely had brands or eccentric features. This girl wasn't that tall, but was slightly more so than Ash and I, and definitely older. The moonlight landed perfectly on her fairy blonde hair, which was cut into an intense style that swept sideways only just reaching her pale blue eyes at the front. Muscles bulged out of her folded arms as she looked down at us. She appeared to be about twenty in Midgardian years and had developed an aura of delicacy, which I could tell to be fake by the dark edges of her scuffed nails.

'Miss Frost?' I asked the washed out version of August.

She bit the corner of her lip thinking. 'And you two are?'

'Blaze and Arrow.' I gave her our titles.

'How do you know me?' she asked, her voice having the same concealed composure as August's did when she was thinking.

'We found the dark side of the sun.' Ash remembered to say the code phrase.

August's sister looked around and signalled for us to be quiet, gesturing for us to follow her. We stood and let her lead us deeper into the dark woods. Each tree looked identical. Just a tall trunk that only began to branch out after two or three metres, though I couldn't see much else. If it wasn't for Overlegen's moons I would be walking into the trunks as the wood gradually got denser. Just as the gaps between trees became even more limiting, Nora swerved to the left and led us into a small clearing. The small break in the woods was only large enough to fit a wooden hut with a small garden. The grass was slightly overgrown and flowers, unlike any I'd seen on Asgard, climbed up the sides of the hut. The air in the clearing hung with a strong scent of damp moss and dying embers, which was an unpleasant shock for my lungs.

'Sit.' Nora pointed to a circle of tree stumps.

A burnt out fire had been strategically positioned in the middle of the circle. Ash and I sat next to each other while Nora opted to sit on the opposite side of the circle. We watched patiently as Nora struck up a fire. Once she had finished, and the orange element burst to life, she sat back, folding her arms and spoke.

'What is the cause of your arrival?' Her question was phrased rather weirdly.

'Asgard was attacked by Overlegen. We fought them off but Azar kidnapped two of our Gods,' Ash explained, in a minimalist way.

'So why does a nation of warriors send teenagers to save their Gods?'

'Our best warriors are needed on Asgard,' I explained, aiming to avoid giving her the idea that Asgard was weak.

'If you survive this you'll be Asgard's best warriors,' Nora offered.

The three of us paused for a minute not sure where to take the conversation next, when Nora suddenly tensed in her seat. Her pale eyes set in a glare aimed over my head.

'Well isn't this cute.'

I recognised that voice as I shifted to see Lavita, Sian, and Pierre heading towards us from the edge of the clearing. Ash and I stood immediately, ready for a fight. Pierre and Sian, however, were also ready. They raised blowguns to their lips almost as soon as we had stood, aiming them at our heads. Knowing that if I made a move there would be a poisonous rock shard embedded in my head, I did the only thing I could do and shot a cold glare at Pierre.

'Sit.'

We were ordered to take a seat for the second time this hour. Once Ash and I had complied with her order, Lavita shifted her focus to August's sister.

'Nora, hand over the Segredos drive and the boys will live, for now.' Lavita held out her hand expectantly.

'Sorry, I didn't quite catch that?' Nora asked Lavita coldly, shooting Ash and I, a *don't worry* look.

'I want the Segredos drive. Duh,' Lavita responded rudely to Nora's stalling.

Pierre and Sian took a couple steps forward so that they were now standing right in front of Ash and I. The blow darts pressed into our foreheads. Twisting slightly I locked eyes with Ash. One, I blinked. Two, he blinked. I reached my hand towards Pierre's side, our slight connection alerted me to the silver in his earrings. Perfect, strong conductors truly made life easier. I moved my fingers around in the air warming them up with the weak connection from the planet's electric field. Using this field to channel my telekinesis I subtly unhooked his earrings and brought them towards my fingers. Pierre, thankfully, was completely oblivious to what I was doing, his attention on Nora. Holding his silver earrings against my charged fingers I looked back to Ash. Three, he blinked, confirmation before we both acted. I shoved the silver and my fingers into Pierre's side, pushing the current charged in my fingers into him. He jolted, shrieking from the shock and dropped the blowgun into the long grass. There wasn't nearly enough charge to cause him any real damage so I sent my fist upwards striking him hard under the chin. With an expression of horrified shock on his face he fell unconscious onto the ground. Taking a glance over at Ash to check that he was okay, I found him sending the same glance my way. Due to Ash's intense speed and strength it wouldn't have been too difficult for him to remove the weapon from Sian who, like Pierre, now lay in the grass.

'Nice party tricks boys,' Lavita mumbled, as we turned on her.

She tried retreating back into the woods but Ash was too fast. He easily reached her before she could break into a run and threw her up against a pine tree. Nora and I headed over to Ash as he made sure Lavita was unable to free herself from his grip.

'What's going on with your antics?' Ash asked, as his hand curled around her throat.

She laughed, Ash clenched his fist and she choked. He released his grip and Lavita began her response.

'In case you haven't noticed, Azar wants the Segredos drive and he has a lot of people helping him.'

I faked punching her and she screamed flinching away from my non-existent strike.

'Arrow was referring to August's vision, the sudden title you helped give her, and Freyja.' I spoke harshly, hardly recognising my own voice.

'Well, Freyja has a little crush on Azar so we used her to get intel and found out Odin took a holiday.' She smiled after that sentence but then continued talking when she got a glimpse of my face. 'The truth is Azar is more focused on pleasing his superiors on Krone than he is on hunting down you lot. I'm not about to reveal anything of importance, you'll just have to figure the rest out on your own.'

'The Segredos drive is just information, how will that help you kill your enemies?' Ash spat his words at the twisted fairy.

Her face went dark, a wickedness rippling through her pupils.

'Information is all you need to kill people.' Her words were barely a whisper as Ash's hand slowly clenched around her throat.

The planet felt as if it had gotten darker and it appeared that even the moons no longer wished to be present for this conversation.

'You see everything has a price boys and there are consequences for all actions. I suggest you talk to your Gods, *if you can.*' Her mocking words were accentuated by the raging fire that cast violent shadows onto Lavita's face.

'What did you show August when you prompted her on her title?' I growled.

'Just a little rock in the Mediterranean.' Her face was growing paler as Ash slowly cut off her circulation.

'Forn Ljós.' Nora Frost spoke for the first time in a while. Her voice overcome with worry.

133

'And the vision of Azar on Undeva?' Ash questioned.

'I did that.' Lavita admitted proudly.

Ash smiled a 'thank you' then smashed his elbow into her temple, leaving her a crumple on the woodland floor.

'The hunt for the ancient runes has started, that's interesting.' Nora spoke more to herself than us.

'What do we do with them?' Ash asked, looking at crumpled Lavita.

No one answered.

'Blaze, I'll give you the Segredos drive. But if it comes to having to give it to Azar, destroy it.' Nora said, not displaying any reaction whatsoever to hearing her sister's name in our interrogation.

Ash gave her a nod, which encouraged her enough to disappear inside the hut still mumbling about Forn Ljós. Ash and I waited in silence enjoying the brief break in chaos and conflict until Nora finally emerged with a small Midgardian flash drive in her hand. For all the drama over it, it didn't look like much. Just slightly rectangular, small, and definitely from Earth. Nothing compared to the tech used by more advanced planets.

'Wonder why they used Earth tech?' Ash muttered, half to himself.

'Protection, not many species can use Earth tech due to its differences,' Nora reminded us.

'Bless their cotton socks.' Ash smiled, knowing full well that Nora was from Earth.

'What is Forn Ljós?' I asked, but was denied an answer.

'Where are you two heading now?' She swiftly changed the subject.

'Undeva,' I answered, annoyed that I'd just answered her question.

'Azar has Thor and Loki there. We're meeting Firestorm and Riptide,' I said, using my friends' titles in case we had any more uninvited guests nearby.

'Why would Azar dare go to Undeva?' Nora spoke hastily.

'Why?' Ash asked, 'What's the big deal about Undeva?'

CHAPTER EIGHT

Alice – Gale

I wasn't prepared for the Antarctic air, not after Asgard or Vanaheim. The bitter chill stung my lungs as it went in. The cold pain in my throat caused me to hold my gloved hands close to my fabric wrapped neck in an attempt to take the edge off as Anakin, Alec, and I started wading into the snow. The amazing Heimdall had provided us with a spacecraft upon our brief return, just as Alec had suspected he would. How I wished I'd thought to wait in the ship. The inhospitable winter land spat snow and ice at us as we trudged through the wicked winds. Next to us, as far as I could make out, was a frozen lake, the dim lights from three houses just ahead of us lit its surface.

'So where is it?' Anakin asked quietly.

'Probably in the fourth house,' Alec answered.

'A fourth house?' Anakin voiced my question.

Without a word Alec led us towards the bland, abandoned hut at the end of the row. Its pale colour and lack of lights made it extremely difficult to spot. Barbed wire had been angrily positioned around the house to stop visitors. Tufts of fur, fabric, and ice weren't the only things keeping the wire fences company.

The walls were plastered with blaring yellow signs that carried morbid messages to ward us off.

'I don't think they put up enough signs,' said Alec sarcastically, reinforcing the fact that I didn't want to be here.

This house especially gave me the shivers, or maybe that was the weather. It was a ways away from the other houses and judging by the footprints someone had been here recently, despite the signs. I circled the house, leaving Alec to fiddle with the wire while Anakin stood shivering. The house was made of old wood and was badly painted blush pink. The same pink Freyja had on her castle's floor. The colour was subtle enough to allow the hut to be swallowed by the snow. As I made it round to the back of the house I spotted a small golden plaque. Despite the blizzard I struggled forward to read the tiny writing etched onto the plaque.

'Many tried, many died.'

As I wiped snow from the plaque my gloved fingers connected with sticky red liquid. *Oh no.* I stumbled back suddenly scared. I became rather aware of my heartbeat as I looked around, but I couldn't see anything except white. My ears were starting to buzz and my veins were freezing. I was stuck in this unbearable place with two people I'd just met, who were on the other side of this spooky house, and possibly a dead body was lying around. I took a deep breath trying to calm myself down. I was immune to most physical injuries anyway (thanks to my power). I started to relax.

Drip. Drip.

The sound of water falling onto the compact snow came from behind and I freaked, falling back into my overwhelmed panic. If someone cut my head off I would die, there's no recovering from that! I tripped in a daze and hit the hard snow upon landing, my world swimming. Thoughts grabbed me with their Siren hands and pulled me deeper into the snow. My influence of the breeze was more of a sick joke, some higher power having a laugh because I was an outlaw and completely harmless.

Drip.

Concern for my own safety got me up off the ground and breathing normally. I wasn't completely harmless. I had survived thus far.

'I am going in,' the voice of Anakin called from the other side of the house.

'Ah, screw it,' I said to myself. If I died an honourable death I'd go to Valhalla in Asgard and I had liked Asgard.

'You sure you want to go?' I asked Anakin, once I had gotten back to the front of the house.

He had approached the first fence and was currently eyeing it suspiciously.

'It would be easier for a smaller person to get through.'

'Actually yeah. Alec you're shorter, you should go.' Anakin chickened out.

'Alice is the shortest,' Alec reminded Anakin, hugging himself for warmth.

I turned toward the fence. I was wearing warm grey pants which meant I had more movement than the two boys. Both of whom had layered up as much as physically possible. Unlike them, the only thing keeping me warm was my oversized, puffy yellow jacket. My power meant I didn't have to wear so many layers.

'Alright I'll go,' I volunteered, before they did that for me.

Focusing on the hut, I ran up and jumped the first fence, including its barbed wire. Thankfully it wasn't too high and I made the jump with relative ease. The next row of wire was too high but wasn't pegged into the ground. I squirmed under it and only just managed to pop up the other side. The next barricade was plastered with spaced out signs and there was no way I could get over or under. I pulled out Leaf, the leaf shaped blade Heimdall had given to me. *Oh I missed Asgard.*

Focus. I scolded myself as I finished cutting a gap in the wire.

Nerves hit me as I approached the spooky house and gripped the door handle. Locked. I crouched down to get a closer look. The key hole had frozen shut with ice that was spread thinly over most of the wooden door. The parts that weren't frozen were practically disintegrating. This hut was old. Very old. Placing my gloved hands on the door I gave it a sudden shove. The snapping noise that came as the door broke open was rather pleasant. However, the darkness that met my eyes as the door opened was not. It took my eyes a minute to adjust from the blaring white to the unlit interior. From what I could tell there was only one room inside the house. It was almost completely empty and covered in enough dust to coat a small moon. My eyes fell to a small, grey smothered box that sat on the floor in the centre of the room. I cautiously walked towards it. Worried that there would be some sort of trap, I opened it slowly. When nothing happened I reached into the box pulling out a small electronic drive. It had a white plastic label taped onto it that read *plug into a computer*. I grabbed the drive and ran out of the house, through the barbed wire, and back to Anakin and Alec. *I thought this would've been better protected.*

'Good, you're back,' Alec acknowledged, as I held up the drive. 'Let's get out of this creepy place.'

Alec, Anakin, and I were thinking the exact same thing so we wasted no time hanging around. The guys put on a fast paced walk back to our ship, which thankfully, I was able to keep up with. Yet, the further from the hut we got the more intense my spooked feelings grew. It had been far too easy to get the drive. Each crunch of snow under my feet made my heart fill with nerves as we got closer to the ship. I felt like we were being watched. Wanting rid of this place I sped up until my shins were on fire. Alec and Anakin keeping pace. Eyes stinging, and limbs freezing, we were finally steps from our ride off of Midgard.

'I'd stop there if I were you.' A low growl entered the cold air and the three of us halted, terrified.

Once again I found myself scanning my surroundings desperately, but the weather was doing a brilliant job at hiding the owner of the voice. I looked towards Anakin and Alec but neither of them seemed to have found the source either. *Crunch.* The startling sound of footsteps behind us got close enough to reach our ears.

'Who's there?' Anakin spun around the fastest, his voice showing no sign of the fear in his trembling hands.

The voice didn't respond but we were finally able to make out the shape of a man as he got closer and closer to us.

'Who's there?' Anakin repeated.

'I am.'

The dark figure stopped before us. He had short grey hair which was the only feature of his that blended in with the weather. He was dressed entirely in black and carried a walking stick, that he gripped like it was a weapon and not an aid for walking. Despite his obvious age he held himself with the confidence of an arrogant boy. His aura fully believing that he could handle the three of us in a fight. I gulped. A fight was the last situation I wanted to be in right now.

'Give. It. Back.' The man spoke again before Anakin could retort.

The dark figure didn't need to specify, we all knew what he was talking about.

'Not. Going. To. Happen,' Anakin responded, with the same tone.

Well that's just going to make this worse.

'And just who do you think you are?' The man took his time with the long sentence, stretching each word out until it became uncomfortable.

'Who are you?' Alec fired back, obviously not fussed about having to fight this old man.

'My name...' He prompted making sure we knew this was our last chance.

None of us responded. He let out a tut as before taking a step closer to us.

'My name is Daymein. I hope each of you have done everything you wanted to do in this life.'

He took another step forward, not putting any weight on his walking stick. I watched his face as he began to frown, his eyebrows moving closer and closer to his eyes. I continued to stare, horrified, as his wispy grey eyes swapped sharply into a deep blood red. *Wait a minute.* My mind began to swim with my childhood memories. My parents had told me stories about a man with angry blood eyes. This was him. *How had I forgotten he was here?*

'Amolt.' His eyebrows shot away from his eyes as I surprised him. 'Daymein Amolt?'

This man had been banished from Overlegen. He, other than August, was the only one to escape the fate of Anden. Amolt's vengeance had nearly wiped out Overlegen. The corner of his lip turned up when he realised I knew who he was, but just as quickly it dropped into a scowl.

'You're from Overlegen,' he spat, and I realised my mistake.

Overlegen guarded their history and secrets closely, no outsider would have heard of him. I was definitely going to die.

'So that's why they are trying to kill you, Alice.' Anakin's words saved my life.

My eyes were still on Amolt as he paused taking in what Anakin had said. After a moment he pointed at the drive I was holding.

'Azar,' I answered, hoping that he would sense the urgency in my voice.

He winced at the name.

'I have a bone to pick with him,' Amolt scoffed.

'When you say bone to pick..?' Anakin's voice was full of curiosity.

Amolt turned his grey eyes on my friend.

'I mean it literally.' Amolt's words were a gruesome promise that even scared Anakin into reining in his curiosity.

'So this is all great, but we still didn't get your names.' A new young voice spooked me once more, as a green haired kid emerged from behind Amolt's shadow. The kid's pale eyes flicked towards each of us expectantly.

'This is my apprentice, Ray,' Amolt introduced lazily.

'Gale, Devil, and I'm Chameleon.' Alec pointed as he spoke, quickly introducing us.

'You are on your way to Azar now?' Amolt asked, and I nodded, getting too cold to talk.

'Ray and I are coming,' he informed us, not giving us a chance to say otherwise, as if we would.

We all walked silently up to the ship and I was glad when the door opened engulfing me with the warmth of the ship's heaters.

'Where would you like to go?' came the sound of the ships' programmed voice, as Alec pushed the engagement button.

'Undeva.' Anakin's voice was sarcastic. 'We don't even know if it is an actual place.'

'Yeah it is,' Ray commented knowingly. 'I found a map of it once.'

Amolt looked at him puzzled.

'Undeva,' Ray repeated.

Amolt grabbed a nearby chair to stabilise himself. 'Undeva?' Ray's mentor clarified again.

The kid nodded.

'Oh, for the love of Asgard.' Amolt lowered himself shakily into a chair, ignoring our confused faces.

'What?' I asked, desperate, we didn't have any information on this planet and my two best friends were already there.

'Don't worry girly, just stick with us and you'll be fine,' Amolt said, but it was clear he didn't believe his own words.

What was that supposed to mean? I thought to myself, feeling slightly offended and worried for August and Anjelica.

CHAPTER NINE

August – Riptide

'Good to see you again,' a feminine voice called out.

I looked around but all I could see were buff men holding guns.

'You should've known better than to come here.' The woman continued from her hiding spot.

'Show yourself,' Anjelica requested.

I looked back at the blue guy with bat wings and then at the man beside him, not wanting to get caught staring. The lightning thrower that reminded me of a gun, had a purple symbol etched into the side, but I couldn't make out what it was.

'I will burn you all,' Anjelica threatened, giving them a warning.

'Fireproof miss.' One of the armed men patted his chest plate with his free hand.

'I'll burn your hair dummy.'

The man didn't respond but, with a smile, reached up and pulled the black beanie off his head. He was bald. The others did the same, casting their now irrelevant hats to the floor. I patted her on the shoulder, we'd figure something else out.

'Can't you freeze them?' my friend whispered to me.

'With my current level of control? No.'

Anjelica spun to face me, taking away any subtlety our conversation had. 'Why not? My control isn't much better but I'd still burn them.'

I frowned, turning to face her. 'Freezing all of them would drop my body temperature too low.'

'And burning all of them would burn my skin.' She crossed her arms.

Our debate seemed to be making our attackers more uneasy.

'Only if it gets too hot. You could easily sweep a flame around everyone without causing yourself damage.'

'Damn. Next you'll be saying my telepathic skills are unreliable.'

I almost broke into laughter as those words left her completely serious mouth.

'And you'll be suggesting I just flood the city, with the abundance of water present.' I gestured around sarcastically.

Her huff turned into a slight smile as we both turned back to the people surrounding us. Several worried glances were being passed around the group, only the mysterious blue man was not participating. Taking a step forward, I caused the man next to bat wings to turn his gun toward me. Just as I had hoped.

'H,' Anjelica read, as I stepped back with my hands in the air.

'You mean Hagalaz ᚺ ?' I whispered.

'No, I mean H with a *slant*,' she responded, and I sighed.

'Kill them,' the woman said.

I looked at bat wings who wouldn't meet my eyes. *H. Helena!*

'Helena, we know it's you,' I called.

There was a pause and then the men surrounding us stood down. It took the lowering of their weapons to mean I was right. I may have been mistaken but a slight smile flicked quickly across bat wings' face. Helena emerged from the shadows behind him, she was four years our senior and had the same long, perfectly straight, violet hair as she always had. Her grey armour matched her heart and her eyes perfectly, though the revolting colour was not doing her skin tone any favours.

'How's your days of stabbing randos going?' Anjelica asked her bitterly, obviously they had a lot of history.

I only talked to Helena once on Overlegen. She was a friend of Azar's and my sister had introduced me. Helena didn't bother responding to the petty comment as she emerged fully from the group and walked towards us.

Anjelica tried again. 'Freyja, Lavita, you. How many-'

Anjelica was cut off by Helena punching her in the face. The attack was swift, not giving either of us time to react. I watched as Anjelica spat blood all over the ground. Helena's expression smug, as my friend slowly recovered.

'My man over there, Nox, is going to take you into that building beside us and brutally murder you. Then I will capture your friends, upon their arrival, and feed them to the locals,' she spoke coldly, and pointed at bat wings when she mentioned Nox.

What sort of planet were we on? Cannibals? Multiple questions floated through my head, but I didn't have time to contemplate them.

'Oh, so Nox is your boyfriend, not Azar.' Anjelica giggled, earning herself another hard punch.

'You're more my type,' Helena said, with a vile smirk towards my coughing friend.

I tried not to laugh as Anjelica looked into her eyes and smiled, red blood oozing out of her mouth and pouring down her chin.

'Lovely,' she said, spitting in Helena's face, as blood coated her teeth.

'Take them away!' Helena screamed at Nox as she stalked off, probably to clean her face.

I took a gander at the tall, grey, rectangular building next to us, two broken windows were the only things of interest. Then, without warning, two men grabbed my arms tightly.

The Overlegenians released us into a large concrete room. Warm yellow lights swung from the bland ceiling casting shadows in multiple directions, as the extra men left. Nox stood on the opposite side of the room to us, rolling up his jacket sleeves. It was two against one. He tilted his head at me as if he knew what I was thinking.

'Let's see what you're made of ladies.' His voice was deep and somehow calming.

I tied my hair out of my face so that I wasn't going to have any issues, and waited. I prefer not to make the first move against an unknown opponent. Finding it best to know what game your enemy is playing at first. Anjelica, however, has always preferred to make the first move. Not wanting to wait any longer she sent a wave of fire straight for his face. He didn't move. It passed over him crackling and sizzling. He didn't even flinch or catch a light. Anjelica, who was already pissed from being punched by Helena, went to influence his thoughts, but whatever she tried to do backfired and she slipped back onto the hard floor. I looked at her, as she glared back at me and pointed.

Fine. Finding the cold I stuck out a hand to freeze him. With minimal effort he swiped his hand through the air creating a horizontal line and I watched, amazed, as the ice melted and collapsed in a puddle at his feet. I hadn't seen any source of water on our way here and I could hardly feel the rivers on the surface so that wasn't an option, not that it would have been especially useful right now. So instead, we both ran at him. Once within distance I brought my leg up to send a front kick into his stomach, or so he thought. As he brought an arm up to block I swapped into the position for a roundhouse, bending my knee slightly as I crashed my leg into the side of his knee. However, as I hit he swept his leg with the motion of my kick, taking away any proper impact before bringing his leg back into mine rather painfully. While I tried to process how he'd had time to do that, Anjelica sent a well-aimed fist towards his nose. Despite his eyes being fixed on me he managed to catch her fist. A completely impractical move, but he'd done it. She screamed as he put pressure on her bones pulling her hand out of a fist and into a nasty looking lock. In an attempt to help Anjelica I fired a compound attack in his direction. I succeeded in getting him to release her. Both his hands attempted to deflect my strikes and elbows, whilst he brought his leg up to soften the blow from my kick. With a perfectly placed block, that he switched into a painful elbow, he managed to grab my wrist and wrench me into a wrist lock. My face stung from his elbow as I manoeuvred my feet to roll myself out of the lock. Managing to spin the situation on its head as I locked his fingers. While I had him, Anjelica landed a powerful punch on the side of his face but he didn't even bother to glare. He offered her no reaction, not even a wince upon impact. It was like this guy wasn't even trying. With my eyes momentarily off his hand he managed to free himself, sending a full blown kick into Anjelica's stomach. I heard a thud as she went flying into a concrete wall, definitely winded. I managed to land another punch on Nox's face but he used my arm to spin me into a choke hold. Before I could get out of it he kicked my legs out and I dropped to my knees. *Crap. This guy was fast.* He tightened his choke as I tried to free myself from suffocation.

'Not too bad,' he said, his voice filled with subtle laughter.

I looked towards Anjelica. She was hyperventilating against a wall, blood running out her mouth again, and I was struggling to breathe. *So no, not too bad.*

CHAPTER TEN

Ash – Arrow

'If Azar is on Undeva it means he struck a deal with him.' Nora's quivering words repeated back and forth in my head. *But who was him?* There was no doubt that Ace was having the same thoughts as we stood at the entrance of this underground city waiting for Alice, Anakin, and Alec, to arrive. When I'd asked Nora about *him* she'd mentioned something about Guardians but her words had been too slurred for me to understand.

'What even are Guardians?' I asked Ace, unsure.

I had only heard of them a few times.

'Protectors,' he answered in short, making me the tiniest bit frustrated.

'Really?' I huffed sarcastically at him.

Ace released a quick breath. I'd never seen him this on edge.

'There's a myth that God-like beings called Guardians live on the edge of the universe and watch over a select few. They can pick and choose who they look after. I've heard that those chosen are called fortunates,' Ace explained, nicely this time. 'If this planet is actually ruled by one and we upset them we're worse than dead.'

I looked around, Ace's statement giving me a chill.

'The people here don't act like there is a Guardian,' I said, eyeing the seemingly happy faces from this distance, and even a street fight in the corner.

'And besides, if we have a Guardian then hopefully they will save us.'

Ace smiled at my optimism.

'Indeed, but what if another of your Guardian's select few is in even more danger than you?' He dampened my spirits again.

Our conversation had led to a feeling of worry rising from my stomach to my throat.

'Besides-'

I couldn't take any more of this talk so I punched him lightly in the shoulder. He took the hint and smoothly changed his sentence.

'Geez man chill, they're just myths. We should be fine.'

I didn't believe him, and I didn't believe that he believed him. So we ignored each other and continued to observe the seemingly normal society.

'Guys!' I heard Alec's voice as he, Anakin, Alice, and two people I didn't know, exited the mud stairs.

'Welcome to Undeva.' I gestured to this monochrome, underground planet.

'Arrow, Blaze, this is Amolt and Ray,' Alice introduced us to her guests.

I noticed her use of our titles, which most likely meant she didn't fully trust the newcomers.

'Shall we go find Riptide and the other one?' Anakin asked.

Thinking it was a good idea we all headed off down the dark grey streets. I didn't like this planet; it was gloomy, and dejected. For a society that lives purely underground you would've thought it would be lit better, instead of this spooky half effort. I also could no longer hear the locals, nor could I see them. We walked close for fear of getting lost, with Alice and Ace leading the pack, following the path through a small village close to the outskirts of the city. No one had any idea where we were going to find Anjelica and August, so we planned to look everywhere. I watched carefully as we headed past some beyond pale-skinned kids who played outside of their houses. They were the first locals we'd seen in a while. Just like all the other locals, the kids appeared so unnaturally thin, and the mood was that of misery.

'Who would choose to live here?' Anakin whispered to me.

I didn't have an answer for him as I was asking myself the same thing.

'I think we should head for that path up there.' Ace pointed to a blue path that appeared to be looping around the edge of the city.

'Look, I've known them for the longest and I think we should stick to this path,' Alice said, her voice rising with a growing frustration.

'But.' I shut my mouth, changing my mind.

Alice was a sweetheart and was obviously just worried about August and Anjelica. I watched the locals carefully, a strange distaste building up inside of me. The feeling was odd, and I had no idea where it was coming from. My gut was screaming for me to run, but I wasn't going anywhere alone, not here. Ace stopped walking, halting the group.

'Grace, I'm sorry but we really should take the blue out skirting path.' His voice didn't give away what he was feeling.

'Why don't we split up?' Alice suggested, obviously having no gut warning about this place.

'Who'll stay with Grace?' Alec asked, eyeing up Amolt and Ray, the newcomers.

'Ray and I will.' Amolt smiled at Alice, who returned the smile gratefully.

'Stay safe,' I offered them, with a half-smile toward Alice as they continued on.

Alec, Anakin, Ace and I then began heading up the hill – the fastest route back to that blue path. One of the locals we walked past smiled at me revealing sharp pointed teeth. I gulped and sprinted up the hill the rest of the way. My heart didn't stop pounding once I got to the top, and I kept looking around.

'You look like you've just seen a ghost,' Anakin teased me, which I didn't appreciate.

'Close.'

We all turned to see the local who smiled at me standing behind us.

'Draugr!' Anakin gasped, somehow identifying the locals as Norse zombies.

This was bad. The *man* inclined his head at my friend, a signal that he was right, and we were screwed.

'Not to worry, you would've died faster on the other path.'

He too was bone thin. His skin, faded with a slight walnut tinge, hung off him in shreds, exposing patches of fossil-looking bone. He had long strands of grey hair that also appeared to be falling out. I tried to find his eyes, but couldn't. His pupils, eyelids, and area surrounding his eyes, were a bottomless black.

'What were you?' Alec asked, his distaste lined with panic.

'Human.' His short answer threw me off guard.

'How?' I managed to force the words out.

The *man* sneered at me, his absence of eyes and hygiene triggering my gag reflex.

'The Guardian here cursed us for what we did.'

I gulped, the Guardian was real. Nora was right.

'What did you do?' Ace asked, but received no answer, as the *man* examined his grotesque nails.

'Hey! Answer the question.' Anakin pressured the *man*.

'Don't worry about it, you're about to join us.'

That was our warning. The *man* leaped at us, his long black nails outstretched. I was in too much shock to react as he raked his nails down my face. Panic hit me as he landed on me, and warm blood began to pour down my cheeks. I grabbed his disgusting bones and threw him off me, tossing him to the ground. The world blurred as I used my talents to get to him before he could get up. I punched him in the face repeatedly, no blood appeared, just dents in his skull, but I kept going. My adrenaline taking charge. He tried to block but I was too fast and too strong. I didn't even notice he'd gone limp until Ace pulled me off him. Breathing heavily, I sat back staring at his deformed body, as my friends tore clothing and dabbed at my face trying to clean up my wound. We'd only been here five minutes and I was already in a nightmare. Only this definitely wasn't a nightmare of mine. Mine were filled with fire and torment, not bashed up skulls and the living decomposed. I stared at the dents my hands had caused but couldn't stir any emotions, I'd gone stone cold. A state I was not used to.

'Guys.' It was Alec's worried voice that woke me up from my trance. 'More are heading up here.'

I sprung to my feet. 'We have to run.'

'Here.' Alec thrust a computer drive into my hand and I stared at it blankly.

'You two are more likely to survive so take the Segredos drive.' His brutal statement was aimed at Ace and I.

'We're not leaving you two,' I barked back, furious he would even think of that.

'Well one of you should at least get the drives to safety, Loki and Thor would be condemned if Azar got them. Or if we lost them.' He bit back.

I just stared wide-eyed at my friend. *I was never going to run off on them!*

'Alec, I see what you're getting at, but there's safety in numbers.' I relaxed a little as Ace's words shut Alec's down.

'Good, I'm glad we're not running around in different directions because I hate running and there's not much I can do about those things.' Anakin gestured frantically down the hill at the swarming locals.

'Here.' Ace handed Alec the drive we'd picked up, with a reassuring smile. 'You're not going to die. Same for you Anakin.' He offered our panicking green thumbed friend a sturdy gaze.

'Great. Can we run now?' Anakin screeched, as the locals came up the hill.

❧❧❧

My lungs burned in the cold air and I was growing more and more exhausted. We had been cornered and were now fighting for our lives. We had all been scratched and bitten but so far the four of us were still in good shape. I was managing fine as my speed and strength aided the situation. I had figured out that if I palm heeled them in the jaw they would go flying. Alec was doing his best, this situation was not ideal for his talents. Anakin was in the same boat. There was no natural light down here and no normal living thing in sight, so he had nothing to call on. Luckily, Anakin, Alec, and Ace had brought blades with them. That was one of the reasons everyone was still in good shape. Whenever Ace found a source of electricity he'd use it, but there weren't many so, other than his sword, he was relying on telekinesis, which is difficult when you're being swarmed.

'Ash,' Ace called, as he smashed a woman's head into the ground with his sword's pommel.

I sent the Draugr child in front of me through a wall before responding. 'Yeah?'

'Punch your way through there.' Ace pointed to a narrow path which had only a couple Draugr blocking it.

I tried to spot Alec and Anakin in the mess of skinny, half dead bodies.

'We may have a way out,' I called, when I located them.

They were too preoccupied to respond but I was sure that they heard. I ran over to where Ace had pointed and wrestled with one of the women in front of the way out. She managed to get the upper hand on me and rammed me into the wall of a house. I spat at her and sent a punch through her ribs, grimacing as I felt the bones break around my arm. Conveniently the others were in a line, so I used that to my advantage. I kicked the one in front which sent them all falling.

'Let's go,' I called, and Alec, Anakin and Ace appeared behind me.

We ran through as fast as we could, trying not to think about the bones under our feet as we moved.

'Almost there!' I yelled, as the exit sat a few paces from me.

As we emerged on the other side both Anakin and I let out a curse as we realised just how many unfriendly faces we were being greeted by. I didn't even get time to take in our bad luck as a loud bang filled the air. The sound went off, startling me. I took a quick scan of our surroundings but couldn't spot any source.

'Back,' Anakin called in a panic, and with him and Alec in the front, we turned.

Struggling our way back through the crowded street, returning to where we were before. I was halfway through when I felt strong, fleshy arms grab me from behind and haul me back. It was Ace!

'What are you..?'

I turned to look at him as the roof over the path we were on collapsed in my peripheral. Isolating us. If they were lucky Alec and Anakin would've made it back to the corner where we were before. But just like Ace and I, they would be completely surrounded. We looked around us at the cold, black eyes before locking gazes. I offered Ace my hand; he shook it.

'It's been a pleasure.'

We both agreed before starting our repulsed shove through the enemy lines.

సౌஜೌ

My knuckles were bleeding and worn to the bone. My face stung from before and I was covered in painful cuts. Ace and I fought back-to-back and were slowly trying to push to an empty area. Hands reached at us from every angle. We didn't have time to think. Muscle memory was the only thing keeping us alive, or Human. In my haste to send a crippling blow, through the skull of a nearby local, I was tripped up by the foot of a small child. Unable to save my balance I fell face first onto the muddy ground. Hands worked their way towards me as I tried to get back up. I couldn't. Between the mud and my blood I was struggling to breathe. Someone stood on my back, forcing it to crack, as they dug sharp toes into my skin. There was no getting out of this.

'ACE!' I tried to call but my voice was muffled.

I shut my eyes and focused on my strength. Unfortunately, I had been expending mass amounts of energy and I was running low. Bony hands worked their way up my back, trying to get to my head.

I forced myself on to my side, overpowering the man on my back. Gasping for air, I hit the hands in front of me away.

Suddenly a loud crackle consumed the cries of battle. I forced myself up off the ground to see the Draugr around us fall in unison. Ace stood a ways away from me, his brown hair on end. I could see the sparks flying from his fingers. Pride and relief swelled through me. Ace looked over at me, his blue eyes meeting my green ones.

'Well, at least that wasn't scary.'

I grinned at his sarcasm, feeling laughter bubbling up towards my throat. Imagine my surprise, when instead, I emptied anything I had left in my guts onto the already revolting ground. When I had finished I noticed Ace was at my side with a torn piece of fabric in his hand. I steadied myself before taking the cloth to wipe my face.

'Where'd you get this?'

'Nowhere too disgusting.'

I sighed, desperately in need of food, and rest. Internally I was in dismay, a punishment surely for using the talents of my iniquitous species.

'You gonna make it?' Ace asked, his voice empty of its usual playful demeanour.

'I'll manage, let's go look for the others.'

We dashed off towards the blue path to search for Alec and Anakin.

'Where'd you find the electricity?' I asked, to break the silence, and because I wished he'd found it sooner.

'Turns out the Segredos drive in your pocket is a great conductor.'

I sighed, with a slight grin spreading across my face. 'You took your time.'

Removing it from my pocket I gifted it to him. There was definitely no use in me carrying it.

'I didn't want to fry you,' he reasoned, placing it in his pocket.

We kept quiet the rest of the way, hoping not to draw attention to ourselves. Ace stopped walking when we came to a circular part of the path. To our left was the dirt wall that accompanied the path, and to our right was a tall rectangular concrete building. The blue path thinned out from here, branching into several mud ones. I looked around, my eyes scanning for clues of anything.

'Ash,' Ace called, pointing to the ground.

I crouched down next to him to see a spot of red blood.

'Alec, Anakin?' I asked, looking at the concrete building.

'August or Anjelica even,' he added gloomily.

'Clever boys.'

We stood to see, thankfully, not another Draugr, but a girl with long purple hair, grey eyes, and a wicked smile on her face.

'That would be from the late Anjelica Starr,' she informed us, and I became sick with disbelief and anger.

CHAPTER ELEVEN

Anjelica – Firestorm

'You kill her, I kill you,' I spat the words at Nox, breathless and unsure how I would carry through that threat.

August looked to her side, grabbing the arm that was choking her. I smiled, she knew what she was doing, so I went back to focusing on my breathing. Being thrown against a wall wasn't nice, and all this exercise was exhausting. This is what my powers are for, so I don't have to do physical effort. August used her free arm to elbow Nox and then hammered him in the groin. He flinched. His slight reaction, the only one either of us had managed from him. She got to her feet, stepping her left leg behind his closest leg and smashed her hands into his kidneys and ribs. He crumpled, just a little. She hooked her left hand under his chin and pushed his head back before slamming her bent fingers into his throat. Nox stumbled back, annoyingly not choking. August looked at me to check I was okay. I gave her a smile and a wave, deciding it would be best to stay down and do nothing until Nox had been dealt with. August stopped short of him, I had no idea what was in her head but she just stood there staring at him.

'Have we met before?' she asked the last question I would've used in this situation.

I would've gone for; 'What are you?', 'Who are you?' You know, something helpful. *How come I was the only one of us thinking straight?* Damn, being smashed against a wall does a lot of damage. My breath became shallow as Nox regained his balance and stared right at my friend with a devilish look on his face.

'No, August Frost, you have not *met me* before.'

I couldn't work out what he meant by that.

'Then who are you?' She finally asked a question I wanted to know the answer to.

'Nox Belmore,' he answered plainly, causing a mild anger to spread through me.

Why was this guy being so difficult?

He opened his dark blue, bat-like wings to their full. 'You'll find out who I am soon enough.'

His focus was solely on August, completely ignoring me as I made a fuss of getting to my feet. My friend looked at him. Her face emotionless but her eyes wide and curious.

'So, you're not actually trying to kill us?' I asked.

Nox spun around to face me, revealing two pointy vampire-like teeth. Geez this guy has it all; wings, vampire teeth, weird powers, a horn, blue skin, glowing freckles.

'No.' The way he said his answer confused me.

Was that 'no,' *I am not;* or 'no,' as in, *I am trying to kill you?*

'I suggest you two go save your friends now,' he said, and with that, he took off.

His midnight ocean coloured wings flew him through a hole in the ceiling, leaving us to contemplate what had just happened. Unfortunately, August didn't give me time to do that as she dragged me with her, running out of the building.

'Hey, you know Nox kind of looks like-' I stopped myself. The sentence I had almost uttered making me sound crazier than I was.

August's expression told me that she knew what I was about to say. Despite me being the one who can hear emotional thoughts, she always seemed to know what was going through my head. Red against blue brought my eyes down to the ground, which was stained with my blood from when Helena punched me. I grimaced. August looked at me and followed my gaze to see the blood.

'Really?' she asked, which triggered my exhausted emotions.

'That bitch made me bleed!' August let a small smile slip onto her face, no doubt wanting to remind me that many people have made me bleed.

'I got revenge against most of them,' I responded to her unspoken statement.

'Didn't say anything.' She giggled, pretending to put her hands up.

I looked around. There were two different ways our friends could've gone, back towards the houses or continued around the edge.

'Let's split up.'

I let August come to that conclusion, not wanting to be at fault if it goes terribly wrong.

'Don't die please,' I called, as I turned my back on her and ran along the path that led to the houses.

CHAPTER TWELVE

August – Riptide

I peeked out from behind a corner to see Ash lying in a pool of red on the floor. Sticky liquid was gushing out from a slash on his stomach. Ace was standing over him. The hilt of his sword locked in on Helena's before he flung it forward, catching her nicely just above her heart. He too was scratched up and bleeding, but nowhere near as critical as Ash. If my heart wasn't pounding before it was now. We desperately needed to get Ash to Alice, wherever she was. I retreated back behind the corner taking a deep breath, and hoping for the best, as I focused on the cold feeling. Once I had latched on to the cold I pulled it upward once again.

Hey, I think I'm getting better at using this! With my gift ready I stepped out from behind the corner, extending my fingers towards Helena wishing for a frozen statue. My wish, however, was not granted. *What was the chance of her gifts overriding mine?* Instead of freezing, she was saved by a protective grey haze that seemingly evaporated the ice I'd sent towards her. My feet were lurched forwards a few steps by an icy pull. A strange feeling, similar to that of betrayal, washing over me. Helena didn't even spare me a glance, she was far more interested in fighting Ace than whatever was happening to me right now. I withdrew my extended arm, staring at my hand. Blue lines, laid out similarly to cracks, had formed on my skin. An acute, painful cold began emitting from the cracks, and it took all I had not to scream. Worried, as the pain shot further up I pulled back my jacket sleeve. The tight leather resisted a little but eventually gave in, exposing the same cracks spreading up my arm. In addition to the pain, a severe chill crept through the rest of my body, its intensity increasing. Thinking it best to pinpoint the cause of these blue lines, my attention went back to my hands. Blue and pale white wisps of ice were being pulled from my skin like steam leaving water. Holding onto the thought of warm water and steam I closed my eyes trying to let go of the feeling that drives my gifts, but I couldn't. It was as if my control had frozen over. An off switch that wouldn't budge. Desperate, I decided to give up trying to shove the cold down and instead tried searching for any fiery emotion or feeling. I was greeted by nothing but harsher cold as the excessive use of my gifts dropped my temperature.

A clang of swords shook my eyes open and I watched helplessly as Helena disarmed Ace, ramming him back into a wall before shoving her grey blade against his throat. He didn't make a sound as Helena paused, turning to offer me a sickening grin. The expression Ace had fixed on Helena was just about as cold as my bones were.

'Don't.' I frowned, just as much at the shake in my voice than at Helena, as she fully turned to face me.

There was a pause as we stared each other down.

'Don't what? Cause your stolen power to consume you or slit his throat?' Her voice was mocking, she knew full well what I had meant.

'Don't slit his throat,' I responded bitterly, as the numbness in my shaky hands and arms began to spread over the rest of me.

Channelling ice always caused a drop in my body temperature, but this was a cold like nothing I'd ever experienced.

'Alright then.' Helena respected my wish removing her sword from Ace's neck, but as she did so her sharp edged hilt caught him across the forehead and he dropped as blood spilled across his skin.

Ace! I gritted my teeth as I felt my knees begin to weaken – I hated the idea of being crouched on the ground in this situation. Jolts of sharp ice flashed across my body and my legs gave way to the numbness, as Helena reached me.

'Take heart, August. It is abnormal that you've lasted this long.' She watched my expression as she wiped Ace's and probably Ash's blood from her sword with her sleeve.

'Great. I'll be sure to add that to my list of questions,' I spat at her sarcastically.

'Love lists.' Helena mocked. 'Got an example of your questions?'

'Why is your hair purple and not grey like the rest of you?'

'It's dried blood.' She smiled savagely, exposing almost grey teeth.

Which was not a surprise. *Ew.*

'When was the last time you had a shower?' I struggled to get the words out as my vocal cords started to fail me.

The struggle was well worth the look on Helena's disgusted face. 'You may as well tell me where you stole all this power!'

The purple haired soldier leaned over me, reaffirming her powerful position. How I wish I could respond. I wish my brain was functioning well enough to retort back, or at least move. Instead, I was forced to sit there internally shaking with frustration while I was consumed by hypothermia.

Helena raised her sword to my head. I tried to move, shakily managing to look up at her impending blade, but she faltered in bringing it down. Her grey tipped fingers released the blade, both hands flying to her neck, as shock and suffocation lined her features. Her hands desperately grasping at a thin black lace.

By my luck the sword managed to miss me, its point only managing a slight scrape on the left side of my face. The warm blood that trickled slowly down my cheek acted like a catalyst. As slowly, inch by painful inch, the nasty chill began to leave. Icy wisps had finally stopped pouring from my fingertips. The blue cracks were disappearing, and I quickly rammed the cold source of my gifts deep down.

With Helena still choking, and my movement starting to return, a warm and welcome feeling of revenge flooded through my blood. I fought with each of my shaky limbs, impatiently, until I managed to successfully lift myself off the ground. With her gift off and her attention distracted, I seized the opportunity.

Summoning Vorago, as a knife in my right hand, I swung, slashing the blade cleanly across her face and through her nose. She stumbled to the side, choking harder as blood poured out of her newly destroyed nose, right into her gasping mouth.

Ace! He stood where she had just. A frigid look on his face and a black shoe lace in his hand.

'You had to cut her!'

'I almost died, I was acting on impulse.'

'Next time *you* strangle the psychopath with a thin material and *I'll* do the blade work.'

Our conversation was forced to an end as we watched Helena pull a short sword from a sheath behind her back.

You were right behind her. My complaint was under my breath and yet somehow Ace knew to say something.

'My options were; save you, or remove her weapon.'

Not being able to help it I let out a small laugh. For a reason unbeknownst to me I found our bickering offered me some relief from the tension.

'Thank you.'

Ace didn't bother to respond as he charged forward, beating me to the next blow with the blade he'd just recovered.

'Bastard!' Helena screamed, as Ace raked across her nose wound with the pommel of his sword.

On his arm's way back he lifted his aim and threw all his force into her temple. This time she was the one to drop cold to the floor.

No sooner had she hit the ground, Ace and I turned and ran over to a, still bleeding, Ash.

'August.' He grinned at me displaying the blood in his teeth. 'It's good to see you.'

'Hang in there Ash.'

I couldn't find it in me to return the smile as I dipped my knees into his blood pool on the ground and began to remove his bomber-style jacket. With Ace's help I managed to tie it tight around his wound, hoping it would limit further blood loss.

'Do you know where Alice might be?' I asked Ace.

'No we-' His answer was cut off by Ash's stifled scream.

Both Ace and I snapped our attention back to him. Helena stood over us, fully awake, and with a wicked smirk on her grey face, as her right foot ground Ash's hand into the mud. Her left foot was on the side of Ash's face. He had turned his head to avoid her boot catching his eye.

Seriously? What sort of – Why not just run away? Why risk Ace and I killing her?

Ace shifted his weight onto one leg as he kicked her foot away from Ash's face. I then stood and sent my boot into her left knee. She removed her foot from Ash's hand as she let out a high pitched growl. Her knee, no longer sitting in the right place. Averting my eyes from the gag inducing sight, I summoned my swords. I guess hurting Ash was Helena's version of fair warning. She really should've just yelled or something.

Her violent smoky eyes met mine as she began to swing her blade in an arch towards Ace and I. Both of us, with our swords in hand, ducked, then carefully stepped around Ash. Fixing another glare on Ace, she swung her sword arm out towards his neck, while attempting to kick her injured leg in my direction. I blocked with my blade, taking no pity on her squeal, as Vorago met her shin bone.

Despite having a severely injured leg, Helena was still one of Overlegen's best blade wielders. This meant that Ace and I were at a slight disadvantage. Even though it was two against one, we hardly knew each other and hadn't fought side by side before. So we kept it simple, attacking Helena one at a time. I was the least injured out of the three of us, not that it mattered much, we were all equally fatigued.

With minimal footwork and rather large actions we weaved, parried, and slashed at each other. Helena extended her arm towards my stomach, I parried, she smashed my sword off target before parrying Ace's next attack. While she tried to riposte towards Ace, I brought Vorago towards her sides in a feint. She bought it, changing the direction of her blade to deflect my sword. But it wasn't there. Instead, it was careening towards her shoulders. She screamed as her bone connected with my blade, then again as Ace sent his sword into her side. Golden blood began to ooze out of her wounds.

'I'm surprised it's not purple,' I commented, as I yanked my sword from her shoulder.

Helena responded by punching me in the face with her free arm. Her strike shocked me a bit, and I stumbled backwards with the momentum. Now out of distance, I watched as she headbutted Ace before shoving him away and wrapping her hands around his sword. Pain flared in her eyes as she pulled the sword out of her side. Ace's blade, which was now dipped in golden Overlegenian blood, was thrust toward his stomach. He moved back with her attack, managing to avoid being impaled. But he was running out of room. The square we were fighting in was limited in size by the closely packed brown houses.

I pictured Gelu in my mind causing the sword to come flying towards my left hand. Once I had it I turned it into a throwing star and aimed at Helena's neck. She chose to block it with Ace's blade, giving him an out. With nothing but hatred in her eyes, Helena turned to me. She hobbled over as I tried to keep our distance as it was, but the muscles in my legs hadn't recovered from the freezing quite as quickly as my arms had and, despite her hobble, Helena was gaining on me. My retreat was halted by a wall. Readying Vorago I braced myself for her assault. The scratch of our blades as they met was intolerable.

'You'll never survive this Frost.' Helena taunted through gritted teeth.

'Why's that?' I asked her, through my clenched jaw.

'Cause you're fifteen, I've got four more years of experience than you.'

'Maybe,' I answered, trying to ignore the burn in my arm, as I concentrated on holding my parry she was trying to force down.

'Or maybe, you're outnumbered,' I continued.

On cue, Ace swung Gelu at the back of Helena's head.

'That's for Ash,' Ace whispered to her, as the blade connected with her neck.

The strike was clean and lobbed her head off with one swipe, but we didn't watch it fall as we were far more concerned about Ash's state.

Thankfully, he was still breathing.

'What happened to the others?' I asked Ace, who was looking at me worried.

'We all got separated by the locals,' he said, with distaste.

'Anjelica has gone to find them,' I told him, and he relaxed ever so slightly.

'Just leave me. Go get Thor and Loki,' Ash told us, his hands holding tight to his wound.

I shook my head looking into Ash's green eyes. 'Not going to happen.'

'I'll look after him.' A familiar deep voice came from the shadows in front of us.

Ace stood, Gelu still in his hands, as Nox came out of the darkness. He was wearing a dress suit similar to those from Earth, minus the shirt. The outfit was a similar dark blue to his skin with white hemming and a pink pocket square. The colour pallet accentuating his enigmatic demeanour. This outfit was drastically fancier than the casual blue suit he'd worn when Anjelica and I met him. Both boys gasped as they took in Nox's appearance. Ace bravely didn't hesitate to lock eyes with him.

'You're the Guardian here.' The words coming out of his mouth did not make any sense to me.

'Correct.' Nox smiled.

I was out of the loop here.

'Guardian?' I asked, still confused about whose side Nox was on.

'Dangerous beings with unique abilities,' Ace told me. 'They protect those of their choice.'

I looked back at Nox, his silvery eyes seemingly confirming Ace's statement.

'The locals said you cursed them.' Ace's attention was directed back towards Nox.

'Indeed.' He didn't seem bothered by Ace's questions, as he swaggered further out of the shadows.

'Why?' Ace's voice was full of respectful curiosity, as he entertained conversation with the celestial.

'They laid hands on my partner,' Nox said plainly, his voice resonant.

'Is your partner alright?' Ash croaked, straining his head back to look at Nox.

'They only knocked him out.' Nox's eyes darkened as they landed on Ash.

'Geez you're protective.' Ash tried to laugh but coughed instead, thankfully no blood came up.

'Are you going to kill us?' Ace questioned Nox again.

The navy skinned Guardian's eyes met mine. Neither of us held the look as he turned to survey the scene in front of him. A few moments passed without anyone saying a word. Without any hints to what he was thinking Nox swept his gaze from one location to another. His swooping eyes taking in my crouched position next to Ash and the bloodied sword in Ace's hands. Only when he spotted Helena's severed head did he respond to Ace.

'No, not today.'

A grin spread across Ace's face and he looked at me, I looked back at him, confused.

'He's *your* Guardian.'

The slight smile on Nox's face confirmed what Ace had said.

'You tried to kill us.' I went to fold my arms but remembered I was holding a weapon.

'No, your friend tried to kill me, I just wanted to see what you could do.'

I took a deep breath. 'Unbelievable.'

Hearing this, Nox shrugged subtly.

'If you are my Guardian, why were you working with Helena?' I asked, standing, with a swift glance at the severed head.

Helena's pure purple hair was slowly being corrupted by gold.

'Figured it would be easier to keep an eye on you if Azar brought you here.'

I narrowed my gaze on the single horn on Nox's head before shifting my focus back to Ash.

'Frost, you two go, I'm good here with bat-man.' Ash grinned, knowing that he'd get away with that comment due to his current circumstances.

I wasn't completely sold on the idea of leaving Ash with my *Guardian* but there wasn't much Ace or I could do for him. Azar would also definitely know we were here, meaning we had to get to Thor and Loki, fast.

'Will you look after Ash until our healer gets here?' I met my Guardian's silver eyes, they caught this planet's light, strangely allowing their shade to shift fluidly.

Nox nodded curtly by dipping his head not more than a centimetre. Taking that as confirmation, Ace and I started to head off when Nox's voice stopped us.

'Try the blue building east of here.'

I nodded my thanks to him, as Ace and I headed away.

'August, here.' Ace handed Gelu back to me, once we had the blue path back in sight.

'Thank you,' I said, as I tucked my weapons, in knife form, into my belt.

∽∽∽

Ace and I walked swiftly east, keeping an eye out for any sign of blue, against the brown, and traces of grey. There wasn't a single cannibal to be seen which I guessed meant that the others had their undivided attention.

'How do you know about Guardians?' I asked Ace.

He kept looking ahead as he considered his next words.

'Just stories.'

There was no emotion in his voice, and he wore a blank face, so I couldn't make any assumptions. Not wanting to ask any more questions, we walked on in silence. I was growing bored of the mud, or fully concrete houses, as we headed deeper into the city. The repetitive lack of colour began to hurt my head as I desperately looked around for variation in the form of blue. We were only just entering the posh part of this underground city. Though posh in Undeva just meant less mud and more grey.

'August.' Ace's voice dragged my attention away from our eerie surroundings.

There on the horizon was a large glass and wood building, covered in blue lights. We sped up as we left the blue path and ventured back into the local area. The stench of damp mud, leaving the air slightly, as we became surrounded by concrete.

'Isn't it a bit odd to keep prisoners in the nicest building here?' I asked, and Ace muttered in agreement as we got closer to the blue building.

Almost there, we slowed our pace and approached cautiously. Stopping at the bottom of a set of marble stairs. I spotted movement inside, a man, wearing all navy and carrying a gun.

'I've seen that guy before,' I whispered to Ace.

'Friendly?'

'The opposite.'

I turned my attention off Ace and scanned our environment but, by the time I looked back at where he was standing, he was gone.

Knock, knock. Ace instead stood at the top of the marble steps in front of the blue glass door.

'Who are you?' The man I recognised, scowled at him.

'That's not the line,' Ace sounded, insulted.

He crunched his fingers into a fist and then thrust his hand into the man's face. The man looked relieved as Ace's fist was blocked by glass, but he didn't get a chance to react when the door broke free of its hinges and smashed into him. Ace opened his hand and glided it towards the door frame, palm up.

'After you.' He gestured to me, as I ran up the marble steps to join him.

Ace followed me through the door and into the rather nice building. We were greeted by about five, or so, armed men dressed completely in tormenting blue.

'If I were you I'd leave.' I gave them fair warning.

No one moved, so I extended my hand allowing cold to flow through me. The nice thing about having gifts is that it makes it easier for one to defend themselves, however, it did bug me just a little that I hadn't the slightest clue where I got them from. I really hoped that one day I'd find an explanation.

'Geez Frost.' Ace stood next to me with a huge grin on his chiselled face, he was untouched apart from his eyelashes which had been slightly frosted.

I covered my mouth trying not to laugh.

He glared at me and said sarcastically, 'You froze me!'

I giggled, my hand no longer covering my mouth. 'Do you feel frozen?'

'I bet I look frozen.' Ace batted his eyelashes at me exaggerating his new look.

Still laughing, I left him and went to scout out the building. It was nicely built, large and in a good location. The city's edge sloped upward, giving the largely glass building a good vantage point. The wooden floors were sprinkled with golden sparkles. Most of the exterior walls were made of thick glass that displayed the gloomy blue path around it. Everything else was the same wood as the floor. I went into the main corridor, poking my head into every room I walked past. Most of which had a desk that matched the floor, and a window that looked into the corridor, or room, behind it. Having explored almost everywhere I headed for the large wooden doors at the end of the main corridor. They were considerably heavier than any of the others. The weight of the doors forcing me to use muscle strength I hardly had left. They clicked open revealing a dark room, one singular light switched on. The light swung ominously from the ceiling, casting both light and shadows onto the contents of the room.

'Ace,' I yelled, too quietly for him to hear me.

I was too intrigued to yell again. The room was a storage room full of weapons, but these weapons were unlike any I'd seen before. Some of them were neatly organised on shelves, or hanging from the walls, while others lay on the floor. The walls and the floor were laced with a dark green metallic substance that obtained no temperature from my touch, or that of the icy room. The weapons were visibly old and not too well looked after. The grips on the hook swords disintegrating, multi-ended blades, bent to appear almost as enlarged throwing stars, lay discarded in a pile to my left, and a tall multi-bladed spear type thing was leant up against some other small unrecognisable weapons. I ran a finger across the handles and blades of a couple, surprised by their warmth even in this cold room. Heading toward the back corner I spotted a dark green cloth draped across something. Just in front of the cloth were a group of metallic green darts. Every edge of these darts was sharpened to perfection and even the spikes on the tail end looked sharp enough to cut you if you stared at them for too long. I wasn't sure what weapon Loki was known for but if I had to guess it would be something like these. With that thought in mind I reached down to remove the cloth from whatever it was concealing. A triumphant smile lit up my face as I pulled the cloth away. *They were here!*

I left the room in a hurry, allowing the door to shut itself as I raced down the corridor. I had already searched the rest of the building without finding Thor or Loki, but at least I knew they'd been here. I skidded to a halt once I reached the main entrance. Ace had shown the last of the living popsicles to the door, leaving the main entrance looking like an abandoned ballroom with its glittery floor and low hanging lights. I didn't like that thought. Anjelica, Alice, and I had been to a ball once. It didn't go well.

'What did you find?' Ace asked, noticing my expression.

He was leant up against the wooden wall using it as a brace to take the pressure off of his feet.

'I found Mjölnir!'

Ace rocked off the wall standing straight. 'Where?'

'The storage room down the end of the corridor. I looked everywhere else but I didn't find any sign of them.'

I tried not to think about how much I wanted to sit down, as I spoke. My feet were starting to scream in my boots.

'They must be close then.' Ace reasoned, I nodded in agreement.

'Shall we go?'

'Definitely,' Ace said, as he headed for the front door.

I followed him, without voicing any of the complaints in my head out loud. My muscles felt sore from fighting, and running, and I was absolutely starving. I couldn't even remember the last time I'd eaten.

Just as Ace and I reached the bottom of the marble stairs a high pitch scream lit up in my ears. I looked around not seeing an obvious source for the sound. I'd searched the entire building.

'Maybe they're under the building,' Ace suggested, as he headed along the left side of the house studying the wall carefully.

Doing the same, I headed for the right hand side and started heading around the house slowly. White marble ran along the side of the building, above it the wood began in panels. There was nothing suspicious at all. So I kept walking round until I reached Ace, who was standing staring at the wall puzzled.

'Nothing,' I told him.

'Same.' He sighed, turning to lean on the side of the building.

'We'll find them.' I tried to reassure him.

He stared at the ground, putting his left leg up against the wall to shift his weight.

'I know.' He kept his attention on the mud ground as he spoke, his voice unusually soft.

Click.

The noise came from the wall as Ace adjusted his leg position. Ace lifted his head, as his defining smile spread across his face, and his eyes met mine.

'Imagine that,' Ace said, as he swung his leg forward and then kicked it hard, back against the wall he was leaning on.

An oval section of the wall whirled open. Smiling, I ducked down through the door to see a set of barely lit mud stairs. The further down the stairs went the higher the ceiling became. I started my descent down, trying my best not to slip on the gooey substance. About halfway down I was greeted with a splintering screech. Quickly covering my ears, I tried my hardest to stay standing. The sound was too high pitched to be Thor and Loki, or at least I hoped it was. Ace didn't make a sound as he followed me down the steps. I had no idea if he was even still behind me, but it didn't matter now. The screeching, and the mud, left my mind as a wooden door appeared in front of me. I reached for the circular handle but Ace tapped my hand out of the way before I could grab it. I frowned at him, wanting an explanation. He pointed at the hinges on the door. I understood. He wanted to rip it clean open. Extending my right hand, I let the cold sensation spread through my fingers, and we watched as frost delicately spread across the surface of the rusty metal hinges. I released my gifts when the hinges were completely covered in a translucent white. Ace stepped back up a few steps and I pressed myself to the mud wall beside the door. Watching as he extended his arm and flexed his wrist. The hinges, being frozen, gave way nicely and the door went flying towards Ace. He placed it calmly to the side.

'You ready?' he asked quietly.

I nodded before heading cautiously towards the door.

We were in a gloomy grey room, the same one I had spoken to Azar in. The vision, or whatever it was, had been true to reality. Reflective tiles did indeed cover the floor. The odd set of boxes were present, and the wooden desk and chairs stood in solitude on the left side of the room.

'The key should be on that box,' I whispered to Ace.

'Feel like flying?' Ace had obviously noticed the small rectangular sensors, dotted in low positions on the walls around the room.

They weren't the only things to watch out for. The diagonal lines created by the tiles joining, had sheathed blades in them, and I could only guess at what the reflective tiles did.

'Please don't drop me.'

'I won't,' he promised, and with that my feet were lifted off the ground by Ace's telekinesis.

It still surprised me that his gifts were triggered by the movement of his hands. In most cases that I'd heard of, telekinesis was a mental gift that didn't require physical movement. I'd have to ask him about it when all this was over. It felt as if a harness had been strapped to me as I was hoisted away from the ground. Despite the clear grip Ace's telekinesis had on me, it still took a moment to calm my mind, as I got used to moving through the air with no effort or control. I glided over the sensors and blades, until I reached the box with the key on it. The box was small and low to the ground, making it just out of my arm's reach. Uncomfortably, I bent my knees and reached down. This time, the cold metal rested on my hand instead of passing through it. As soon as I had picked it up Ace moved me towards Loki, who was the nearest of the two Gods.

'What on earth took you so long?' he complained, as I reached him.

'You didn't send us a postcard.' I fired back at him, and he grinned.

Loki was tied up on the wall, so I wasn't sure how this was going to work.

'Ace?'

'I've got both of you,' he responded reassuringly, raising another hand in our direction.

Quickly, I uncuffed Loki, weary that Ace would have to bring the God back to him while holding me here.

'Brace yourselves.' Ace's voice sounded like a whisper, more to himself than to us.

I grabbed onto the cold handcuff that Loki's right wrist had been in moments before. Hoping that if Ace's telekinesis dropped me, the cuff would be enough to stop me falling. Loki swept his greasy hair away from his forehead as Ace pulled him forward and over to the way we'd entered the room. Nothing went wrong as Loki got closer and closer to where Ace was standing. Once the God was successfully on the ground behind him, Ace focused back on me. I let go of the metal cuff and glided towards Thor. Unlike Loki, he didn't make any sarcastic comments. Thor's restraints let off an unwelcome echo as I freed him from the wall.

'Bring us back cousin,' Thor called to Ace, his darting eyes distracting from the full smile he was putting on.

I tried to relax as we were pulled towards the door but even the air in this room felt uneasy. A slight blur of light had my gaze snapping to the right. A blade cut through the air, only narrowly missing me. Time played out in slow motion as my eyes followed the knife. It arched, putting itself directly in line with Ace. Just as Thor and I gradually got closer, so did the blade. It was just out of arm's reach, flying in front of us. Reaching for the cold at the pit of my centre I tried to create a wall of ice between Ace and the blade. But, luckily, Loki beat me to react. He reached across Ace, and with perfect timing, prodded the knife's pommel causing it to flop to the floor.

'You were lucky this time Frost.' The voice of Azar turned my full attention to a doorway on the right side of the room.

I didn't respond to our shadowy adversary as Ace set Thor and I back on the ground. The second our feet connected with the slimy mud floor we sprinted up the stairs.

↜↝↜

'Nice place.' Thor smiled, as we walked through the main door of the wood and glass building.

'We commandeered it,' Ace said with a slight smile, as he quickly scanned around making sure we were the only ones in here.

'All the best things are.' Loki nodded in approval at us.

'So, where is the rest of the gang? I take it you two didn't come alone,' Thor asked, flicking his long hair behind his shoulder as he headed towards one of the hallways.

'Missing,' I responded.

'They'll be here somewhere,' Thor said, thinking that his statement was helpful to us in some way.

'We best find them. Azar's definitely going to try to kill us now and I personally don't feel like dying today.' Loki added another totally helpful statement to the conversation.

'Well, at least the kids should find them. We've been tied to a wall for the last day or two,' Thor yelled, as he plodded along another hallway.

Loki, Ace, and I followed just close enough to hear what he was saying.

'Agreed. We can stay and make sure no one takes back the building.' Loki made the decision for Ace and I, as Thor emerged from a neighbouring room.

'Have any of you seen Mjölnir?' the God questioned, as he walked into another room.

'I swore they put it somewhere around here.'

'It's just down the end of the main corridor,' I offered, pointing in the direction as I spoke.

'Are you sure?' He frowned, as if he wasn't convinced I had the right hammer.

'Yes.' I let my attitude seep into my answer.

Did he not want to have to walk and get it?

'Well, what did it look like?' The sunset haired God folded his tattooed arms, flexing his muscles as he spoke.

'Thor, seriously?' Ace cut in, happy to point out his cousin's strange behaviour.

'Again, I have just been tortured by Azar, one of you could go get it for me.'

I shared a look of disbelief with Ace, his jaw tensed a bit but he didn't respond. Instead, Ace extended an arm in the direction I had pointed and closed his eyes. After a few seconds I heard the loud slam of a wooden door followed by the sight of Thor's silver hammer moving towards us. Ace's gift was pulling it by the strap. Just like all the other times I'd seen it, Mjölnir was smoky grey with varying textures, due to the different carvings etched onto its surface. It had a slightly rounder shape than a normal hammer, and an extra impact point in the middle, which rose up creating a sharp peak. Its handle was wrapped with warmly coloured leather, creating a wrist strap at the end, which I had used to carry it on Asgard.

'August, you were right indeed, this is my hammer.' Thor seemed overjoyed and completely oblivious to the slightly annoyed expressions both Ace and I had.

'Go on now, go find your friends so we can get the Helheim out of here.'

With that, both Gods walked past us. Loki offering a slightly sympathetic smile before heading into a large room to chat with his nephew.

With my stomach violently attacking me, my throat dry, every muscle I had aching, and my feet beyond sore, I walked with Ace towards the missing door to the right of the glass window.

'August, I don't suppose you could conjure some water or something?' Ace asked me, his voice ever so slightly raspy, clearly he was feeling the same as I was.

I concentrated on the cold for a moment, searching, just in case I'd missed a source of water the last time I'd checked.

'I'm sorry Ace, the only sources of water are on the surface and they're just too far away.'

He offered me a small smile to show he understood, before continuing outside and walking down the steps.

CHAPTER THIRTEEN

Alice – Gale

Clutching a blood soaked hand to my stomach, my mind was desperately trying to find a way out of here. I wasn't hurt anymore but I was alone and surrounded. I held my breath from behind a collapsed roof that provided me with a hiding spot for the time being. The boys had been right about this place. A low, growling noise startled me, they were getting closer. I was fighting tears, I didn't want to die like this. *If only I hadn't been separated.* A small voice in the back of my head piped up. I shut it down. I had made it through tougher situations. I could do this. However, the fear circulating my body hadn't caught up with my new mental attitude.

Not a single muscle wanted to move as I watched a decaying arm reach in through the gap. I didn't scream, there was no good that could do. So, instead, I took a deep breath and did the only thing that I could. Desperately, I focused my emotions on the air in an attempt to blow the local's decaying arm away. For a brief moment the arm was pulled out of my sight, probably not due to my feeble attempt, but as quickly as it left it was replaced with the creature's head. I gasped, my hand flying towards my mouth. This local was particularly ghastly in appearance. Hardly any flesh was

199

covering the grey bones on its face and neck. Most of the wretched yellow flesh hung off in uneven strips, exposing strange grey bubbles and splotches of pus. I was too busy trying not to gag as it reached in and grabbed my arm, ripping it away from my face. I tried to reach for the knife in my pocket but the local pulled me towards him. Trying not to think of the bone thin fingers, and other revolting bits of flesh or fabric, that were digging into the skin on my arm, I resisted. Wiggling and flailing in an attempt to hit him and free myself, I felt his bones tighten his grip with each of my movements. Each glance that I took at the partly attached, rotten flesh made my stomach try to exit my body. There was nothing I could do as he pulled me out into the open. The second I was dumped onto the mud floor they all closed in. This time I screamed. *What was I meant to do?* Several razor sharp nails scraped across my face and limbs as I shoved myself violently to my feet. Though I hardly managed with all the revolting decaying bodies drowning me. *This was how I'd die.* That horrid thought shot jolts of fear through my already cowering veins. My desperate desire to live had me wrapping my hand tightly around a nearby local's arm, as others continued trying to scratch my skin off. Thank Asgard they weren't going for my head yet. There was only so much one could heal. Without properly thinking it through I plunged into my fear.

My consuming emotion focused my power onto the creature's cells. As I let myself sink deeper into my despair an imaginary warm yellow light tore through the shaky darkness of my current emotional state. If I had been thinking properly I would never have thought of this, but I wasn't thinking. I was trying to survive. I aimed the yellow beams of my power towards the cells of the local who I had my grip on. Opening my eyes I watched as he screamed and grabbed his nearest neighbour. Yellow light shot through their skin, creating waves as it plunged in and out. The local that had just been grabbed copied this action. Sinking its nails into the shoulder flesh of another, who copied this reaction, until I had a direct line to all of the zombie-like locals surrounding me. They were too far cursed for any permanent healing to be done so that left me one option. I tried to focus my eyes on the ground as the sight was too disgusting. Annoyingly though, the screams of the locals drew my eyes up off the mud floor. The one in front of me was enveloped in a yellow haze and slowly, like the others, began to turn more and more Human. The flesh hanging off their limbs slowly sewing itself back into place. Their skin violently lurching with lumps of red. The black pits of their eyes slowly sinking beneath the skin and into the skull, leaving eyelids and eyebrows to form. But the eye socket wasn't filled. No hair sprouted properly on their heads either, some things I just couldn't heal. Even if I stopped and left them looking like this they would soon return to their decaying form, their curse was the strongest kind. Slowly their amended form started to evaporate into dust.

'ALICE!' I heard the voice of Angelica just as the locals vanished into golden dust, completely disappearing before they hit the ground.

I sighed in relief, as the crazier of my two crazy blonde friends rounded the corner. Anjelica was closely followed by Ray and Amolt. I would've run straight over and hugged my dear friend but I was exhausted. So I waited, glad not to be alone, until Anjelica scooped me into an embrace. She too was breathing heavily as if she'd been running. An unusual action for Anjelica. Neither of us spoke for a minute, just relishing the fact that we were both alive.

'Anjelica, where's August?' I pulled out of the hug suddenly worried about our friend.

'She's alive. I just ran into her and Ace. They're looking for Alec and Anakin.'

I took another deep breath in relief. The exhaustion, from using that much emotion, begging to hit me. Anjelica understood and put my arm around her shoulders to help me walk towards the others.

'What did you do?' she asked.

I looked around. I didn't have an explanation for what had just happened.

'Ash!' I gasped, recalling that Anjelica hadn't mentioned him.

I pulled my arm off her shoulders and gripped them instead.

'We have to find him.' *He could be dead.*

'Not dead.' Anjelica must have heard my thought, I was rather emotional right now.

'He's with Nox, though he is in a bad condition.'

Still worried about Ash, I took a weak step away from Anjelica surveying her. I hadn't noticed before but her nose was severely bloody, and she was covered in scrapes and visible bruises.

'Who's Nox?' I asked, as my friend held up a finger, before coughing a rather large amount of blood onto the muddy ground.

'Something about being a Guardian or something. Not sure.'

I stepped back over to her, placing a hand on her back as she let out another blood filled cough.

'And who did this to you? The locals?'

'Nope. Nox.'

'What?' I asked, not hiding my surprise as I reached for the last of my emotions.

'I'm fine. And besides, I think he's actually on our side.'

I shook my head at my deluded friend as I shot as much of my healing power as I could muster into her.

'Thanks,' Anjelica mumbled, as we both collapsed.

Exhaustion flooding over me completely.

'Are you two quite alright?' Amolt asked, as he and Ray came over to us.

All I could manage was a sarcastic thumbs up, taking another moment to just breathe before I joined Anjelica, and got to my unsteady feet.

'Firestorm, where's Riptide?' Amolt questioned, obviously having been filled in with everyone's titles.

'Big glass building with blue lights somewhere that way,' Anjelica answered, casually pointing back at the way they'd come.

'We'll be heading that way then. Do survive.' Amolt smiled at me, before Ray and he turned and headed off in the direction Anjelica gave them.

How helpful.

⊰⊱⊰

We had been wandering for what felt like hours, when we turned a corner into an alleyway to see Ash lying in a pool of crusted blood. I didn't need to be a healer to know that he was barely hanging on. Forgetting all of my ailments, I ran towards him but skidded to a halt as a tall, blue-winged man appeared in front of me, blocking Ash's body. He tilted his head at me, his eyes threatening.

'Nox, she can heal him.' Anjelica ran to my side.

'You know this guy?' I asked, still looking over the polished blue man.

'Yes, this is the Nox I told you about.'

Nox, this tall, winged, horned, blue skinned, star freckled man, with wavy hair a similar colour to his skin, wearing a sharp suit that was missing a shirt, is a Guardian? If that was an actual thing. Nox studied Anjelica for a second before stepping aside. I ran to Ash and placed my hand on his forehead.

'Come on, come on,' I whispered to myself.

But I didn't feel anything. I was completely drained of emotion, meaning that I was unable to use my power. I tensed, trying to push some form of healing out of my hands, but instead I collapsed next to Ash. All my energy was completely burnt out.

'Alice.' Anjelica was at my side but I shoved her off. 'Help Ash.'

What good was a healer who exhausted her power to save herself? Nox came to stand in front me. Something in his dark silver eyes gave me an idea.

'Can you save him?' I was useless, no help here, but Guardians are meant to protect people so surely that meant he could help.

'I'm fine, don't worry Alice,' Ash's voice got softer as he spoke.

Tears pricked in my eyes. Ash was such a kind soul, he didn't deserve this.

'Don't be stupid, you're only alive because of your powers.' Anjelica retied the jacket around Ash's stomach tighter.

Her scolding voice failed to hide the emotion that not even my tears could summon.

'Don't call them that. It's my stupid biology.' Ash clearly hadn't lost his fight, though I had no clue what he was complaining about.

'It's not stupid if it's keeping you alive.' Anjelica shut him up, as she gripped his hand in support.

I watched, holding my breath as Nox knelt down. He placed a navy blue, pointy fingered hand on Ash's stomach. He then held his other hand up in front of me.

'I need to borrow your abilities,' he spoke ominously, as he waited for my permission.

'I used it all.' I sighed.

Nox shook his head. 'You just exhausted yourself.'

With tears now fully streaming down my face, I poked a finger onto Nox's extended hand.

'Use it.'

He took a deep breath and I watched the single horn on his head change blue, ever so slightly. The crusty blood that was pooled on the ground fully liquefied before working its way back up onto Ash's body. It was as if Nox was rewinding to a time when Ash hadn't been injured. As ever so slowly, the blood sunk into his body. Veins and organs started to reform and close, until eventually the wound started to sew itself shut. Tears trickled faster down my face as Ash sat up, healed.

'Thank you.' Ash smiled at Nox, who kept his poker face on at all times.

Anjelica and I helped Ash to his feet, even though he didn't need a hand up. We were just worried that something else might happen to him.

'Do you know where Alec and Anakin are?' Anjelica asked Nox.

He looked at her but didn't reply. Instead he opened his navy bat wings and flew up out of our sight.

'Who was that?'

The three of us spun to see the owner of the voice. Anakin. He, Alec, Ace, and August stood there alive and unharmed. Another wall of exhaustion smashed into me as I relaxed knowing everyone was okay.

'How long have you two been there?' Anjelica asked.

'Two minutes,' Alec answered, unsure.

'Great, so I looked like an idiot when I asked Nox where you two were,' Anjelica sounded, extremely frustrated.

'My speciality is making you look stupid,' Anakin declared proudly.

August decided to interrupt before a fight broke out. 'Shall we head back to our temporary base?'

⊰⊱⊰

The conversation was a mixture of hilarious teasing and emotional reunions, as we walked at a slow pace. August and Anjelica were at my side, occasionally checking that I was still upright and moving.

'Thank goodness for your Guardian, August,' Ash spoke, dropping his pace to walk next to her.

She rolled her eyes ever so slightly at the mention of Nox, but I noticed a small grin as it fought its way across her face.

'I'm glad he saved you.'

I stopped paying attention to their conversation as I spotted the marble steps of the building that Ace and August had commandeered. The building was stunning. Even more so when compared to everything else in this city. The wood was a brighter brown than that of the mud huts, and the white marble was a nice change from the concrete. But the things that really brought it all together were the glass and blue tinted exterior lights.

'I hope there's food,' Anakin grumbled, as the group of us headed up the steps.

CHAPTER FOURTEEN

August – Riptide

The warm blue light from outside bounced through the window in the large room we were all sat crashed out in. The cooling blue wavelengths sank into the wooden desk that was pressed close to the wall below the window. From the opposite angle warm hallway light flowed into the room. Rays of blue and yellow met in the middle to form a spotlight on the empty box of bread, that now lay torn and abused. Though not even a crumb of the bread remained, the strong musty smell of herbs and honey lingered in the air, reminding me of my full stomach. The soft scent of bread also drew my thoughts to the hut we had stayed in back on Asgard. A soft smile began to form on my face as I realised this was the first time I couldn't wait to return to a planet. This strange train of thought brought with it an unusual feeling, one that I had given up on. For the first time, possibly ever, I actually felt as if I belonged somewhere.

'So, Alec, Anakin, how did you guys survive the locals? Ash asked, his words filling the silent air.

'That's not my favourite moment to relive Ash,' Alec answered, triggering a toothy grin from Anakin as his sense of humour kicked in.

'You make a good cursed man though.' The troublemaker referred to Nox's curse as he nudged Alec in the arm.

'You what!' Alice sounded, somewhere between astonished and horrified.

'I guess, I'll miss being able to scare you with one look.' Alec grinned at Anakin.

'Trust me, your natural face is plenty scary.' Anakin winked, causing laughter to erupt around the room.

The thought of Alec's soft and rounded features being terrifying to anyone fuelled our laughter for a good long while.

'So what do we do with these?' Alec asked, desperate to distract us from laughing.

He held up one of the Segredos drives from his pocket. Ace, who had the other one, had been tossing his copy up in the air and catching it for a while now.

'If we decide to destroy them, I volunteer to be in charge of the destruction.' Anakin grinned, grinding his foot into the floor as he spoke.

'We should probably see what's on them first before we do anything,' I suggested, remembering spotting an Earthian computer in one of these rooms.

Alec and Ace gave me a nod, but before we could leave the room, Amolt spoke.

'I have a question for you lot.'

Overlegen's nemesis pointed a finger at everyone but Thor, Loki, and Ray, who were sitting on his side of the room. When he was sure we weren't leaving, he began.

'I've noticed you kids insist on carrying weapons despite your powers.' He paused as if he was trying to pull in everyone's interest before he spoke again. 'So why don't you channel your powers through your weapons? At least that way you're using both.'

This caused quite a reaction from the Asgardian Gods, who immediately bolted out of their slouched sitting positions.

'Only certain rare metals can handle that sort of energy.' Ash pointed out, as Thor and Loki set cold eyes on Amolt.

'But what's wrong with only using one or the other?' Alec questioned, as Amolt ignored the Gods who were eyeballing him.

'Oh no, nothing,' Amolt answered, as if he meant the exact opposite.

'Just thought you kids should consider it. Might put up more of a fight that way.'

What was that supposed to mean?

'Well, we'd have to find a really good smithy along with tracking down the rarest elements in the universe.' Anjelica pointed out the absurdness of Amolt's suggestion.

'There are a couple good ones on my home planet,' Ash grumbled, his words full of distaste.

The hate in his usually kind voice caught me by surprise.

'You're not Asgardian?' Alice asked the same question I was about to.

Not wanting to speak about his planet again Ash just shook his head in confirmation.

'You know you need more than a smithy and magical metal though?' Amolt brought the discussion back to his point.

At this stage Thor and Loki had visibly had enough of this conversation, shooting to their feet they blocked Amolt from our view.

'You know what, I can't remember what they're called.' Amolt tried to back track but it was too late.

'How do you know about them?' Loki's voice was full of menace.

'I'm Overlegen's biggest threat. What makes you think I wouldn't know everything they do?'

'Is he belittling our threat level?' Anjelica whispered to me, as she folded her arms.

'Tell me Gods, when are you going to tell them?' Still hidden from view Amolt spoke again, defying the Gods' wishes for him to shut up.

'Tell them what old man?' Thor's voice was gruff and thick with his Nordic accent.

'That this is not purely about them.'

I shared a puzzled look with Anjelica and Alice as they joined me standing. We'd only just met Amolt and he seemed to know more than we did.

'What's more than just about them?' Anakin asked, as he and Ash also rose off the floor.

'This war.' The two words broke Thor's self-control.

He picked up Mjölnir and pointed it towards, what I'd assumed, was Amolt's head.

'It's not your place!' Loki's words were dripping in outrage and I couldn't even imagine what was causing such reactions from them.

Ray sat quiet and unbothered as all of this played out. He too had a confused expression on his face but he wasn't fazed by anything else.

'Outside.' Loki turned, revealing he was speaking to us. 'We need to talk.'

Silently, we all followed as Thor and Loki led us out of the room and into the main foyer.

All eyes were on Thor and Loki as we waited for them to explain whatever was going on here.

'Where do we start?' Thor scratched his head as he spoke directly to Loki.

'Probably at the beginning.' Loki fiddled with his long overcoat, as he responded.

'There was a meeting in the 19th Midgardian century.' Thor started slowly, too slowly.

I could feel tension and worry prickling at my skin as the air seemed to get colder.

'The meeting was attended by the contenders for the head of each realm. It was established that Asgard would head this realm, instead of Krone.'

'What does this have to do with us? And who is Krone?' Anakin interrupted Thor, obviously also on edge with the slow pace.

'Krone is the planet that governs Overlegen and Anden.' Loki cut in, taking over from Thor. 'Overlegenians are the ones who are hunting the-'

Anakin cut off Loki this time.

'Yes, yes, we know, they're after the girls and they kidnapped you two to get to them. So what?'

I had to hand it to Anakin. He really had nerves.

'Well.' Loki began to speak again, glaring at Anakin just a little. 'They didn't kidnap the lead Gods of Asgard with the sole purpose of killing some teenagers. This is them, weakening Asgard so that they can take the realm.'

Loki and Thor wore matching grave expressions as Loki finished forcing his words out.

To my left Anjelica let out a laugh, her tone mocking. 'It's taken them nearly three centuries to start their attempt on Asgard's realm?'

'Nearly three Midgardian centuries, yes.' Thor confirmed, pedantically.

'Wait, so by coming to rescue you two we've left Asgard almost defenceless?' Ash's voice was full of worry as he stared at Thor.

'Yes, but thankfully that is not a problem,' Thor answered, bluntly.

'How is that not a problem?' Anjelica threw the next question.

'Because, Overlegen has more reason to send all their forces here,' Loki answered, and everyone went quiet.

Overlegen's army was coming here?

'That's not... There's no way...' Alec gave up what he was saying as his voice faded into silence.

'No way we'll survive this.' It was Alice who finished his sentence, almost as quietly as he had said it.

I couldn't process that, not just yet, we still didn't have the full story. There had to be something else going on. *Why would they not just go for Asgard? Why come here?*

'But what does that have to do with them hunting us? And why come here?' I voiced my thoughts, having a slight feeling that the answers for both questions were the same.

Loki's green eyes met mine as he took a step forward.

'Those are the wrong questions.'

I frowned, not sure how they were the wrong questions. *But regardless, why couldn't he just give me an answer?*

'What does this have to do with August then?' Ace asked, having figured out what Loki thought was the correct question.

Loki straightened his expression into a completely neutral one.

'Aside from the fact that I embarrassed them?' I added, as Anjelica and Alice gave Loki a confused look.

'Think August. It's been brought up a lot lately.' Loki's answer was unhelpful in the usual, higher powers being deflective, way.

Been brought up a lot lately? A lot has happened *lately*. Trying to bury my frustration I set my mind to work. There were always the constant digs about me not having had a title, but thanks to Lavita that wasn't a thing anymore. *Lavita.* She had been working for Azar, same as Freyja, but she'd shown me an old memory of mine. *Maybe it had something to do with that?* My mind then lead me to Anjelica, Alice, and I's arrival on Asgard. Loki had given me my weapons. Heimdall had called them *Mutabilis*. The name didn't ring any bells, but I had a feeling I was missing something that Loki had said. I tried to replay our conversation in my head. *What had he said?* Something about not touching the light in the centre. Something clicked and my mind immediately connected that to what Amolt had said before.

'My weapons.' I started speaking before my mind had fully caught up.

Small grins started along Loki and Thor's faces.

'Whatever Amolt was talking about, it's in my weapons.'

A proud expression was now fully present on Loki's slender face.

'Something to do with that rune I found in the Mediterranean.'

Thor nodded, folding his arms while still holding Mjölnir.

'Correct.' Loki's voice was still tense but his tone had lightened.

'You gave me the weapons..?' I didn't properly finish my question as my voice trailed off into thought.

'Turn the weapons into throwing stars.' Loki didn't bother to explain himself.

Doing as he said, I pulled Vorago, in knife form, out of my belt. Imagining a throwing star, the knife shifted with ease into the other form. I brought it closer to my face so that I could make out the shape of the warm blue light that was being emitted from the centre. I had not really paid attention to this feature before. It had been much paler before, as if it didn't want me to discover it until now.

'Recognise it?'

I nodded at Loki's question, it was the same rune.

'Laguz ⌐,' I answered, with the name of the rune that had now appeared in my life for the second time.

'But I put it back into the water, how did it get here? How did *you* get it?' I tried to get an explanation out of Loki again.

'I was paid to look after the weapons and give them to you when you got to Asgard.'

His answer was not what I was expecting.

'By who?' I had a feeling I already knew the answer to my own question.

'Not someone a God would like to mess with.'

The bland description was enough to confirm what I thought. Only one person fit that description along with the whole, 'looking out for me part'. Nox. From what I could tell Guardians seemed to outrank Gods.

'So, Overlegen was hunting the girls because they thought August had...' Ace connected the recent discovery to our situation.

'Yes. They only just found out August had come into contact with one of the Forn Ljós as she left their planet.' Loki's statement opened up even more questions.

One of the Forn Ljós? How'd they know? Instead I went with, 'What do the Forn Ljós do?' If I really did have one it would be good to know.

'Enhance.' Loki's one word reply was enough, I understood.

They enhanced the gifts of the wielder through the weapon, and probably the weapon itself as well. Before I, or anyone of my friends could ask another question Thor took over the conversation.

'It is vital that Overlegen do not get their hands on the Segredos drive or the Laguz rune. If they do, we will lose our home.'

I winced at the thought of Overlegen desecrating Asgard. It's lovely green and sunny lands would run with Asgard's red life force. The bodies of the Asgardian people would litter the pristine planet, and my newly found friends, and myself, would likely be no more.

'We'll leave you to process.' Thor stopped my dark train of thought, making it clear he was done as he headed back to the room where Amolt and Ray were.

Loki stopped in front of me wanting one last word. 'There is more but this is enough for now. Heimdall will be sending forces to help us find a way to survive the battle. Then we'll talk.' And with that, Loki stalked past me and headed back to the room behind Thor.

With the severity of the latest complication sinking in, I took a deep breath hoping I could exhale this situation. I finally had a planet, and people to fight for. But, in traditional Overlegen fashion they were about to take all of that away from me. I looked around our group, suddenly gripped with a protective sort of anger. I would not, under any condition, let anything happen to anyone here.

Apoint, Duana, and Azar would not win this. They couldn't. I had too much to lose if they did.

'August. Your sister knew about the Forn Ljós.' Ash's voice interrupted my thoughts.

'She did?' I don't know why I was surprised my older sister seemed to know everything.

'Of course she did.' Anjelica let her voice run sour, she wasn't Nora's biggest fan.

Nora had never been there to help us, or me, out of trouble even if she had every opportunity to. Anjelica resented her for that. If she wasn't my sister I would almost definitely feel the exact same. But, at the end of the day, she was family. So I held onto the hope that she'd return to what she was like when we were younger.

'Anyway.' Anjelica moved forward. 'Surely they didn't just spend our entire childhoods trying to kill us because they thought August had an ancient power rune. I mean they almost killed me several times!'

Anjelica sounded like someone had stolen her thunder.

'Of course not.' I grinned at her. 'They wanted Alice's healing power and-' I was cut off by her as she grinned back at me.

'They couldn't handle having someone with my capabilities as their enemy.' Anakin snorted, but Anjelica was probably right.

They had gone for Anjelica and Alice many times without me there. They definitely hated all of us.

'What are we going to do about this fight?' Alice moved the conversation on, her green eyes clouded with worry.

'Frost, your ideas have kept us alive thus far, got another one?'

Something about the way Ace said that brought a smile to my face and I let my worry slip to the back of my mind. We could win this. We had to.

'When did everyone start calling me Frost?' I was unable to remember when, and who, decided to refer to me by my last name.

A large grin appeared on Ash's cheery but extremely guilty face.

'I was dying.' He shrugged.

'And it is more fun than us calling you Aug.' Anakin reasoned proudly, and I let out a laugh.

'Fancy a nickname Anakin?' Anjelica offered as innocently as she could manage.

Bless him, Anakin had no control as his ego took the reins from his logic and he fell into her trap.

'Duh. Let's see what you got?'

'Perfect.' Anjelica rubbed her hands together displaying a toothy grin.

'But only if I get to give you one too.' Anakin recovered a little bit of his wit.

'Preferably come up with short ones.' Alec chimed into their thoughts. 'It's already a mouthful to yell your names in a crisis.'

'Thank goodness we don't go to them for help much.' Ash's statement triggered a series of giggles or, in Anjelica's and Anakin's case, sarcastic snorts to display their lack of amusement.

'Anjelica's fire has its moments though.' Alice lightly defended Anjelica.

'Shame she can't aim it,' Anakin refuted.

'Well at least I can do something helpful.' Anjelica winked at Anakin.

'Hey! I can do more than Ace's telekinesis when he gets swarmed.'

Ace didn't give Anakin the pleasure of responding defensively. Instead he smiled to himself and changed the topic swiftly. 'So nicknames?'

'Ana.' Anjelica let the word fall out of her mouth. 'I'm pretty sure it means graceful.' The addition of sarcasm in her statement wasn't subtle.

Anakin badly mimicked a smile and tilted his head, pretending to find it funny. 'J, that's yours.' He folded his arms.

'Did you just pick a letter in my name?'

'Sure, but it's better than that.'

'Do elaborate.'

'The J is for jackass.'

Anakin levelled Anjelica's sharp smile with his glare. She held it and both of them just stood there silently arguing, as if they'd forgotten everything else going on around them.

'And I thought Anakin alone was trouble.' Alec's words were fond as he folded his arms, watching as Anakin and Anjelica stopped glaring at each other and turned to look at the rest of us.

'What's that supposed to mean, Alec?' Anjelica softened her tone as she said his name.

The matching smirks on Alec and Ace's faces were enough to answer Anjelica.

Anakin took a step away from her. 'We're not trouble.'

My mind was only half paying attention to the conversation that seemed so good at distracting everyone else. We were going to have to come up with a brilliant tactic if we were going to have any chance of surviving, let alone defeating, Overlegen. Asgard was known for being a warrior realm, but they'd be stupid to spare half of their warriors to help us, even if the most important fight was here. They were missing three Gods, and the most capable members of their younger generations. Plus, the honourable dead were on the wrong side of the planet to offer any aid. So we needed a plan that compensated for our lack of numbers.

'They're just as bad as each other,' Alice whispered to me, and I smirked, but didn't really pull myself out of my thoughts.

There were several strategies I'd stumbled across on Earth, Overlegen, and Krone, but it might not be wise to use one they were familiar with.

'Why don't we just unleash them on Overlegen?' Ace's statement was a joke, in reaction to their bickering, but he was onto something.

Anakin was adamant and unyielding, while Anjelica was persistent and a bit pesky, and together they seemed to create a chaos that was hard for anyone other than them to understand. Overlegen wouldn't have a clue. They'd have to throw their precious schooling out the window. I knew full well they'd never do such a thing.

A warm feeling lit up my face. 'We should.'

I looked at Ace as his blue eyes flicked down slightly to meet mine. A sly grin formed exaggerating his cheekbones.

'What's this?' Anjelica asked, noticing that Ace and I were up to something.

'Would you and Anakin hold off annoying each other long enough to piss off Apoint?' I asked.

They both took a moment to side-eye each other before shrugging.

'Does this mean I get to lead the operation!?' Anakin exclaimed.

'We.' Anjelica corrected, as a subtle trace of excitement crept into her tone.

Without another word they both turned and began walking briskly down the hallway to plot.

'What have we done?' Alec asked anxiously.

'We won't survive this. Anakin alone isn't very tactically advanced, them together...' He trailed off staring down the now empty hallway.

'Couldn't one of you have made the plan?' Alice, to my surprise, joined Alec's team of dread.

I smiled. 'Technically this is our idea. But mainly Ace's.' I added, jokingly shifting the blame.

He dipped his head at me. 'You're welcome.'

'I might go and oversee what they're up to.' Alice started backing away from the remaining group of us.

My inner laughter tugged the side of my lip upwards. If I was calculating, and Anjelica was unpredictable, then Alice would be the reasonable one. The three of us had gotten pretty good at keeping each other in check, probably the only reason we'd survived thus far. My eyes pricked with a tiny bit of water as I thought about just how far we'd come together. I met them when I was ten. Alice's family had taken in Anjelica when she was seven or eight. We'd had a decent year of friendship before I realised I was going to be banished to Anden. The prison world. Knowing I'd never go they said they'd escape with me, and we survived together running from planet to planet, until we finally escaped the

Kronevian Empire's branch and made it to Asgard. Now here we were, fifteen, and about to run towards the people we'd spent four years running away from. To make things worse, we were doing it on their terms, not ours.

'I'll join you.' Ash sped to join Alice as she got further down the corridor.

I took a deep breath before turning towards Alec and Ace. We were going to survive. We all were.

'Shall we go check out the Segredos drives?' Alec asked, as he and Ace each held out the matching black flash drives.

The only difference being that the one in Ace's hands had a white label on it.

'Let's find a computer.' I agreed, sounding more eager than I thought I was to see what was on the drives.

It didn't take us long to locate the room that had the computer. It was just left of the second hallway. There weren't any windows in this room and it was relatively smaller in size. The wooden walls had the same flecks of gold as in the rest of the building. Ace sat down on the chair and turned the computer on. It was slow to start up but eventually he managed to pull up the contents of Antarctica's drive. Unfortunately the files were encrypted, not really a surprise, but it could make life a bit difficult.

'Does anyone know the password?' Alec asked, but he needn't have.

Ace had already typed in the phrase I'd given him to tell my sister. It worked. Alec and I watched silently as Ace clicked on the closest file: Forn Ljós. I barely breathed when several documents popped up. It appeared as if most of them were written in Icelandic and no pictures were available. Ace scrolled down each of the documents just in case we could read any of it. We couldn't. Leaving this file, Ace opened another one. This one was without a title. Again, we couldn't read anything, except for one word.

'Halion.' I read out loud, not recognising it.

The word before Halion was *skapari* but I hadn't a clue what that meant either. Maybe I should learn Icelandic, it seemed rather prominent in this realm.

'I think *skapari* means creator,' Ace sounded, slightly unsure at his translation.

'As in, she created the Segredos drive?' Alec asked.

'Why would she have a document about herself in here?' That didn't make any sense to me. If she had made the drive why would she have something on herself in here? Though we couldn't read it so we couldn't be totally sure.

'I think it's written in two different languages.' Ace kept scrolling down.

'Yeah, but Portuguese and Icelandic are an interesting combination.' Alec recognised the second language.

'Is Halion a Midgardian name?' Ace asked, turning to look between both Alec and I.

'No,' Alec answered. 'In neither language.'

'Alec, are you from Earth?' I wondered.

He nodded, releasing a warm grin.

'How did you get your gifts?' I stared, just a little surprised at the Earthian shapeshifter.

'Odin. You?' Well at least one of us had met the real Odin.

'Not sure yet.' I turned back to look at the computer. 'What's on the other drive?'

Ace swapped the drives. The new one, just like the other drive, required a password, and just like the previous one it had files, one of which was called Forn Ljós. Confused as Alec and I were, Ace opened it. Nothing. It was completely blank.

'So, it's not two drives, it's one and a fake,' I said, partly under my breath as I realised that was actually rather helpful.

'Bleep.'

Something went off in Alec's pocket. He pulled out a flat device that I didn't recognise. The majority of it appeared to be a screen but I wasn't sure. Overlegen didn't use a lot of technology, and Earthian technology was not like anything in Asgard's branch, so I was clueless. Alec frowned as he eyed the screen.

'What's wrong?' I asked.

He positioned it so that both Ace and I could see as two saffron dots moved toward a blue planetary shield.

'There are two heat signatures heading towards Undeva.'

CHAPTER FIFTEEN

August – Riptide

It was midday, I suppose, by the time we met Azar in the central courtyard of this strange city. Heimdall had sent us enough aid for our plan to work, but we were frighteningly small in number when compared to the bloodthirsty, cruelty hardened, army of Overlegen. They had hardly even bothered to wear armour. Their mistake, but still their arrogance was infuriating.

'I guess we owe you thanks for removing the locals,' Azar spat at us, through his disgustingly coloured teeth.

I ignored him, focusing on wearing my feigned calmness without falter. Inside my heart was roaring like a waterfall. All my worries were hurling into me before pooling at the pit in my stomach. Keeping an eye on two people in a battle was one thing, but six! I briefly closed my eyes. Nerves and worry were not the ideal head space to be in before a battle. I desperately needed to cool my emotions. Focusing on the cold feeling that was, as always, waiting for me. I took a deep breath as I felt the cold embrace wrap itself around me, ready for use.

'August.'

A new voice brought my eyes open and I watched as the owner emerged from the ranks of our enemy. All of whom stood uniformly guarding their side of the courtyard. The bald head of Apoint appeared, making its way towards the front.

'None of you will last 'till nightfall.'

'It's Riptide now, and you wouldn't know if it were night or not, this city is underground.' I mocked his failed threat.

He didn't respond. *What would the dimwit even say to that?* I watched, satisfied, as his lungs grasped at the claustrophobic air that he wasn't yet used to.

'Hand over the Segredos drive, Riptide.' Azar let a growl resonate in his throat as he spoke. He extended his pasty thin hand as he took a few steps away from his forces and towards ours. 'Last chance.' *For your sister.*

He said his words quietly, aiming them right at me. He didn't need to voice my sister's involvement in this, we were both thinking it.

I pulled my blades from their sheaths in my brown, leather-like armour. Alice had discovered the armour hidden in the room where I'd found Mjölnir and the darts. There was just enough for the seven of us, and Ray, which meant that Amolt and the Gods weren't wearing any, not that they needed to. The armour was surprisingly comfortable and, dare I say, looked quite cool. It consisted of a couple pieces; a corset which included built in sheaths for weapons, some buckles and straps that I couldn't place the use of, along with similarly detailed bracers for my wrists and forearms, and the same leather-like material in a sort of wrap that covered just below my knees until my boots took over. My friends were all dressed similarly.

'You'll kill us regardless,' Alec objected, noticing I'd drawn my weapons.

'August.' Azar's tone changed into a startling friendly one as he used my name instead of my title. 'Did my girlfriend not give you a title?'

The stench of Lavita's primrose smile entered my memory. If my blades were not in my hands I would've been lulled into reaching for the drive hidden in one of my sheaths.

'You owe me. No more will you end up in any of those *situations*.' He paused as he said the word carefully.

From the look on his face it was clear he knew I'd get the reference. I did not want to send my mind there. The bile rising in my throat put Lavita's magical stench out of my mind. As her strange influence cleared an idea popped into my head. Pretending to still be in the trance I sheathed Vorago and took a few steps towards him, pulling out my sister's drive just as I stepped clear of my group. Not considering that this was rash, I offered it to Azar's open hand, but it slipped and landed under my boot. Azar's horrified face was worth it.

'I owe Lavita then,' I said, as I ground the fake drive into the floor. *Sorry Anakin, I know you wanted to do that.*

Not turning my back, I watched Azar's horrified expression as it slowly morphed into a glare. I felt Anakin's eyes on me as I merged back into our ranks. Expecting to be greeted with another glare I sent him an apologetic look. I couldn't help myself. But Anakin's green eyes weren't lowered menacingly, instead his features carried a wicked smile.

Tension was now almost sweltering as everyone was waiting in anticipation for someone to start the fight. Azar was the only one unmoved. He stared at the broken flash drive, where I had stood.

'For your sake I hope that was a fake.' There was no real threat in his words, which was just as surprising as his volume. Like before, he was speaking so that Apoint was out of earshot.

I didn't acknowledge him.

'I'll get the real one after, maybe if you lose some friends it'll steady your hand.' Azar finally looked up from the ground and turned to head out of the courtyard.

But he didn't make it very far as Anjelica had other plans for him. He hissed as one of his jacket sleeves caught alight. Calmly he shook it out until the flame was gone.

Azar then swung around, locking eyes with my friend, a minacious expression on his face. 'You'll regret that lassie.'

234

'Idiot.' It was Anakin's turn to scold her. 'He was leaving!'

'I know that,' she replied unconvincingly. 'I just wanted him to stay.' She reasoned, more realistically.

'Well, if we die because you did that, I will come back and kill you myself,' Anakin growled at her.

'If we die because I did that, I'll be dead too,' she fired back.

Anakin leant forward, a murderous look in his eyes, but thankfully Ash intercepted the situation before it could escalate. Redrawing Vorago, I shifted both weapons into their katana-like form.

'You ready for this August?' Anakin asked me quietly, sounding slightly worried.

I nodded at him, his fringe for once well away from his green eyes.

'Are you doubting the plan?' I asked teasingly.

He snorted. 'Of course I am, I made it.'

Both his hands were gripping tightly to the hilt of the great, double headed axe he'd pulled from the storage room. With the flat part of my blade I tapped the metal on his axe. A soft ding was released into the warm air and I heard Anakin let out a huff-like laugh.

'You know, you're not the worst, Frost.' I wasn't sure what Anakin meant by that, but the way he phrased it sounded like a compliment.

'That would be Anjelica, right?' I responded fondly, as she flashed her teeth at Anakin and I.

Distracted, I hadn't noticed the cause, but an Asgardian roar erupted from Thor as he leapt forward into Overlegen's forces. A series of loyal soldiers followed him into the stationary army. Swords and gifts flying as blood from both sides started pouring.

'Time to pay up.' Loki too joined his nephew's vengeful attack.

'All you have to do is hold them here,' I said to Anakin, hoping to sound as reassuring as possible. 'We'll do the rest.'

He gave me a determined nod as Apoint's voice was the next one to cry out. 'To war!' His delayed command finally commenced the madness.

Naturally, chaos erupted from the tangle of bodies, weapons, and gifts. Still within the ranks of Asgard, I didn't have to parry too many blows as Anjelica and I moved towards Ace and Alec who were waiting for us to reach them. There were no words exchanged, nor emotion displayed by any of us as we all shared a look. Without any further delay we snuck back to the edge of Asgard's forces. Making our way over to a side street that, if followed correctly, would lead us behind Apoint's forces. We didn't check to see if we had been spotted, or if we were being followed, as the four of us slipped behind the building that stood at the corner of the path.

CHAPTER SIXTEEN

Anakin – Devil

'Hurt yet?' The impatient voice of the large Overlegenian scoundrel, dragging me across the deceivingly sharp ground, asked.

I frowned, trying to wriggle free. Anjelica and I had devised a wicked plan that had consisted of pure chaos in every known direction. Yet, somehow, Alice had thwarted our genius with her common sense. Leading me to be in the worst position anyone could be in a battle. Being raked across the ground towards your enemy's recently dropped weapon. At least this moron hadn't the intelligence to just kill me with his abilities, whatever they were. No wonder Anjelica and Alice weren't the brightest, their planet was just the stupid leading the stupider. Unfortunately for me they were actually good at fighting. Both the girls and my enemies.

My wiggling wasn't getting me anywhere and I had lost my axe, Thor knows where. If it wasn't for my armour, my clothes and my skin would be no more. The unfortunate parts of my skin that were exposed gave into new tears for every inch that I was dragged. With each freshly opened cut I reached a level of discomfort that I didn't know was possible. I was going to die out of agony before he even reached his weapon. The only grace in this situation was that Anjelica wouldn't be here to witness my untimely doom. Although she would probably, knowing my luck, be alive to laugh at my dead body. I growled, that was not a pleasant thought.

My attacker changed his angle ever so slightly, his grip drawing out more bruises on my ankles. My sorrowful thoughts were cut off as I heard a clunk and felt warm blood unleash itself across my face. *What in the..?* I craned my neck at an odd angle to spot the latest object of my abuse. My eyes locked on a wooden handle that extended upwards and erupted into two beautifully shaped blades. *My Axe!* My hope was crushed with the betrayal of my own weapon causing me bruises, blood, and pain. My chin was raked over a rock which somehow managed to knock some sense into me. I was being daft.

This idiot soldier was giving me so many opportunities to live. Returning to the axe, I glared at it wishing I had Ace's telekinesis or August's summonable weapons. Despite mentally reaching for the weapon, which was slowly getting further away, my body refused to move. A weird fogginess clouding the connection to my limbs. *Where did this come from?* I didn't have time to ponder that, all I could do was fight. My ankles crashed to the floor sparking even more pain.

He'd reached his weapon! Grinding my teeth and tensing every muscle I had I managed to wiggle my fingers. That was a slow start.

I felt the ground move as my heavy footed attacker came back towards me. *Crap.* Letting out a hopefully menacing scream of frustration, I managed to throw my arm above my head. My fingers were now only a centimetre from the axe. My neck ached from the angle and my jaw was still clenched.

'Any last snarky comment?'

I thought I heard words leave his mouth but I didn't respond. I was too busy reaching for my life. My bones felt as if they were full of metal and time felt like it was having a laugh. I managed to grip the axe but couldn't find the strength to do anything but roll over. So I did. Which was a mistake. Greeted by the sight of a large silver sword held high into the air above my neck. I swore. I should've stayed facing away from death. The Overlegenian re-did his footing making sure he was in the correct position to lop my head off. Or just cut me in half. I furiously tried to engage the muscles in my arm. Still only being able to roll, I had a desperate idea. Rolling onto my side, so that I could no longer see the sword or its wielder, my axe wielding arm moved with my body. I knew my axe had met its mark when I felt bone resistance and heard a sharp outburst of pain. Suddenly released from my inability to move, I scrambled to my feet. *Oh, that's his ability.* I tugged my axe free from his ankle and sent a quick remorseless swing. My strike led another pain filled scream to enter the air. Large bulging eyes met mine as I cut him down.

'Devil,' he whispered, his last words as his head fell.

I gulped as I fully processed what peril I had been in. My soul had almost been torn from my body and then Gods knew what would have happened to me. *Devil.* The Overlegenian's last words reminded me that I wasn't the one who was lifeless. Surprisingly, I'd never minded it when people compared me to destructive spirits. In fact, to make my enemies lives easier, Thor had granted me the title of Devil. Just for a good old laugh really. Any plans beings had of messing with me often disappeared when I introduced myself. I didn't know what they did in other realms. Not having titles was a strange idea, one that made me feel unprotected. There was no way I was going to go to one of those realms anyway. I laughed out loud to myself. It would be more than a good life if I spent it on Asgard. After this I was going nowhere else.

'Laughing to ourselves are we?' The graceful and entirely unwelcome voice of Freyja brought my attention back to my violence filled surroundings.

'Of all the arrogant twats in all the realms,' I muttered to myself.

The displeased look on her face told me that the lack of joy I felt towards her was mutual.

'Thought you weren't going to show,' I spat, wishing she'd just vanish.

I didn't even have the use of my abilities here and she was a Goddess. The smile, dripping in two-faced charm, that greeted me, made clear that she had not been threatened by our visit.

'Don't you have a fight to run along to?' She shooed her hands at me, flashing her rather long nails as she did so.

I adjusted the position of my jaw. It was feeling rather uncomfortable after being clenched so tight. Taking one more sweep of my previous attacker, as I adjusted my mindset for dealing with a Goddess. The dead soldier's golden blood had almost all been absorbed into the mud and rocky ground. His pupils had rolled up to the back of his head, like a shark's does before they bite.

'If you take a moment longer, Devil, I'll kill you.' The thick layer of charm was still tightly coiled around Freyja's words.

I was about to take a step away when a flash of dark gold caught my eyes. The swinging yellow light far above us, highlighted a rectangular golden plaque that was half out of his pocket.

'Say, you wouldn't happen to be trying to rob a dead man?' I asked Freyja, flashing her my most charming grin.

Her sudden flinch told me one of two things. Either, I wasn't as charming as I thought or she was trying to rob a dead man. Freyja's deceptively warm brown eyes looked down on me with pity.

'I'll play nice with you Devil. We both know I can't smite you.' She paused to make sure I felt the relief that sank into me.

Being smited by a God was widely acknowledged across the universal tree as being the worst way to go. Supposedly, it felt like suffocation, burning, and something else I'd purposely forgotten. Although no one was too sure. You can't be with this sort of thing, no one has ever survived to describe it.

'You're welcome for that,' she spoke kindly, her words desperately trying to lull me into a relaxed and compliant state.

I snorted. She'd rudely asked for our titles knowing August didn't have one. She hadn't done it for us, she'd done it to belittle and threaten our friend. It was a miracle that August hadn't already been smited, actually. With the amount of disguised troublemaking Gods out there. A sudden realisation clicked in my head. She was actually quite smart. I couldn't even imagine how Alice and Anjelica survived as long as they did, let alone how August did. In regards to the smiting she'd probably been handing out fake names. Though I'm not sure if beings could sense that sort of thing. I know I couldn't, or hadn't, if she'd lied about being called August.

'So, I propose to just impale you instead.' Freyja's words distracted me from admiring my new friend's intelligence.

The shock of her sudden words triggered me into throwing my axe backwards. Which was stupid. Ish.

'No, please Freyja, you can't kill me.' Though my words were pleading they didn't come out that way. My tone was of a more aggravating one. A secret talent of mine. I didn't even need to try to be infuriating.

'Why can't I kill you?' She feigned boredom. 'This realm would be grateful to be rid of your annoying mouth.'

I placed both my hands together in a prayer position, pressing my lips to the top of my fingers before speaking again. 'It's all I've got.'

She shot me a puzzled look. So I continued, gesturing around to the bloodshed and violence, as my people battled Overlegen for our home.

'It's a miracle I'm not already dead. I can hardly fight and my abilities are useless. Not to mention I'm fifteen!' I belittled myself in a frighteningly convincing way.

She folded her arms, tilting her head at me as if she was re-analysing my threat level. I tried to reign in my inner voice, which was cackling at her for considering this.

'Please let me grab my axe and I'll be on my way.' I pointed behind me.

Unaware of my strategic positioning she gave me a nod. I dipped my head remembering that I'd seen people do that action to seem polite before. Swiftly, I turned around and with my left hand I grabbed my axe, while my right smoothly yanked the golden plaque from the dead man's pocket. Slipping my hand into my trouser pocket I quickly ran off into the thick of battle hoping

Freyja hadn't noticed my slyness. Once I was sure that I wasn't about to be attacked, by anyone, I took a quick glance at what I'd stolen. The plaque was blank other than a symbol that had been scratched carelessly onto it:

I'd seen that somewhere before. I was certain of it. Taking another glance at the rune, similar to the letter F, Asgard came to mind.

'DEVIL!'

I crammed the plaque quickly back into my pocket. Freyja was looking for me. If our plan was to work I'd need to get rid of this unwelcome Goddess.

'Thor, Loki, where are you?' I grumbled, as my eyes started darting around the courtyard trying to spot either of the three Gods.

CHAPTER SEVENTEEN

Anjelica – Firestorm

My ears rang as metal clattered against the concrete wall next to my head. I dropped into a squat before springing upwards and catching my bulked up attacker in the groin. Some of Apoint's soldiers had managed to sneak into the side street we were taking towards the back of Overlegen's troops and the exit. So Ace, August, Alec, and I were now being forced to fight our way through instead of my preferred idea of sneaking past. The others had made it a little bit further ahead than I had, but so far I'd had to deal with more.

'I'm gonna kill you for that.' The guy I was currently fighting stuttered in pain.

His emotional words stinking up my thoughts. If this guy could calm down that would be lovely. Fighting without the thoughts of others in your head was hard enough.

'And how do you plan to do that?' Not sure why I was entertaining this conversation with him, I responded, as I ducked another set of his punches.

I was already bored of this fight and wanted to get on with getting out of here. As lovely as Nox turned out to be, I sneered at that thought, I really hated this planet.

'Easy.' The Overlegenian had the guts to smirk. 'I have the strongest punch on Overlegen.'

I snorted. *That was unlikely.* 'And how do you suppose you're going to hit me?' I teased the smug soldier as I fired a foot into his knee cap.

'You're going to let me.'

He had the most arrogant voice that I'd ever come across that, paired with the smug expression he wore so well, made me think he was right.

As he stumbled from my knee shot I readjusted my guard, leaving it slightly open just so that he was easily able to send a clean blow into the side of my face. *How dumb was that?* But I was determined to prove to him that I wouldn't die from his punch. Blood roared down the side of my cheek and my ears screamed at my stupidity.

The narrow side street began to spin as I gripped the wall with my nails. Thankfully the pain was brief, but it was horrid, I'd give him that, though not out loud.

'I'm pretty sure that Devil can hit harder.' My voice was mocking, despite the fact that I definitely didn't believe my words. Anakin looked strong but he wasn't bulk like this prat.

'You sure about that?' His words reminded me of how much I hated the Overlegenian accent.

I had spent four years trying to talk myself out of it, but I don't think it had worked all that well.

'Drop your guard completely, let's see how many hits you can take.' His words played nicely into my desire for a fight and I found myself lowering my guard.

That's it. His thoughts were full of so much ego as they echoed into my head. I was glaring at him before I even realised why, my hands back up high.

'You're a Charmer?' I asked, feeling a little hysterical, most likely due to fighting his influence.

He wrinkled his nose at me and anger began to rise up in my throat. I narrowed my eyes on his hair and pointed two fingers at his head.

'What do you think you're going to do?' He was trying to mock me into forgetting.

'I'm going to burn you.' I spelled it out for him.

His gasp was priceless as he stumbled backwards. 'Not my hair.' He desperately placed his hands over his swooping russet locks.

'To Helheim with your precious hair.'

Charmers were the worst. Even the most aware or powerful beings had trouble detangling themselves from their words. I had the advantage of hearing his distracting thoughts.

'Why not pass me that sword and we can fight this out like the honourable warriors we are?' He coaxed all the charm he could into each painfully convincing words.

To make matters worse his tension had stopped all thoughts echoing into my mind. Before I could fight it I chucked an abandoned sword at his hands and retrieved my own. To my distaste he caught the blade smoothly and extended his arm towards me. Then he charged. I side stepped and swung my blade out to parry him. But his sword wasn't there. Instead he had hunched over, cutting me unevenly across both my shins as he charged past. Trying not to scream from my latest injury, I managed to catch him in the back with my sword as he stood up. *Why wasn't I wearing the same shin armoury thingies that August was*? I halted my thoughts in time to charge at him as he ran for a pile of stones stacked up next to a nearby building. I was too far behind him and he managed to get there before I could stop him. A rounded, well thrown stone crashed straight into my ribs. The force of the impact shocked me, almost knocking my breath away as I kept moving forward. I did my best to parry the stones thrown at my head, but I had to take the ones thrown anywhere else, as I was in too much agony to dodge. By the time I reached him he only had one stone left.

'You wouldn't kill me.' There he was with his sickening powers again.

Once again under his influence I was forced to change my mind. My arms lowered my sword and I gave him a sweet girlish smile. Just before I stepped out of distance my rebel side broke through his control and I spat at his feet. His face went still and his eyes met mine before looking around in panic. I smiled, though I knew none of his own saw. What I had just done was the greatest dishonour in our culture. By spitting at his feet I'd practically told him that he was not a soldier enough to be respected or killed. Even if no one saw to discharge him he'd have to live with this. Pinning me with such a glare he aimed his sword at my stomach. This time he drove it straight and simple towards my gut. Obviously not paying my armour any mind. I checked his blade and turned side on to be sure. I remained in this stance as he fell into his momentum, running himself into my waiting sword. He wasn't even wearing any armour. Ignoring him as he dropped to the ground I set my attention ahead. Thankfully, there were currently no incoming threats.

⚜⚜⚜

Having finally managed to catch up with Ace and August, I took a breather as they finished dealing with a small group of attackers. Other than some painful ribs, a blood covered face, and cuts in my shins, I was doing pretty okay. August and Ace were both scratched up but seemed in much better shape than I was. Obviously they weren't giving out free targets to hard hitting charmers.

'Where's Chameleon?' Worry I couldn't hide slipped into my voice. His abilities were great for espionage but not this. Besides I couldn't help but develop a soft spot for him. He just had this likeable quality to him that he couldn't shake. Even when he tried to be mean.

'Why do you sound so worried?' A roughed up Alec appeared from around a twist in the path.

He was only a little bit less injured than I was, but had no wounds that hindered his movement as he made his way back to us.

'No reason.' I shrugged, though very relieved that everyone in my group was alright.

Alec eyed me like he was going to say something that would back me into a corner but August swooped in changing the topic.

'How many are up there?' She used the corner of a mud wall to scrape the blood from her blades as she spoke.

'None anymore,' Alec responded with a proud grin, his cheeks becoming slightly chubby as he did so.

'We've made it to their back line.'

I watched as August did a quick scan of everyone, no doubt checking our injuries before unleashing a cunning grin. I couldn't help but feel the same as she did. Freedom was inching closer. Once

Overlegen had shrunken back into a loathsome, unthreatening blob in the distance, we could do what we wanted. We could live. Whatever that meant.

August, Ace, Alec, and I walked in a tight group round the rest of the street. The cries of the battle sounded distant thanks to the buildings that managed to block a bit of the noise. I could see the courtyard's other entrance and the backs of Overlegenian soldiers as we rounded another corner. A twinge of excitement entered my fingertips, this was almost over.

'DEVIL!'

A desperate wail had me looking left towards the very edge of the battle. Anakin was backing away from someone. His back was to me as he walked himself, and his assailant, into a corner. I couldn't see his face or hear his thoughts. The others had noticed him too. Alec and August were trying to figure out how to get to him, while Ace watched our backs. We could see Anakin through a small gap between two buildings but, due to the secluded path we were in there was really only one proper exit at the courtyard, that was too far from Anakin if he needed help.

'I'll deal with this.' I shooed them away. 'Go to the courtyard and continue with the plan.'

They all shot me a concerned look which took me a minute to register the meaning of.

'I won't let anything happen to Anakin.' Though that's not quite what they meant it seemed to assure them, so I continued. 'Go, my telepathic powers are more use here.'

Ace and August surveyed the gap that showed Anakin, making sure they wouldn't be of use, before both giving me a nod and running off with Alec towards our enemy.

'Devil,' I called out to him when he'd stopped backing up.

As he looked to see me I spotted who he was running from. Freyja. Surprisingly worried I looked back at his face, but his expression was not what I expected it to be. A slight smile curved his lips upward and he even offered me a wink, so quick I questioned whether or not it had just happened. When Anakin turned back to face Freyja my eyes followed. Narrowing my gaze on Azar's *girlfriend*. She didn't see me but if she had it wouldn't have changed her course of action. She gave Anakin a devious smile before rolling her eyes into a strange position. Before I could witness anymore a blinding light was unleashed from Freyja. My reflexes dropped my gaze as heat and a pale white colour seared themselves onto my closed eyelids. My hands flew over my eyes as the scorching light got brighter. I felt my face redden, probably burning, as the full force of what felt like a star hit me. My fingers and closed eyelids did nothing so I spun putting my back to the light and Anakin. I tried to mentally reach out to him, hoping he was doing the same. A crackle and a scream scratched into my ears as the blinding light seemed to subside. *Anakin!* My legs spun me back around but I was dizzy and seeing coloured spots so was unable to make out anything.

'Devil!' I shouted hoping to hear a response. 'Please don't be dead, you self-important...' I couldn't even bring myself to finish the insult as tears pricked at my unseeing eyes.

The only response I got from my shout was a high pitched, feminine laugh. Anger prowled at my stomach, *if he thought he got to die before me...* I frowned as my stinging flesh distracted me. I had decent fire tolerance. If I was burnt Anakin would be fried. Blinking, I tried to see but the green, yellow, and blue, splotches in my vision blocked out almost everything. I kept blinking as they slowly began to shrink in size. When I finally managed to clear most of the colours I could only make out two figures standing behind someone who was kneeling on the ground, obviously in pain. *Don't be Anakin,* I willed as if that would change anything. Other than those three figures I couldn't make out anything else. I wanted to unleash my fire, or torment everyone's thoughts, but I didn't know which one Anakin was. Hope had me believing that he wasn't the one on the floor and loyalty had me not wanting to put Anakin through anything painful. So, by my own choice, I was useless as I stood desperately waiting for all of the splotches to disappear.

Another painfilled grunt and then a scream entered the air. Louder than that of the other cries of battle. The noises didn't sound feminine which crushed my hope that Anakin was okay. She'd got him and she was killing him. Another figure stood blocking my view of the person, Anakin, crouched on the floor. Desperately, I swatted at my head with one hand and traced the wall with the other as I ran, seeing only splotches and blurry black shapes as I headed towards the courtyard entrance. I had to get to Anakin. I brandished my sword like a wand, hoping it would keep everyone at bay, as I kept clinging to the wall. Each step felt heavy as dot after dot slowly faded. I was closer now and, with my vision cleared, I could make out the unmistakable physiques of Thor and Loki. A little relief crept in. If they were there surely Anakin was alive. I hit a wall of dizziness as I got to where the Gods were and backed myself up against the wall hoping to stay upright. Unlike Midgardians, I hardly ever got dizzy so I had little to no clue what was going on or annoyingly what to do to get rid of it.

'Firestorm?' A familiar voice entered my head as I fought to open my eyes, that had shut on their own. Hands gripped my shoulders fiercely as the speaker tried again to reach me. 'What are you doing?' The owner of the voice was furious.

'Devil?' I grabbed onto his hands that were still on my shoulders, blinking my eyes until they managed to remain open.

He released his grip on me seeing my eyes open.

'What in Helheim are you doing?' I glared at him for being so stupid.

'Are you kidding me? I had a plan. You nearly got killed.' He frowned right back at me.

'Where is Freyja?' I questioned, looking past Anakin at Thor and Loki.

'Gone.' This was definitely Anakin I was speaking to.

His voice was full of its usual smugness. Thor and Loki noticed me staring at them and so decided it was best to re-enact what had just happened. Loki extended his hand dramatising Freyja shooting out light from her eyes. Thor dropped to the floor, being Anakin, before standing and pointing to me. He took a few paces back, flipped his red hair then covered his eyes mockingly with his hands.

Man, I really wanted to hit someone right now. Preferably him. However, I could hardly stand so I settled on folding my arms. Surely he could tell that I wasn't amused. If he could he didn't care as he went back to Loki, who acted out stabbing him several times before making weird firework like actions with his hands. Sighing and preparing to grab onto Anakin if I fell, I took several steps away from the wall. My vision had now almost completely returned allowing me to see my friends as they cleared out Overlegen's forces. With the dizziness easing I put more distance between me and the wall. It was time to join the real battle.

'How's your side of the plan going?' I questioned Anakin, who seemed to no longer be concerned about me.

'Better than yours is.'

Ignoring how wrong I found his answer, we both turned towards the fight.

This was going to be fun.

CHAPTER EIGHTEEN

Ash – Arrow

My head was spinning and I was on the verge of throwing up. But that was the price my species paid for being able to whizz around at insane speeds. Once again I let my vision blur as I sprinted around the battle saving Asgardians from death blows and sweeping the enemy off of their feet in the least romantic way possible. Far too frequently I had to come to a stop and catch my breath, hoping the break would be enough to spare myself from regurgitation. I bent over gripping my knees with my hands. I was running rather low on energy. Food and water would be nice right now.

Focused on fighting my reflux and my starvation I was paying little attention to my surroundings. My saving grace was the quick swishing sound that alerted me to a sword. Jumping out of the way I realised an Overlegenian was standing in striking distance bringing his sword down towards where my neck was. My hasty jump to escape, however, cost me energy that I didn't have. If it hadn't been for the building next to me I would have doubled over. The sword wielding Overlegenian was covered in a mix of bloods but wasn't anywhere near as exhausted as I was. He swung again, still aiming for my neck. My legs gave out with impeccable timing. I hit the floor just as metal scraped cleanly through clay. I forced myself past the fear of puking and sent a powerful punch in between his hips. The only food I'd eaten recently surfaced as he screamed and dropped to the floor with me. Both of us puked onto the mud before recovering to glare at one another. A rather long minute passed as we both recovered. If I wasn't on the verge of dying I would've felt bad about what I'd just done to him. But I just didn't have the energy to feel pity for an attempted child murderer. He was at least twice my age and carried a scar for each year on his face alone.

'You deserve worse than torture for that.' He spat in my face, causing me to return to vomiting.

'I know,' I responded, in between gagging, 'but you were trying to murder a kid.' I finally countered him as I managed to sit up straight. His brown eyes were harsh as he judged my face, looking for Odin knows what.

'And that's just rude.' I shook my head at him as I slowly prepared myself.

The Overlegenian sharply tugged a knife from his boot, having no idea that wouldn't help him. I gave him three seconds to stand and run but he didn't. I let out a tut before punching him in the throat. It wasn't a particularly hard punch from me. I didn't have the energy for anything that would kill him quickly, so I had to try and ignore his chokes as my body lurched me back towards the ground. Attempting to throw up anything else. I really needed this to be over. It was my first proper battle, other than the one on Asgard, and I was in desperate need of training. *I mean how am I meant to survive if this goes on for another day?*

'Looks uncomfortable kid.'

I didn't even need to look to know another murderous maniac was standing over me.

'It was a noble fight for your realm. Now allow me to end your misery.' She phrased it like I was doing Asgard, the planet that saved me, a great favour by dying in my own puke.

In my head I was already on my feet kicking and punching but, in reality, I was done. My muscles felt like they'd been glued in place and the aching in my joints was hardly bearable. Too exhausted to move, or even gag, I just sat staring at the disgusting ground in front of me. All I could do was wish for help.

'One moment.' My murderer gave me another second to curse my species and therefore my talents.

Managing to twist my head, I saw her turn to face three Asgardians who were running toward me. Tears brimmed my eyes as I realised they were coming to help me. My tears of joy left my waterline and began streaming down my face as the Overlegenian began to cut them down. She smashed one of my rescuers in the throat while slicing off the other's ear and landing a kick in the groin of the other. She made messy work of them, her fighting style as grotesque as the other Overlegenian's. My rescuers were not granted clean deaths, as hatred incarnate displayed her desperation for power. I was unable to make out what her ability was exactly but it had something to do with a purple smoke that hovered below the noses of the three Asgardians.

'Don't,' I croaked, before she stabbed the last breathing one through the neck.

Preferring the sight of my own guts, than the blood of loyal Asgardians, I turned away. She didn't say another word as her footsteps got closer to me. I felt so angry but at the same time I felt as if my sorrow could drag me underground. I didn't even know what to do with my feelings as they overwhelmed me. If only I had known how to conserve my energy during this sort of battle. If only they hadn't seen me weak and vulnerable. I choked back tears and harsher emotions as my mind strangled me. If only they hadn't died. I didn't deserve to breathe if I couldn't even protect the people fighting with me. Absolutely drained of energy, yet overflowing with nasty thoughts and feelings, I hung my head accepting my untimely demise. There was nothing more I could do.

The universe, however, didn't agree. A sharp feminine scream pulled me out of my downward spiral to see a foot appear next to her head and a blade sticking through her rib cage. Saving me from having my neck torn apart. The rather sharp sword twisted before being removed. Two strong hands wrapped around my back pulling me out of the way as my would-be murderer collapsed into a pool of stomach acid.

'Arrow, are you alright?'

I smiled warmly at my rescuers, as Ray and two other Asgardian warriors gazed at me.

'Thank you.' I met each of their eyes then grabbed Ray's outreached hand.

He was surprisingly strong for a kid his age. Once I was on my feet the Asgardians gave me a couple pats on the back before heading off into the chaos, which I was glad to see was thinning of Overlegenians.

'Anytime.' He gave me a rather large grin, his blue eyes in deep contrast with his green hair.

I couldn't help but let out a small laugh as I realised he was hardly injured at all. 'I see you're doing much better than I am.'

He shook his head, tilting towards the ground as he did so. 'I wish. Amolt says I'm too young to be left to survive alone. He's always two steps behind me.' Just as Ray had said, a red haze reached out behind him choking several of our enemies as Amolt stepped towards us.

The fact that he was as old, if not older than he looked, and was still able to wield without consequences as obvious as mine, was astounding. I gave Ray an encouraging pat on the shoulder, unable to tell him that he had something I wouldn't even dream of.

'Ray told me you were hurt.' Amolt's sentence was neither a question nor delivered like a statement.

'Better now.' I surveyed the nearby fights as a couple got uncomfortably close.

At least August was right about Overlegen not knowing what to do with chaos. That was definitely our advantage as our forces did the unthinkable. We weren't overwhelming in number but we had strength in other ways.

'Come on Ray, we've got more evil to clear.' Amolt gave me a subtle nod before unleashing his dark talents once more.

Ray continued looking at me as if he was unsure I would be alright on my own.

'Go kid, I'm alright.' I smiled, encouragingly.

I watched to ensure that he had reached Amolt safely before heading towards an approaching Overlegenian. I wasn't sure how much energy my brief break had restored to me so I was going to have to be careful.

'The name's Anders.' The soldier who was at least two head heights taller greeted me.

'Why do you feel the need to tell me your name?' I asked, to give myself more time to breathe.

'Just so you know who killed you.'

I screwed my nose up as he said that. His stench making me feel sick. I could tell that this guy was a rambler. You can usually tell by the stream of putrefied boredom that encompasses them. But I could use his love of speaking to my advantage.

'And how do you intend to do that?' I asked.

'Do what?'

'Kill me.' I reached one arm across my chest and caught it with the other one. I was in desperate need of a stretch.

'Well first, I'll separate your head from the rest of your body and then...'

I let his voice zone out as I focused on counting seconds before I swapped to a different stretch. The tight pull of my muscles made me wince but it had to be done.

'...then I'll grind you into crumbs and then mash you into saw dust. Then I'll add some water and pour you into a cupcake holder, bake you, and then feed you to the birds...' Anders' dumb brown eyes followed my movements as he tried to showcase his creativity in destroying me.

Since my recent encounter with doom I had developed a strange cavalier attitude, at least for now. Which was a little concerning. I had no clue why I had suddenly stopped worrying.

'Stop,' he wailed, stumbling backward just a little.

'Stop what?' I asked, grabbing my ankle.

'Stretching. It is rude.'

I tilted my head at him, pulling my leg tighter against itself.

This guy was hilarious.

'How so?' I swapped legs.

'This is a battle for one, the proper etiquette must be followed.'

'What etiquette?' I asked, swapping back to my arms as I pulled my bent arm across my head ever so slightly.

'Overlegenian etiquette.'

I could now hear the crisp frustration in his deep voice.

'No stretching is permitted in the battle for the first realm.'

'And secondly?' Once again swapping to another arm as I pretended I was paying him little attention.

'I'm a storyteller. I need, no, I demand your full attention.'

'How about a deal?' I offered.

'Anything, this is not etiquette.' He folded his arms against his chest awkwardly whilst still trying to grip his three-bladed axe.

'If you lean on your axe, making yourself seem less menacing, then I will stop warming up and start conducting proper fight etiquette.'

Anders didn't respond but he complied, leaning on his axe. I too complied and stopped stretching.

'Now back to your demise.' His eye twitching obnoxiously as he spoke.

With one swift motion I pulled his axe towards me, not even giving him time to regain his balance I swung his bloodied weapon of grime at him. After I was sure he was finished I snapped his axe and dropped it in the mud. Thankful that that had gone smoothly and rather quickly.

'Anders,' came a voice from behind me.

Not another one!

'Poor Anders, he was-'

I cut her off. 'Too stupid?'

Her glare caused shivers up my back as I slowly turned to face her.

'To die.' She finished.

She carried no weapon and had her back to a rather large group of her own forces. I hadn't realised there were so many more Overlegenians that we had to survive. I gulped, taking a step backwards as she exposed her not so well aligned teeth, as if to show me that I needn't worry about anything other than her. Her lack of weapons meant that she had a talent that was extremely practical. She could probably kill me by blinking. I took a deep breath as I prepared myself for the physical exertion I was going to have to do. I was not going to let her kill me. Even if that meant exhaustion took me, so be it. But before either of us could act a bold flash grabbed our attention. Just then, like a welcome sunrise after a tormenting night, streaks of colour shot through the ranks of

Overlegenians causing an equal amount of cheers and screams to erupt. Two different forms of electricity shot out from either side of the exit side of the courtyard. Flashes of blue and white petrified the Overlegenians, especially those in the most advantageous positions, while flames licked their way through the others. More colours joined my friends as other Asgardians joined in.

We could win this!

'Arrow!' someone yelled, tearing my attention away from the beauty.

Anakin and Alice stood a few metres in front of me. *Right, fight, don't stare at the colours.* I crashed my foot into the chest of the Overlegenian who was still standing facing me despite being totally distracted. She crumpled onto the floor gasping for breath that my strike wouldn't allow her to get back. I headed past her towards my friends.

'We've got to find Azar and Apoint.' Alice's voice was the coldest I'd ever heard it.

Obviously she was better at controlling her emotions during a fight. Joining them, I scanned the remaining Asgardians that I could see until I spotted Ray and Amolt. They didn't appear in need of aid any time soon so I turned back to my friends.

'Right, I'm coming.'

We ran at their pace towards the Overlegenian soldiers who were now mainly fighting fire. Spotting Alec, Ace, and August, we headed towards them. I mentally adjusted to thinking of my friend's titles instead of their names as we entered the thick of where the last remaining Overlegenians were battling it out. Rather viciously. I doubted that there were any mind readers on Overlegen's side but you could never be too sure. Despite being rare, Firestorm was the second one I'd met, which meant they weren't as uncommon as they used to be. Supposedly, there used to only be one every hundred years, according to my father. Moving away from thoughts of my father I fixed my gaze on Riptide. Watching as she ducked Azar's slash and flicked the blade from his hand with ease. She stood, moving her sword towards his throat as he scampered away from her. His robes were torn and dirty as he attempted to fend off my friend. Her black boots reflected the blue light of her swords as she moved and her golden hair flew out behind her. Though it remained away from her eyes as she slashed and ducked below a new attack from Azar. He was desperately trying to turn the tables on Riptide but without any luck as he was still staggering backwards. Azar's attention was so focused on Riptide that he didn't even realise that Firestorm had now also set her attention on him. *Good luck Azar.* I smirked, he was going to need it.

'Apoint.' Gale pointed to the scoundrel who was frantically trying to sneak away from Blaze and Chameleon.

'Let's go.' Devil grinned, charging axe first towards Apoint.

Several shadows fell over the ground around us before Gale and I could follow him. I looked up to see several extremely tall Overlegenian soldiers. All of whom were built like bricks and weren't carrying weapons. I held back a panicked yelp. Alice and I were in serious trouble. Focusing on my breathing, I prepared myself for another energy draining situation.

CHAPTER NINETEEN

Alec – Chameleon

My hands held tightly to the shaft of the spiked flail I'd grabbed from the weapons room before we left for the battle. Surprisingly, I'd managed to hold on to it the entire battle and was becoming more and more fond of it. Studying the soldier facing me I watched, waiting for her to send her sword towards me. I'd been fighting the same girl since I had re-entered the courtyard, and both of us were growing increasingly sick of each other.

I'd spent the majority of our fight ducking behind other Overlegenians and hiding in plain sight while she tried to change my state. Many of her own side had been melted into a golden pool of gore. Luckily for me her gifts seemed to dehydrate her, which seemed to be causing her a great amount of pain. With the fight on slightly more even ground I'd given up hiding. I needed to get rid of her anyway, she and her friend were the only ones blocking us from getting to Apoint. The arrogant orchestrator of this battle, who was doing more talking than fighting, barking out orders in a language I couldn't understand. Finally, she swung her sword sideways at my head. Adjusting my feet I brought the shaft of my weapon up to parry her sword. There was a screech of metal, followed by her scream, as the chain connecting the metal shaft with a spiked metal ball flipped on its own accord. The second that the sharp points implanted themselves in her flesh I moved her sword with my weapon. Giving myself the perfect opening to land a punch into her temple. Not being built like anything remotely close to all of Overlegen's weight lifting crazies my punch wasn't hard enough to knock her out. But I didn't need it to be. Ripping the spiked ball from her wrist, I swung it up and towards her forehead. Despite the several distractions I'd provided, she saw it coming and pulled her head backwards managing to lean out of the way. Very aware that I couldn't safely stop the momentum of the flail, I winced as I saw what was about to happen. *She should've run backwards.* The Overlegenian didn't even get a chance to scream as the ball landed its spikes in her throat. I didn't feel any resistance as it raked across her flesh and finished its arch back towards me. Man, this thing was scary. I quickly stepped over her body, avoiding looking at the damage I had caused as I got closer to Blaze. His opponent was distracted by the sight of her friend's mangled throat allowing Blaze an open strike. Having an ounce of honour he went for her legs making sure her attention was back on him before he moved for a more fatal blow.

'You two will die for that,' she spat her hate at us.

'Isn't the whole point of you being here, to kill us?' Ace asked, as he rammed the pommel of his sword into her gut.

His initial strike with the blade had been deflected but his second attempt, be it less fatal, hit its mark. She bent with the attack, her long nailed hands grabbing his hair. I readied my flail as she pulled his head back exposing his throat.

'I'll slit you open with my nails.' Her words came out sharply.

I stepped forward raising my flail towards the back of her head. *No one was going to slit my friend open with anything!*

'That's not very hygienic.' Ace's voice was devoid of worry as he met my eyes.

I paused my attack, he had this. As I lowered my flail, Ace swung his sword arm, which was pressed against his body, in a close arch slicing her stomach open with the edge of his blade. He stumbled backwards away from her as she realised her mistake.

'Apoint.' I reminded the both of us, noticing the path to him was clear.

Riptide had given us a run down on Apoint before we'd all left. She'd said he no longer had gifts but was exceptional with any weapon and rather good at escaping. So we'd have to be alert. From where we were positioned I could see the upward slope that led to the exit of this dreadful city. The exit was calling me and I had to fight to turn my attention onto Apoint. Blaze, unlike me, was completely in the zone for a fight. He extended his arm, pulling Apoint towards us. I flicked my flail into his ribs as Blaze pulled him full force into my attack. Apoint struck out with a knife, which must have been concealed, as I hit. He crumpled but his blade managed to slice Blaze's arm. Neither my friend nor Apoint let a sound escape them as they winced from their injuries.

'Help!' I heard the unmistakable yell of Devil as Blaze slashed at Apoint, and I delayed another swing.

Apoint was unconcerned about Blaze's slash and sent a foot straight into my face. Stumbling out of the way, just enough that it didn't hurt too much, I flicked the flail up into his calf muscle. Though more as a reaction than on purpose. A scream, not belonging to Apoint, filled the air as I quickly scanned our surroundings. *Where was he?* Blaze parried Apoint's stab and stepped in with his riposte.

'He's been cornered.' I finally spotted my friend who was being manhandled by several tall Overlegenians.

'Let me introduce you to my guards.' Apoint gave us a ghastly smile but Blaze remedied the expression on Apoint's face.

My friend plunged two fingers into the flesh exposed on Apoint's wrist and gave him a good shock. I knew that Ace had hardly any access to electricity so Apoint would only be stunned for a brief second, but at least Apoint's face was now cleared of his horrid smile.

'Get Devil,' I said, watching Apoint as he rummaged through his cloak pulling out another knife.

'Be careful.' Blaze placed a reassuring hand on my shoulder before dashing off towards Devil.

'So this is how you'll die.' Apoint extended his arm towards me.

I jumped back swinging my flail at him, I had longer reach. All I had to do was stay out of distance. But Riptide was right. Apoint was rather good at fighting. Regardless of us being slightly distracted, Apoint had held us off without help or gifts. He flung his blade across his body, to swap hands as he ducked and threw a knife towards me. I primarily focused on dodging and staying away from his near unfollowable actions, only managing to catch him with my spikes occasionally. I side stepped the most recent knife to be flung at my head and spotted my opportunity as Apoint reached into his cloak again. I charged forward, bringing my flail down towards the back of his skull. But just as the spikes connected I was wrenched up and away from my attack. Two strong arms plucked me from my jump and flung me sideways. Unsure what had just happened, I narrowly managed to avoid the rebound of my own weapon as I hurtled through the air. My time in the air was cut off with a hard slam as I felt a wall, that definitely wasn't mud, at my back. My breath was displaced from my lungs as my head and neck smashed backwards into the wall. My eyes were already closed and I slipped into darkness before I even got to feel the pain of landing.

Not only was I thrown into a wall but I was also thrown into an old unwanted memory. If I didn't recognise my surroundings, and what was about to happen, I would have thought I was in a dream. I knew better than that. I was back on Earth. The legs of my younger self carried me away from the bathroom and back into the large wooden meeting room of our archery club. This had come on too suddenly for me to prepare myself. So, without any choice, I relived my least favourite memory.

❧❧❧

As I entered the room I saw my older sister, Lexine, waiting there for me. Our parents had disappeared a week ago. The local authorities thought it had something to do with the case they were working on and had made arrangements for the two of us to move to Iceland, while they looked into it. Supposedly we'd be safe here. The kind people we were staying with had suggested we pick up a sport to distract ourselves. To be fair to them the archery helped. It had given me something to pour my emotions into. A release that would carve a nice gash in the wooden targets.

'Alec.' Lexine's voice was on edge as I entered the room, startling me, she never used my actual name.

Having already lived this moment there was nothing I could do as my eyes took in my sister's tense stance. Her long brown hair was still tied up in a ponytail and her freckled face and hazel eyes were facing the opposite end of the room. Looking past the furniture and the archery stands I followed her gaze to see Gunnar, the star student.

'Nice of you to join us.' He smirked at me, as I walked slowly over to my sister.

'What's going on? Can we go home?' I asked her, tugging gently on her jacket sleeve.

She didn't respond, just kept looking at Gunnar.

'You can't seriously think that I'll just let you leave?' Gunnar remarked at me, his fair eyebrows folding into a scrunched frown.

I shrunk back a bit. I'd done rather well today, hitting dead centre every time. Every time, that was, until Gunnar's buddy had tried to sabotage me. Gunnar hated being out shot. Their plan had gone terribly wrong for them though. I had released my arrow as Gunnar's friend slammed into me. My arrow went off course. Really off course. It had found its target in the flesh of Gunnar's hip. Our instructor had told me it wasn't any fault of mine. Gunnar obviously didn't feel the same way. *I didn't respond, what was I to say?* He grabbed his bow and an arrow that were leaning against the wall behind him. I squinted, not really understanding what he was planning to do. He took aim, his arrow pointing straight at my head. I was too shocked to react. *Surely he wasn't actually going to shoot me?* Lexine didn't think the same. I hadn't seen her grab it

275

but she stood next to me with her smooth wooden bow. Gunnar fired, and my sister being my sister, fired too. I didn't react. I didn't even think about moving as Gunnar's arrow cut through the air towards me. My sister, four years older than me at fourteen, wasn't wired to freeze in deadly situations. She shoved me and I fell, like a rock to the concrete floor. It hurt but I scrambled to my feet as two screams crashed into my ears causing my eyes to pool. Looking straight ahead I saw that Lexine's arrow had pierced into Gunnar's skin and I watched as his white shirt quickly ran red. He cried for help but I wasn't listening.

'Lexine,' I whispered, turning to check on my sister.

The arrow meant for me had hit her in the stomach.

'I'm fine,' she lied, smiling at me.

I took off my shirt and tied it tightly around the wound.

'Please stay with me.' I cried, tears pouring down my cheeks. I pulled out my phone and dialled 112.

'Please don't die,' I whispered on repeat.

She rolled her eyes at me. 'Don't be so dramatic.'

I kept pressure on the parts of the wound that weren't covered by the arrow head. Trying my best to limit her blood loss.

'Why didn't you just move?' I scolded myself.

'Sorry, this line is currently unavailable.' A voice from the phone informed me.

Panicking, I dialled it again.

'Al, it's alright.'

I didn't look at her, I couldn't.

'No it's not!' I mumbled through tears.

She was all I had. I kept staring at the phone as the ringing stopped, hopeful that someone had picked up. They hadn't, my screen was black, the blasted thing had died.

'Don't die,' I told my sister, as I discarded my phone and ran out of the room.

There was no one around. I tried to scream for help but my voice was weighed down with tears. So I turned and ran back inside, stopping as I reached Gunnar. He watched me stand over him with a sneer on his face. My saddened state twisted into an angry despair. He had tried to kill me and in doing so had shot my sister.

'Help,' he croaked, finally letting go of his wicked expression.

Gunnar lay at my feet in a worse state than Lexine. His blood pushed out regardless of the arrow head in its way.

'I'll help.' I glared, salt water overflowing my eyes.

I crouched down and gripped the arrow's tail. Before I could pull it out, and let his flood drain, I felt a firm hand land on my shoulder.

A deep voice spoke soothingly into my ear. 'Let's not do that my dear boy.'

Not releasing my grip I turned to see an elderly man, unlike anyone I'd seen before. He had spectacular silk coloured hair, that was the same length as his beard, which stopped abruptly at his collar bone. His eyebrows flared at the ends and he had one sparkling blue eye that seemed to be reading things I couldn't. His cloak was long and hid his physique. The black fabric ran into red before settling at a golden rim. In the hand, that wasn't still firmly holding my shoulder, was a beautiful bronze spear that had a hat sat over the pointy end. His skin was of similar appearance to thick ice which also sparkled just a little like his eye. His right eye was covered by an eye patch that, like his cloak, ran from black to red and into golden flakes.

'Please do not rip that arrow out of him, son. His death would be most unfortunate for me.'

I frowned, Gunnar's death. I couldn't care for it. I just wanted revenge for Lexine. Lexine. I let go of the arrow and shot to my feet. The magnificent looking man rose with me.

'How so?' I barked through my emotions as I stormed back over to my sister.

'He is hardly honourable, but if he died as a result of battle I'd have to do an awful lot of paperwork to remove him from Valhalla.'

I frowned, which forced more water to stream down my cheeks. *Who was this guy?*

'I'm here to take your sister to Valhalla.'

I choked on my own tears.

He couldn't take my sister anywhere! I needed her. I looked down at Lexine, the blood in her wound had stopped midflow and her eyes were flicking between the both of us. *What was going on?*

'I won't let you, she's staying here.' I put myself between her and the strange man.

His blue eye looked upon me with pity.

'She cannot stay.' His words were slow and though he didn't mean them to be I found them aggravating.

'Why is that?' I growled, not knowing what I was meant to do.

'My name is Odin, I watch over war and death. I'm afraid Lexine can't stay.' His tone was gentle, and although I could see both of his hands it felt as if he was holding onto my tense shoulders.

'You're taking her to Asgard?' I questioned the God, still standing between them.

He nodded, his blue gaze turning from pity to contemplation.

'You may join us if you'd like?' My tears poured even more.

'Will that mean I can still see her?' He didn't voice a response but gave me a comforting nod.

❧❧❧

My mind chose that moment to swirl out of the memory leaving me sick with teary emotion. Despite our enjoyable five years on

Asgard, that included Odin giving Lexine a place among the Valkyrie, and giving me my gifts, I'd never been able to lose the guilt that she'd been removed from Earth because of me.

I woke up. Light swinging back and forth in my eyes, as my mind scolded itself for reliving that memory.

'Alec,' came August's hushed voice.

She was knelt in front of me. Her arms, for some reason, resting behind her back. Slowly, I sat up, giving myself time to take in my surroundings. Somehow we weren't in the main courtyard. If I had to guess, probably the street nearest the exit but I couldn't be sure as all the landmarks looked the same. Apoint and Azar stood just far enough away to not be immediately threatening. I swivelled in my position and spotted my friends. Alice looked ruffled and furious as one of Apoint's dreaded guards held a dagger to her neck. He was holding it deep enough that blood was seeping out of the wound. With the blade pressed into her neck she couldn't even heal. *He was bleeding her out!* Next to Alice was Anakin. Two large guys had him pinned in an uncomfortable position. With a third guy standing over my wiggling friend. In his gloved hands was a nasty looking branding stick. I could easily see the red hot metal from where I was, but it got worse; in the centre of the symbol, at the end, was a spike. Sharp and hot enough that Anakin would feel everything as it was rammed into his skull. I flinched, hating this situation as I looked to see Anjelica next to him. This was too much for me. Enduring the memory of my sister's death, only to wake up to my friends about to be tortured and killed. It was too much. I grabbed August's arm to steady myself.

'It's alright Alec, they won't hurt them until they get what they came for.' Her whisper was calm but her blue eyes gave away her fear.

Just like me she had no idea what to do and I could tell she hated it. I heard a grunt from Anjelica which brought my eyes back to her. She had a blood covered scarf tied tightly around her neck, her limbs were bound and the angriest expression covered her face as she tried not to choke. I really didn't want to see what state the rest of my friends were in but I forced myself to. I needed to know what we were up against. Ace was gagged and bound, but as that was obviously not enough, his arms and hands seemed to also be wrapped as he knelt on the muddy ground. The man behind him, who was holding what looked like a Midgardian taser, couldn't see the defiant look on his face. Guessing that what they'd wrapped him with disabled his connection with any electric fields, he probably wouldn't be able to use either of his gifts. Which meant they could easily electrocute him.

How did they know so much about our gifts?

'Lavita,' August whispered to me, somehow having guessed what I was wondering, 'She can access memories.'

Well that's just great.

'Is she here?' August shook her head before double checking our surroundings.

Finally, I forced myself to look at Ash's predicament. I could see the exhaustion on his face and from the way he was holding himself. But regardless, he refused to let himself fall to the floor. He stood leaning against a wall for support as three men looked ready to impale him with a variety of different weapons. This was worse than bad. The only thing that was stopping my friends from pain and death were two objects that August was hiding on her person. Staying seated next to her I watched Azar and Apoint talk intently about something. I felt the same despair I had when Lexine had been shot. It was a wretched, helpless feeling, and this time I knew Odin wouldn't step in. I didn't even know where he was. Or the other Gods for that matter. Though I presumed they were still busy with the rest of Overlegen's army.

'What do we do?' I asked, hoping August would have an answer.

'I don't know,' she whispered back, the same worry pleated into her voice as in mine.

'They've already asked nicely, what happens next won't be pleasant.' She twisted so that she could get a better look at Azar and Apoint.

Noticing she was bound behind her back I subtly started picking at the knots. She went still, realising what I was doing.

'Thank you,' she whispered, as I slowly managed to free her.

Azar left Apoint and came toward us as I managed to pull the thick rope free of her wrists.

'Let's start with water's opposite shall we.' Azar's words weren't a question.

Reading the situation faster than I thought possible, she stood, moving swiftly to put as much distance between herself and me as she could. I realised why as Azar pulled out a distinctively Overlegenian grenade. Dragging myself off the ground I made it to my feet as Azar's scrawny arm threw the explosive at my friend.

'NO!' I thought, as Anjelica screamed it.

In my mind I saw myself where August stood, unsure what to do. I became Lexine as the grenade morphed into an imaginary arrow. I threw myself forward, lunging toward the grenade. All I had to do was touch it. Thankfully, the street hadn't given August a lot of room to get away from me and I reached her with ease. With one finger I reached towards the destructive favourite of Overlegen and with the other hand I gave August the hardest shove I could. Hoping she'd fall out of the way. My finger connected with the warm metal of the grenade as I felt a hand wrap around my other wrist. Damn August for not just falling. *Why did she have to pull me out of the way with her?* With only a seconds worth of contact with the grenade it morphed into the only thing that was in my head. A Midgardian grenade. Admittedly, it was much better than what it originally was but still not great at all. Thanks to

August's grip on my wrist, and her forward momentum, the grenade didn't hit me directly as it exploded. But we were far too close for safety. I felt heat slam into my back harder than the wall before. This time I managed to remain conscious long enough to feel my body hit the ground. The world went quiet for a moment, nothing moved or made a noise. Not longer than a breath later the peace shattered back into pain and buzzing.

'Alec.' August's voice was more of a rasp and was difficult to hear through the beeping in my ears.

My vision was the definition of blurry as she crawled towards me, also having been thrown by the explosion.

'Thank you.' She managed as she reached me.

She looked a mess, which was very much unlike her usual put togetherness. Her golden hair was slightly singed and muddy and she looked like she'd just walked out of Helheim. I dreaded thinking about what I must have looked like. With the scent of blood making me feel sick, and the deafening beeping in my ears, I closed my blurry eyes fighting to stay conscious. The rest of my body was in so much pain I could no longer feel it. But I didn't regret it. A small sense of pride fought out from under the lava field that was my emotions. I hadn't frozen. I had managed to save my friend. My fingers dug into the mud as I remembered the situation my other friends were in, but my body failed me as I tried to move, darkness suffocating my senses.

'Save them,' I whispered, as August grabbed my hand giving it a squeeze as I fell into darkness.

ஓஒஓ

I felt like I was falling down a midnight tunnel, but unlike any other tunnels, I couldn't see the light at the end of this one. I was trapped in isolating blackness with no sense of anything as I plummeted. I saw spots of pink and brown weave their way into the darkness. Their surface area slowly increased until it overwhelmed the black. I felt a jolt as I connected with something warm and solid. Everything went still for a brief moment before something gripped me harshly and tore me right out of the tunnel. The shock from whatever had just happened knocked me out before I could think anything of it.

CHAPTER TWENTY

August – Riptide

'This will be the first and last time I offer anyone a third chance.' Azar scowled at me as I forced myself into a sitting position.

Everything hurt to the point where I could hear my own pain. The shadowy hitman angled his long sword at my neck as he spoke.

'Man, I'm so grateful you're close with my sister.' I dripped sarcasm as blatantly as I could hoping he could feel the hate in my eyes.

He called this a third chance? He'd kill my friends if I gave it to him and I'd already lost... I forced my thoughts to shut up before I broke the dam protecting me from tears. I was alive and breathing because of him. I had a chance to do something because of him. Yet as soon as the warmth had left his skin I couldn't bring myself to look back at him. Noticing my inner torment Azar smirked, smacking the side of my head with the blunt part of his blade forcing my head to turn towards *Alec.*

I fought back my tears being adamant that I would not cry in front of these wretches. My voice was too croaky to even say his name as my eyes absorbed his appearance. His fluffy, light blond hair was charred, triggering visions of dandelion seeds being burnt before they were able to fly away. Blood was still running down his face from his hairline, crushing my hope as each droplet fell from his muddied face onto the ground. His clothes and armour were in bad shape and he was lying in an uncomfortable looking position. Closing my eyes, I tried to banish thoughts of the loyal and stubborn guy Alec was. I would cry my heart out later. Right now I had to find a way to save my remaining friends.

Manipulating my deep sorrow I turned it towards the cold instead of anger. Emotions would do me no good right now. My body temperature had dropped quite a bit during the battle though the grenade had likely warmed me up enough to freeze Azar. I was going to make him hurt first. My hands hid behind my back, subtly summoning my weapons. *Wouldn't it be funny if he was killed by the very things he wanted the most?* Gripping tightly to the Mutabilis, which were concealing one of the Forn Ljós, I contemplated what my best course of action was.

'If you think I'd give you anything after-' I paused, even though each word bought me some time. One glance at Alec and I couldn't say it, '-you're wrong.'

Azar didn't seem to care about my refusal to cooperate.

'I'll take it from your corpse then.' He rotated his body, swinging with his blade.

Reacting quickly, I parried with my blade against my forearm. Swinging my other blade at his throat as I stood. I caught him in the throat but nothing damaging as he stepped away from me. I went to attack again but was faltered. Something felt very wrong. Just like that I stopped breathing. My lungs squirmed as I felt lumpy liquid start appearing out of nowhere. Thick foam began to rise uncomfortably up my throat and into my mouth and nose, completely cutting off my access to air. Dropping my weapons, I doubled over trying to expel the liquid by gagging, but it wasn't working. The suffocating gloop stuck to my insides as my body went into an internal panic. I couldn't let Azar's gifts kill me. Unfortunately, my brain was no longer functioning, unable to come up with anything to save me. Muscle memory didn't serve me in this situation either. So I continued gasping and gagging as my world shut down.

'Your friends will die with you.' Azar must have been close to me as his words were barely a whisper.

I fought to shut out his voice, and my thoughts, as the shouts and screams of my friends began. The sound of their pain was enough to kill me even without Azar's gifts. It couldn't end like this. Not after all that had happened. I wanted so desperately to fight back, to get even, but I had no air to deliver my justice with. Overlegen really was taking everything from me. My sister, my freedom, my friends, most of whom were only guilty of being Asgardian and meeting me. Now they were trying to take my life, so that they could take my belongings and overpower the Asgardian

Realm. As I suffocated, my thoughts and feelings were overrun with malice. I couldn't let them. They didn't deserve what they wanted. Asgard was a wonderfully welcoming place full of honourable and pure-hearted people. Overlegen was deceitful and conniving, full of people who thought themselves superior to everyone else. If will itself was enough to save me, I would be on my feet and throwing everything I had at Azar and his planet. But sheer will did nothing for me as I choked once more. Slowly, the surrounding environment faded into silence. Leaving me helpless and frustrated. I didn't even have the energy to throw a weapon at Azar. All I could do was collapse completely onto the ground and watch Azar's smile grow wider with each molecule of oxygen that I lost.

A flash of deep sea brought my attention back to Azar, halting my drifting off. The thin shadow of a man toppled out of my sight as a small hole opened up in my lungs. My chest heaved, desperate to reclaim as much oxygen as possible, panicked energy refilling my system. As my airway opened up, I sat, gasping uncontrollably as I noticed what was happening. A set of magnificent, dark sapphire wings blocked Azar from seeing me. The wings were flapping, gently wafting air in my direction. The extra momentum fed it straight into my lungs, easing the work I was having to do. *Nox!* I'd recognise his uniquely exquisite appearance anywhere. A small grin spread across my face as I realised what else my Guardian was up to. He had his fingers spread out on each of his hands, pointing a star-speckled finger towards each of the men looming over my friends. Each of Apoint's guards seemed to be having the same problem I had just recovered from. The goop in my lungs had disappeared without a trace and was now flooding theirs. *Nox was redirecting Azar's gifts!* I took, the slight glow from the horn to the left of his head, as confirmation of my theory. Not wanting to sit around any longer, I grabbed my weapons and got to my feet. Apoint seemed to have disappeared and Nox was doing a splendid job at killing the men near my friends, so I headed over to Azar.

He was crawling away from the dark angel as he spotted me approaching. His bony hand grabbed a jagged rock and he threw it towards my throat. I deflected it easily with my katana. My parry gave him time to stand. Although he was now weaponless, and Nox was using his gifts, I had him. Azar snarled at me, obviously realising the same. I kicked him in the knee and swung a katana toward him as he fell.

'August!'

I hesitated as I heard my name. I lifted my eyes away from Azar to be greeted with the sight of Nora running towards me. She held no weapon and was not dressed for combat.

'There's no need to kill him.' She placed a hand on mine, trying to force me to lower my blade.

Warily, I let my sister lower my blade from Azar. Although there was no way I was going to let him get away that easily. I tapped into the cold at my core and wrapped a few thick sheets of ice around his ankles. Nora smiled at me, not noticing what I'd done.

'I got here just in time.' She seemed rather pleased with her timing.

I wasn't. My heart hurt as I recalled Alec alerting me of her arrival ages ago. *Where had she been this whole time? And why was she intent on saving Azar?* Knowing I wouldn't be able to get the words out if I asked her what she thought this murder's redeeming qualities were, I instead questioned her whereabouts during the battle. Azar was silently trying to move his feet as I waited for Nora to reply.

'I had to pick someone up.' Nora turned from me to beckon a young girl, probably around my age, over to us. 'Ashia this is my sister Au-.'

'-Riptide.' I corrected her bluntly before she gave my name to a stranger.

The girl had long, straight brown hair and hazel eyes. Her build was rather frail and told me that she lived a completely different life from me. Ashia wouldn't survive a day in my life, and yet Nora had brought her here.

'I can help.' She spoke to me, her eyes ignoring Nora.

'How?' I didn't care if I was being rude, I had other things concerning me right now.

'I can locate people on this planet by touching the ground and cause small earthquakes.'

What? My calculating brain jumped at the opportunity.

'Can you find a man named Apoint?'

She nodded, not taking offence at my blunt tone.

'Nora.' Azar was back to speaking with his sly words.

My sister met his eyes with a kind gaze before noticing the ice wrapped around his ankles. 'August, let him go.'

My gut clenched, feeling like it was being twisted. Sorrow floating into my throat as I tried to keep it from my eyes. He can kidnap Gods, spend years trying to kill me, succeed in killing my friend and hurting my others, all while trying to get hold of two of the most influential objects in the universe. Yet, despite all of that, she stood, just as she had when I'd left Overlegen, right there at the shoulder of my enemies. A bitter realisation broke my emotional dam. Nora was always going to choose her own goals over me.

I tore my thoughts from Nora as I noticed Azar's expression. The look he was giving me was full of malice. His grey eyes seemed to flare at the hope that he could still achieve his desires. Nora had been waiting, stepping in only when it suited her. She hadn't come here to help or to fight. She'd come here to teleport Azar out of danger.

'Why?'

Nora gave me a puzzled look as I gave her the opportunity to explain herself.

'Why do you want me to let him go?' Surely she had a good reason. She had given us the Segredos drive after all, not him. That had to mean she was on my side. *Right?*

'If you must know, Azar is helping me research the Forn Ljós.'

I looked up at her, through my squinted lashes and frowning eyebrows.

'I know you found one. I was learning what I could to help you.' As she finished answering she turned grabbing Azar's blade.

The one he'd hit me in the head with. Not giving me a chance to stop her. I realised something else as she shattered the ice, freeing Azar, who pulled the weapon from her hands. I laughed. A short sarcastic chuckle. My sister, with all her power and influence, was an idiot. Azar was using her. Yet, she thought it the other way around. Instead of just showing up she'd thought she could help from the sidelines, a mistake Azar was all too happy to abuse.

He gave her a rough shove as he swung his blade at my neck. I dropped, allowing his blade to make an empty sweep of the air above my head as I brought my swords across to the opposite sides of my body. The katanas tore flesh and cut through bone as I slashed his stomach. Green gloop formed over the wound. It probably wouldn't save him but its stickiness would be enough to keep him going for a while longer. I wasn't fazed by his next sloppy attack, my cold mental state had returned. Parrying with both my blades I poured in my strength as a sound similar to shattering glass interrupted our silent battle. I had to duck and take a few steps back as his blade splintered into multiple pieces. Sharp stinging erupted in my left shoulder and I spotted a glinting shard sticking out of my skin. Caught off guard, I winced as blunt agony hit the right side of my face. Azar had taken advantage of my distraction but in doing so he'd stepped unarmed into close quarters. Without allowing hesitation to cost me another chance, I plunged Vorago into his heart. He stumbled backwards, his hands and his eyes shooting in shock to his chest. His golden blood was the only colour I'd ever seen him wear.

'Gold really brings out the murderer in your eyes.' I took a verbal jab at the dying man.

'Well played.' He wrapped his hands around my weapon, noticing the glowing rune displayed below a clear part of the blade. His eyelids fluttered and a small grimace appeared on his lips. His ghost grey eyes meeting mine as his pupils dilated.

'Thank you August.' He seemed to be appreciative of the irony in his downfall.

For the last time I took in his smudgy appearance, his long and lean features managing to be both pale and dark at once. His very appearance had haunted my nightmares and days for far too long.

Never again would he drain the life from a person as good as Alec. Never again would he manipulate, torture, hunt, and kill. He was gone. My tears tore down my face fast as I turned away from the falling body of my childhood demon and towards where Alec lay.

'Is that the Guardian here? Who's side is he on? What is he?' My sister's voice drew closer but I didn't need to look at her to know she was asking about Nox.

Deciding that, for once, I'd like to be the one with all the answers, I replied unhelpfully.

'He's a Fylgja.' I grinned, as I remained turned away from her.

Nora knew less than nothing about Norse folktales. It would be funny when she realised I was having her on. The being was close enough to what Nox was that she'd have to actually think to figure out the difference.

'Why did Azar thank you?' Nora was full of confusion as I summoned Vorago.

This time I offered her no response as I headed away from her.

⊰⊷⊱

Alice and Ash were helping Anjelica, Ace, and Anakin get free of their bonds but I couldn't bring myself to walk over to them. Not after Alec. So instead I headed towards Nox, his expressionless face watching my every step. He stood in front of my friend's body shielding Alec's face from my eyes. As I got closer I realised that Nox was actually glaring at me. My feet failed to move any further as I reached him. My Guardian had a youthful appearance but I could sense his ancient aura radiating off his skin, judging me for whatever reason. We stood in silence for far too long, as tears pooled in my eyes, and Nox remained still and quiet. I really disliked crying but this was getting too much. I'd lost people but I'd never had anyone die saving me before. I did not like the feeling it left with me. If this was the universe trying to teach me something, they could give him back. I didn't want to learn anything if the price was a friend's life.

'You can stop crying,' Nox finally spoke. 'He will be fine.'

He twisted, standing side on so that I could see Alec's face. This was too good to be true.

'But he's-' The warm look in Nox's light eyes cut me off.

'He was caught.' Nox's smooth voice was trying to hide an edge as he corrected my assumption.

'He was what? How? By who?' The questions came tumbling out of my mouth.

Nox shook his head at me as if he was sad that I didn't already know.

'The most difficult feat in this universe is catching someone's soul before it leaves their body.' Unease awakened in my gut as

Nox explained vaguely. 'She'll never recover, but he will.' Nox folded his arms thinking that was enough detail.

It was. As long as Alec was alive. I'm sure we'd have to face the consequences of that later, but for now I didn't care. I looked from Alec, to Nox, and then to the faces of my friends, Ace, Ash, Anakin, Anjelica, and Alice, as they headed over. I could've lost everything. But I hadn't. I hadn't because of Nox. He really was a Guardian.

'And August, please do try to avoid near death situations. You almost gave me a heart attack.' Nox set a navy hand on his heart as he continued to hold his glare.

No doubt because I'd scared him. I took two quick steps towards Nox and crushed him with a quick hug before I retreated back. The shock in his wide eyes made me giggle as my tears dried.

'Thank you,' I said the words slowly, wanting Nox to know how much his rescue meant to me.

After what felt like a long moment, Nox's composed resting expression broke into a warm grin. His star-like freckles rose up with his smile giving the impression that the universe itself was grinning down at me. Offering me a dip of his head as goodbye, Nox opened his wings to their full length and took off. I couldn't stop from smiling, despite all the bad, I'd somehow found people who had my back. For the first time in years I actually believed to my core that everything would be okay, and if it wasn't, I had people to face the bad with.

'Alec.' Anjelica's voice was broken with emotion as she reached my side.

Stopping her before she could break down completely, I placed a hand on her shoulder.

'Nox said something about soul catching. He'll be okay,' I reassured her as the others made it over to us.

Anakin had Ash's arm slung over his shoulder helping our exhausted friend over. Fatigue was also blatantly apparent on Alice. Her posture was more slouched than usual as she headed over. Once she reached us she bent, placing her hands above her knees and started taking deep breaths. Ace came to stand on the opposite side of Alec to me. His hair was swept left and flopped down over his eye. While the right side of his face bore a cut that wove from his jawline up to just below his eye. He looked a bit like a Midgardian pirate in his rugged state. Anakin's appearance was ruffled and his fringe angrily attacked his forehead as dried blood splattered parts of his face.

'We still need to deal with Apoint.' Anjelica grabbed my arm.

She was definitely covered in the most blood. Her tied back hair was clumpy with red and gold droplets, while scratches and large bruises covered her arms.

'My sister brought a girl with her, who can supposedly locate people by touching the ground.' Before I could gauge my friends' reactions I noticed Ashia come running out of the courtyard towards us.

'Riptide.' She skidded to a halt, out of breath. 'I'm sorry, I can't – it's not working.'

I was prepared for this answer, having grown sceptical of anything and anyone *my sister* thought was helpful.

'We'll just find him the usual way.' I offered her a small smile as I turned my weapons into knives and tucked them into my belt.

'Gale, Arrow, stay here with Chameleon and rest,' I ordered, not giving them a choice.

I looked over at Ace, Anakin, and Anjelica. None of them were ones to want to miss a fight but I wasn't sure about leaving Alec unconscious with our two most fatigued friends.

'Riptide, we'll be fine.' Ash picked up on my use of their titles around Ashia and my unease about leaving them alone.

I gave him a nod as the rest of the group began to head towards the courtyard, weapons ready, and shoulders tense. We paused as we got to the edge, taking advantage of our view of the battle grounds. I could see Amolt and Ray on one side fighting side by side with a large group of Asgardian warriors as they boxed five or so Overlegenian soldiers in. Towards the centre of the battle, Thor and Loki surprisingly fought back to back. Darts and Mjölnir flying around as soldiers made moves against them. Asgard's forces had pushed Apoint's forces back almost all the way.

'I can't see him.' Anakin voiced what we were all thinking.

I took a step back and spun to check on Alec, Alice, and Ash once more before we left them. A feeling flared in my gut urging me to stay with them. It was probably just worry that something else would happen to one of my friends. I probably would've ignored it if the nerves in my hands hadn't flared up at that moment, spreading the unease.

'You know what guys, go ahead. I think I'll stay with them.' I gave in as I took one last sweep of the battlefield. 'Go get him.'

Anjelica shot me an *'are you sure'* look but didn't say anything.

I gave her a reassuring smile, they didn't need me with them to get Apoint. Spinning back around, I walked away before I could change my mind. Ash and Alice sat with their backs to me not yet noticing I had returned. Azar's body lay just inside my peripheral, reminding me that I'd left Nora there. I wonder where she'd gone. Maybe she found a weapon and went to fight for once. I ought to cut her some slack though, this was the first time since leaving Earth that she'd actually shown up. Even if it was only partly for me. As I reached Ash and Alice a swishing sound broke off my thoughts. Instinct had my knees buckling before I even processed why. My reaction was so fast I lost my balance, falling back onto my hands as the tactically dressed Apoint stepped in front of me. *Where'd he come from?* Sooner than I could get my act together, or Apoint could strike again, a silver spiked ball appeared in the otherwise empty air. It flew smoothly into the temple of Overlegen's right-hand man. Apoint's golden blood fell with his body as I shuffled back out of the way. Relief clattered through my heart, taking away any of the tension I had in my muscles as the fair, freckled, and slightly rosy appearance of Alec appeared in front of me. Before I could acknowledge him, the dying voice of Apoint startled me.

'Dead walking.'

I barely caught the words as they left, along with his energy, but I knew exactly what he'd meant. Duana was coming for us.

'It's good to see you August.' The cheery voice of Alec distracted me as he offered me a hand up.

I grinned back at him with my warmest smile as I gripped his hand and he hauled me to my feet.

'Alec!' Anakin alerted us to his arrival as he charged past me crushing Alec in a hug.

I was so happy to see Alec alive and well. I didn't realise Ace, Anjelica, and Ashia, were back until they stood right beside me. It was a good thing they weren't the enemy. My senses were now completely burnt out.

'He's gone!' Alice sprung up to her feet from where she and Ash were still crashed.

'I feel like I can breathe again.' Anjelica joined Alice in her joy.

'Isn't it a shame your first free breath is in this claustrophobic underground city?' Anakin sounded only half sincere as he released Alec.

'How am I alive?' Alec asked, before Anjelica and Anakin could get started with their usual bickering.

'Nox said someone caught you.' I told him what I knew which landed him as confused as I was.

'Children!' A shout had us all spinning towards the courtyard with our weapons ready.

'Whoa, it's just me.' Amolt walked over accompanied by Ray and Nora. 'Your Gods are double checking but we should be pretty much done here.'

He had developed a new limp and had earned a nasty looking wound in his stomach but Amolt didn't seem to mind as he rubbed his hands together and stared at the exit.

CHAPTER TWENTY-ONE

August – Riptide

The mud under my boots slowly turned to soft damp grass as I made my way out of the underground city. I took in a deep waft of fresh air as my eyes adjusted to the darkness. A large silver moon glinted above me occasionally disappearing behind the passing clouds. Stars speckled across the visible patches of sky adding to the tranquil beauty. I couldn't see the forests or mountains, that I'd seen when we first arrived, as the moon's light only fell on the ground before me. Anything past the light was so dark it may as well have not existed. What I could see was in shades of deep emerald or royal blue and faded into the darkness. I could hear the creaking of the trees in the wind and the slow crashing of water against rocks. The sounds were as welcome as the grassy smell carried with the refreshing wind. My feet carried me up the hill, where I stood enjoying the battering of the wind and the serenity of the twinkling stars.

Thor and Loki were escorting their warriors to the Bifröst's connection on Undeva. My friends and the others were probably still in the underground city. Not wanting to stay for another minute of Nora's rambling about her research, I'd left after she'd finally introduced Ashia properly. As it turns out, Ashia was also from Earth, and Nora had been mentoring her on controlling her gifts. This discovery had convinced me to give up trying to understand my sister and her motives. Ashia claimed to have been cursed by someone. Nora seemed to think this also explained my gifts. I let out a quick snort just thinking about it. *Why would someone curse me with a means of surviving?*

My feet ached in my boots but the rest of my ailments were soothed by the refreshing night and the adrenaline that was still flying around my veins. Alice had healed my more serious injuries but instead of healing my lesser ones I told her to save her energy. There were people with more pressing injuries and I had earned all of my cuts, bruises, and sore muscles. For now I wanted to wear them as a medal for surviving my childhood. Besides, these ailments were rather light. Having grown up without gifts I'd had as much martial arts training as I could, which still served me well, even with the added benefit of gifts.

'There you are.' Thor's deep voice alerted me to his and Loki's approach.

I stayed silent as they made it up the hill, not sure what they could want now.

'Glad to see you're alright.' Loki's words were far from empty. Though probably more so because of an ulterior motive than actually caring.

'Let me guess, you two need something.' I wasn't offering, more like teasing, which earned me two sarcastic smiles.

The moon's light was present just enough that I could make out their expressions, but was unreliable thanks to the wind and the clouds.

'Did Nox put the Forn Ljós of Laguz in the weapons you gave me?' I asked, before they could start speaking, giving myself a higher chance of receiving an answer. I suspected that Nox had, but I just wanted to know for sure.

Loki sighed knowing his answer would dictate how open I was to what they were about to say.

'Yes. He split the rune in half. Now can we get to the point?' Loki's voice was as tired as what I could make out of his appearance.

I gave him a nod.

'We feel it is only fair to warn you that some bad people will still be after you.'

'As opposed to nice people?' I muttered to myself, although Thor's uneasy shifting in his position made me wonder if they'd heard.

'And seeing as they think you have one anyway...' Thor continued carefully, like he was worried about the outcome. 'Well, as you do have one, more like.'

307

I remained silent, lost for words as I watched the mighty Thor stumble over his.

'What he's trying to say is.' Loki decided to take over, his confidence in his words much higher than Thor's. 'How would you like to do the hunting for once?'

I couldn't help but smile at Loki's silver words, he definitely knew how to spin this.

'You want me to collect the Forn Ljós runes?' Both Gods nodded, seemingly relieved that I hadn't shut them down yet. 'Why don't you do it?'

'Politics,' Loki responded bluntly, 'and besides, why do you think you have a Guardian?'

I frowned at him, trying to make out his expression in the darkness. I don't even know where my gifts were from, let alone why I have a supernatural Guardian.

'What does that have to do with this?' I crossed my arms, suddenly feeling the wind chill.

'Everything.' Loki seemed to be fond of one word replies.

I definitely wasn't.

'Please August, at least consider it. We can't risk people like Apoint, Duana, and Azar getting a hold of and using runes like these.' Thor let his plea enter his voice, surprising me as his words came out soft.

I stayed silent, unsure what to say. There was a strong pull in my gut to say '*yes*', but my head was still calculating what doing this would mean, and it was a lot to take in.

'What have we here?' Ash's playful voice startled me.

As I scanned behind me I made out six dark silhouettes and guessed that my friends had stealthily made their way up the hill. An opportunity to change the subject, if ever there was one.

'Thor, Loki, what should we do with this?' I unzipped the hidden pocket in my jacket and pulled out the Segredos drive.

I personally would like to have a good look through all of its folders and learn more about its origin, but my friends and Asgard had also shed blood to protect this so it definitely wasn't up to just me.

'You can't be serious?' Loki's grin was almost wider than his face and the moonlight hitting him front on made his expression even more menacing. 'You'd trust me with that?'

'I'm not giving it to you, I'm asking for your opinion.' I recoiled my arm.

'I know.' Thor reached out, taking it from my hand.

Wrapping his hand in a tight fist a swift crunch was let off, as Loki shut his eyes.

'Probably better nobody has anything like that.' Thor stood a bit straighter, seemingly very proud of his moral high ground.

'That could have been useful Thor.' Anjelica's voice carried the same emotion I assumed Loki was feeling.

Thor tilted his head to the side, questioning her in silence.

'Knowledge nephew, knowledge.' Loki's voice a gruff whisper.

'Mother always taught me that strength was the most effective gift in my arsenal.'

'That's because intellect isn't in your arsenal.' Loki turned his back to us and his nephew, taking a few moments to recompose himself. 'Thor, I could use a word.' Loki's voice was a sharp hiss as he began walking back down the hill.

Thor appeared pretty jovial despite the sharpness in his uncle's tone. The fiery haired God gave a mock salute before following Loki back down the hill.

'So what did they want August?' Anakin redirected my attention with his wonderfully blunt personality.

'Just another situation I'm slightly involved it.' I didn't expect to meet his sharp green eyes as I looked in his direction.

'Well that's hardly surprising. You girls come gift wrapped in problems.' His words were fond as he tilted his head at me.

It appeared from Anakin's appearance, along with what the moon was lighting of the rest of the group, that everyone had been healed by Alice.

'Thor and Loki want me to track down the other Forn Ljós.' I relaxed as I filled them in on the situation.

'Sounds like fun.' Ace surprised me with the eagerness in his voice.

'Yeah, and I was worried we were going to be bored now that Overlegen isn't after us.' Anjelica grinned, her teeth catching the moonlight.

'Well we've still got Duana though.' Alice reminded us.

'So where do we start with these rune things?' I looked towards Alec as he spoke.

'We?'

'Of course, you three didn't think we'd leave you to have all the fun did you?' Ash put his arm on Alec's shoulder as he made clear I wasn't doing this alone.

My only response was a warm grin, I didn't have the words to describe how grateful I was that I met these people. Before we could continue the conversation, Nora and Ashia made themselves known as they joined us.

'I'm going to leave Ashia with you. I've got some things to see to.' Nora ignored my friends and stopped walking right in front of me.

Hang on. What? 'Nora can I have a word?' I gestured further along the hill top.

'Oh no, no need. You can trust her, I trained her myself.' Nora was pushing buttons I didn't know I had.

311

'It was good to see you though.' She beamed at me before reinforcing that she was an idiot.

I responded to her two sided smile and offer of a hug with low set eyebrows and a harsh glare. I was done. She kept too many secrets and had the strangest ways of *helping me*. Plus she'd chosen to help a stranger over me. It seemed I'd finally come to grasp that the old version of my sister was long gone. Whatever her title *Honora* meant, that's who she'd become. The darkness itself moved away from Nora's outstretched arms, repulsed as the moon reappeared. Despite my current feelings toward her however, I couldn't bring myself to leave her with nothing but a glare so I offered her a curt, 'and you,' before turning back toward my friends. I didn't spare her a glance as she headed away, I'd seen her leave enough. This time I had turned my back first. She'd have to earn a place in my life now. Our paths were different and I had no room on mine for someone who wouldn't make an effort with me. I was worth more than her half-hearted attempts at being in my life. I had a purpose, a goal, a team, and the coolest Guardian anyone could ever ask for. I had learnt a lot from my days running from Overlegen. I'd survived them and now I had a job to do. As dangerous as it may be.

'Ashia.' I turned to face her silhouette. I didn't like the idea of having her with us but she had just been abandoned by Nora.

'What we're all about to do may lead to our deaths.' I told it to her straight, at least then she knew what Nora was getting her into.

'That's okay, I've nearly died twice in the past six months.' She shrugged, brushing off the danger in a naive way.

'She's got a lot of catching up to do,' Ace whispered.

I smiled at his silhouette, which was to my left.

'Yeah, twice in six months sounds quite relaxing,' Anjelica added, from somewhere to my right.

'We all nearly died at least a hundred times in the last day.' Anakin spoke directly to Ashia.

To her credit she didn't reveal how she was feeling inside.

'I'll do my best to help.' She gave me a weak smile.

'So where do we start?' Ash took the attention off of Ashia as we began to stand in a circle.

The moon wasn't doing too well at highlighting who was standing where so I had to rely on my recognition of voices to know who was speaking.

'There's actually something I need to check back on Asgard.' I caught a glint of gold in the hands of who I was assuming was Anakin as he spoke.

'We'll send you a raven to let you know where we are.' I recognised Alec's voice as he responded.

'Stay safe.' We all offered, as Anakin made his way around the group saying temporary goodbyes.

'Try not to get killed without me around to save you all.' Anakin's words carried an arrogant grin as he approached me.

'Try not to cause too much trouble without us,' I returned, as we shook hands.

He gave me a wink as he responded, 'No promises.'

We waved him off as he trekked down the hill going after Thor and Loki.

'Wonder what he's up to?' Anjelica sounded slightly disappointed as Anakin's outline disappeared.

'What happened to Amolt and Ray?' I asked, despite also wondering about what Anakin had to check.

'They left with the rest of Asgard's warriors,' Alice responded, from a position opposite me. 'Said to tell everyone they say goodbye.' A pause followed Alice's words as everyone was suddenly unaware of what to say.

Finally Alec broke the silence. 'We should probably split up, it'd be easier to scout that way. We can send each other ravens to keep in contact until we all purchase interbranch coms.'

Alec's plan was pretty sound.

'Good idea. But make sure to alert everyone if you find anything or need help.' I added, as a pale yellow light began to line the horizon. *It was dawn already?*

'Who do we contact first if we find one?' Ashia asked a fair question.

'Contact whoever's closest,' Alice responded.

'But in a crisis turn to Anjelica,' Ace teased the unsuspecting Ashia, who gulped after one toothy grin from Anjelica.

The first light making it easier to see everyone's expressions.

'I do handle crises the best,' Anjelica confirmed, but when we all broke into hysterical laughter she added, 'provided the problem can be solved with fire.'

'I would like to visit Portugal on Midgard.' Alice picked the first location. 'Admittedly there probably isn't a rune there but it is where the Segredos drive was named so we may as well have a look around.'

Something told me Alice also just wanted to go to Portugal.

'I'll go with you.' Ashia volunteered, tucking her hair behind her ears to stop the wind moving it across her face. 'I'm not too confident with other planets, just yet.'

I locked eyes with Alice, checking that she was going to be okay with this. After all, since we'd met Anjelica, Alice and I had stuck together, and Ashia was a stranger. She gave me a subtle nod that was more in her eyes than her head.

'Be safe then.' Anjelica wrapped Alice up into a hug before Alice came over and gave me one as well.

She shook hands with the boys and then left, leading Ashia towards the Bifröst. Hopefully Heimdall was still at his post to get us out of here.

'Alright, so August and I are going to Iceland.' Anjelica decided. 'It's where they were named and also Heimdall told Thor to tell me that Pebbles might be there.'

She referenced the fake stone Jotnar that had attacked Asgard.

'Why Pebbles though?' I asked, she hadn't even met him.

'I've got one of those gut feelings.' She nodded as she spoke, trying to add severity to the statement.

I smiled at her before turning to Ace who was still standing to my left.

'Let us know where you three end up.' I offered him my hand.

He offered me a warm smile as he shook my hand, his grip as firm as mine.

'Try not to make any more enemies while you're there.'

Playing along with his tease, I responded, 'Don't worry, I'll let Anjelica do the talking.'

We held each other's serious stares for a moment before humour broke our blank expressions. I shook hands with Ash next, as Anjelica went from Alec to Ace with her goodbyes.

'Stay safe.' Ash's eyebrows tilted up slightly making his words into a challenge.

'You too.' I challenged back.

As I got to Alec he wrapped an arm around my shoulder bringing me into a one armed hug, which caught me off guard.

'Stay away from grenades.' He released me as he spoke.

'Hey, you too.' I looked at him seriously for a moment before giving him a smile goodbye.

Without further delay, Anjelica and I began walking down the hill and towards the Bifröst's anchorage.

CHAPTER TWENTY-TWO

August – Riptide

'Are you sure Duana is coming for us?' Anjelica questioned, sounding slightly excited as we reached the end of the Bifröst.

Heimdall had let the bridge down on a small peak in the middle of an Icelandic meadow.

'Yes,' I responded, as I quickly scanned our surroundings.

Many rocks lay scattered across the landscape, disguised by moss and long green grass. Just below the hill was a smooth flowing river that reflected the colours of the rising sun as it ran towards a village sitting a ways ahead of us. There was no obvious threat, for now.

'Great. You take Pebbles, I'll get Duana.'

'What if I don't want to fight Pebbles.' I wasn't a fan of the fake Jotnar, there was no skill in his fighting and it was Anjelica's idea to come after him.

'Because, in the case they both turn up at once I have more reason to want Duana dead.'

Right.

We hadn't been walking towards the village for too long when the Earth beneath our feet started to shake.

'Earthquakes,' Anjelica grumbled, but kept walking.

'Or a giant.' I pulled one of my blades out of my belt's sheath.

'Could be.' The deep sounding words made my heart jump as I spun around. There he was. Pebbles sneered at us as Anjelica too turned pulling out a sword. 'Asgardians come to die?'

Anjelica cast me a confused look, obviously Pebbles had no clue who we were. The fake Jotnar's eyes were wide with the opportunity to kill in the morning. This look was precisely what encouraged me to put my blade away. It would be a great opportunity to practice fighting with my gifts. Using the fresh Icelandic air, I locked onto the cold feeling, ready to throw some ice. Flame roared to life in Anjelica's sword free hand.

'That's not normal,' Pebbles mumbled, looking between us, but he wasn't talking about our gifts.

He was referencing a tight blue line that had wrapped itself around his body. Taking his attention off of us he tried to pick the line off but his fingers were too large. Anjelica and I shared a quick glance as the unmistakable zap of electricity filled the air. Pebbles' eyes rolled back into his head and he fell forward onto the ground. Looking past the collapsed giant I noticed a young guy, probably about twenty, approaching Pebbles. He wore a brown leather jacket and blue jeans. Not paying any attention to us he continued forward, brushing his burnt hay coloured hair out of his blue eyes. Anjelica and I approached cautiously. This guy was definitely a fighter and was heavily armed. He had strong features and stubble adding to his threatening appearance.

'That is not a weapon from Earth,' I spoke to Anjelica, but raised my voice so that he could hear.

'He took something of mine.' The guy kept his eyes on Pebbles, the strength in his voice matching his walk.

Still not looking at us he reached into a black shoulder bag, pulling out a pair of tongs and a small clear box.

'That was an Asgardian weapon.' Anjelica realised as he crouched down next to Pebbles and pried his hand open.

We just watched as he used his tongs to grab the object clutched between Pebbles hand. Which, looking at it now, was black in colour and full of painful looking cracks.

'Something was burning through his hand,' I thought out loud, quiet enough so that only Anjelica could hear me.

My breath caught as the tongs revealed what was in his hand. A small glowing shape, definitely a rune, was clutched tightly by the silver coloured metal. Swiftly, he placed the rune in a container, and both it and the tongs back in his bag. *What are the chances?* Surely it wasn't going to be this easy to locate all of the Forn Ljós runes.

'Lasses.' He gave us a quick glance as he turned to leave.

Had Pebbles had that on Asgard?

'Ow.' The sound came out of my mouth even though I didn't feel any pain from Angelica's elbow.

Not needing to be elbowed from my thoughts again I sent two feisty globes of water from my hands towards the guy's feet. Freezing them upon impact. He twisted to glare at me as he was literally stopped in his tracks.

'How do you know about the Forn Ljós?' I asked, as we got nearer.

'What makes you think I know about them?'

I couldn't quite place his accent. Parts of it were definitely Scottish but occasionally something else filtered through.

'You said Pebbles took something from you,' Anjelica reminded him.

He lowered his glare so that he was staring at us through his eyebrows, his nose crinkling just a little.

'That thing is called Pebbles?' His voice carried both humour and horror as if he couldn't quite make up his mind. When we didn't reply he spoke again. 'I am not inclined to answer strange questions from you lasses.'

His tone was mocking, trying to get a response out of us. Though what kind of response, I wasn't sure.

'Who are you?' I asked, before Anjelica could cut him with a remark I could see her preparing.

'Sage Marek.' He finished his blunt response by raising his eyebrows and tilting his head towards me, silently asking me back.

His lack of a title meant that he either hadn't spent time in the Asgardian Realm, or wasn't concerned about dark gifts or being smited. By the way he held himself, even with his feet frozen in place, I figured it was probably the latter option.

'August Frost.' I decided to give the same detail he had.

'I'm Firestorm.' Anjelica introduced herself, definitely not comfortable with giving this guy her name.

Which was probably smart but I doubted this guy could smite.

'Off worlders huh.' He didn't look surprised.

'What are you doing with a Forn Ljós?' I tapped the ice with my foot making sure it was still solid.

'I'm a Forn Ljós hunter. Or, as Heimdall put it, the keeper of Othala.' He grinned as he pulled the clear box out of his bag.

My eyes landed on the glowing symbol:

'Well, Heimdall sent us here to relieve you of stone duty,' Anjelica stated, holding her hand out.

Sage paid her no attention, placing the box back in his bag. Motioning to Anjelica, we put our backs to Sage.

'If Heimdall gave it to him then maybe he can be trusted,' I whispered to her.

'I guess it will take some attention off of us.' She sighed, beginning to agree with me.

'And we can always steal it off him later.' I nodded in response.

'Can you prove that Heimdall gave you that rune?' I directed the question at Sage, as we turned back around to face him.

Without responding, Sage pulled his right arm out of his jacket's sleeve. Tugging his shirt sleeve upwards he revealed the Valknut symbol on his deltoid. The three triangles had bold enough margins that small writing fit inside:

Varðmaður Othala eins og eftir orð Ásgarðs.

I looked at Anjelica to see if she understood the words any more than I did. She didn't.

'Alright, you can keep the rune.' Anjelica gave him permission he definitely didn't care for.

I liquefied the ice at his feet as he returned his arm to his jacket.

'You wouldn't happen to have come across any others?' I asked, knowing the unlikelihood of that happening.

'Sorry, I haven't.' He spoke kindly as he moved his feet, checking he was actually free.

'Ahh.' Anjelica let out an exasperated groan. 'Do you know where we could get some food?' She questioned Sage who let a laugh escape his composure.

'There's a hot dog stand near the beach, I'd be happy to escort you there.'

'Lovely.' I smiled at him as Anjelica started trudging ahead towards the dark sea and colourful village before us.

The sight of pristine dark sands running seamlessly into the wispy blue ocean came with the dreaded feeling of an unseen threat. Anjelica's instincts were currently being overrun by her hunger and she hardly spared the ocean a glance as she charged at the hot dog stand further down the beach. The sun's pinkish yellow light cast spotlights onto the small waves and I scanned each one, my sense of something bad growing with each peak.

'When did you get your rune?' I hadn't even realised Sage was still stood next to me.

I broke my reconnaissance to see that he too was scouring the area, though not the ocean.

'How'd you know-' Before I could finish speaking I was rudely cut off by a high pitched screech.

'August!'

I turned back to the ocean just in time to see a disgruntled woman wading out of the water. *Duana.*

Her pink cat-eye glasses were nowhere to be seen, and the bow around her neck was torn and water logged, just like the rest of Duana's ridiculous outfit.

'August!' she bellowed again, wiping straw blonde hair away from her eyes.

'Did she swim here?' Sage asked, not sounding bothered that there was an angry woman screaming my name.

I opened my mouth to respond but thought better of it, snapping it shut as she rolled her eyes up into her head and pointed at Sage. *Crap!* There was nothing I could do as she forced his actions. Wading into the frigid looking waters she made him drop to his knees as a large wave came crashing over him. He choked, shivering just as violently as the water swept the black sand around him. I focused all my will power on the next wave forcing it to break around him. *Let him go Duana.* I yelled in my head knowing she'd be able to hear my thoughts. *What do you even want?* I fired the question at her as I broke another wave around Sage.

'You know me so well,' she scoffed, also shivering despite the sun's rays reaching us. 'You ruined my people's reputation! You and your friends killed my two most highly ranking officers and pranced away with everything I deserve.' Her voice was shrill as she made her way to me. 'I'm here to kill you. Painfully.'

I snuck a quick glance in Anjelica's direction but she hadn't noticed our situation.

'Get in line!' Sage yelled sarcastically from the water.

Duana glared at him.

'If he says another word, he'll stab himself.'

I ignored her threat and drew Gelu.

'Come on, August. Let's not be pathetic. Fight without all the props.'

If she thought neither of us using weapons or gifts would give her a fair fight she was delusional. I complied, but took the opportunity to make the first move. Which was unusual for me but I knew the tone of this fight. She was here to kill me. That wasn't going to happen. I reached her with a snappy punch to her nose as I swept my leg behind hers. Using the arm I'd just hit her with, I rammed her shoulder and she fell back onto the sand. She spat hair and sand from her mouth as she tried to recover from the impact. Not wanting to be kind, I sent a leg into her side as she scrambled up. Once on her feet she staggered back to give herself a moment to breathe. As soon as she'd managed to remove the wince from her face she attacked, sending a leg crashing towards my face. I ducked and then responded similarly. Misunderstanding my response, she side stepped in the wrong direction. Leaving her stomach open for my incoming boot. Huffing from the impact she pulled a knife out of her belt and lunged at my neck. Feeling slightly panicked I ducked under the blade and came up with a foot towards her knee, but her blade free hand connected with my face causing my foot to miss. My world spun in pain as I tried to gauge the right distance I had to be at to avoid her next knife attack. The point only managed to catch my cheek on its way past. Her arc with the weapon was rather large so, taking advantage of this, I sent my boot down hard on her one shoeless foot. Multiple bones crunched and she forgot about the knife for a moment, giving me time to stop my world from spinning. With my head once again free from pain I focused back on my gift. If she wasn't going to play fair, nor would I. This was life and death after all. Concentrating on the stunning waves I let them increase in size before I sent them crashing towards her. She didn't have time to try anything else as the water grabbed her with its icy arms and pulled her out to sea.

'Help!' She tried to grab Sage as she was swept past him.

He grabbed her arm and let relief spread across her face. Just as she relaxed into his grip he smashed an elbow into her nose and gave her back to my current.

'What is this?' she shrieked, as the current picked up dragging her down and out.

It's a Riptide.

I didn't look to see Duana's fate as I gave Sage a hand out of the water.

'You know some real interesting people,' Sage huffed sarcastically.

'That wasn't even notable behaviour.'

'Why has Asgard sent two teenagers to collect the most dangerous objects in existence for them?'

I shrugged, not sure what to tell him.

'Actually, they've sent eight.'

'That's so much better!'

He shook his head as we walked over to Anjelica.

ACKNOWLEDGEMENTS

I have the deepest appreciation for all of the people who have supported and guided me with publishing my first book.

My family; Mum, Dad, and Sidney, your endless support means more than the world. Mum, thank you for helping me through this self-publishing journey. I am very thankful for your hours of research while I wrote or did my studies. Dad and Sidney, you both have keen eyes and I'm grateful for your perspectives.

Scarlet, words cannot do you justice. I am beyond thankful for your friendship, support, and creative insight into the characters and plots. I hope Anjelica Starr makes you proud and I can't wait to see what trouble the gang gets into next.

My English teacher, Tracey Allen, I still want to call you Ms. Allen. I greatly appreciate all of your support and encouragement with writing when I was younger. Thank you for also being my editor.

Author, narrative book designer, video game designer and design professor, Dr. Zach Dodson, thank you for being my editor, mentor, and bouting partner in the sport of fencing.

Ms. Sonia Visser, I thank you for encouraging me to use your English lessons to write my first stories. Both your English class and your support helped me realise my love for storytelling.

Author, artist, and my grandmother, Margaret J. McMaster, thank you for your publishing advice.

Thank you to my readers, librarians and booksellers.

ABOUT THE AUTHOR

Wynter Tickle

Wynter Tickle has released her debut novel in the Forn Ljós fantasy fiction series, influenced by her fascination with mythologies, legends, folk tales, chemistry, martial arts, languages and culture. Wynter has long been intrigued by the scope of characters and colourful imagery of this genre, and has woven her own blend to delight the reader's imagination and curiosity.

www.wyntertickle.com

Printed in Great Britain
by Amazon

46638833R00198